T0279124

"A wild ride of a paranormal thriller with a will they/won't they romance that will keep young adult readers turning the pages and wanting more." —*School Library Journal*

"Liv and Liam's alternating perspectives construct an intriguing mystery . . . a satisfactory addition to the meta of fast-paced paranormal adventures." —*Publishers Weekly*

"Give this to your diehard *Supernatural* fans." —*Booklist*

"Everything I want in a story—Monsters, family, romance, and humor. Don't hesitate to one-click this one!" —**Wendy Higgins, *New York Times* bestselling author of The Sweet Evil Trilogy**

"Fans of *Supernatural* will not be disappointed with *Hunterland*. Dana Claire knocked it out of the park." —**Lynn Rush, *New York Times* and *USA Today* bestselling author**

"*Hunterland* delights in every way. Both the intrigue and the romance are deliciously dangerous." —**Eva Pohler, *USA Today* bestselling author of The Underworld Saga**

"In *Hunterland*, danger lurks everywhere. This coming of age adventure is filled with murder, mystery, the paranormal, and lots of thrilling twists and turns." —**Cameo Renae, *USA Today* bestselling author**

"*Hunterland* is an angsty, action-packed adventure. In Dana Claire's world every kind of creature is causing trouble, and the possibilities are as fun as they are dangerous." —**Jennifer Ann Shore, Amazon bestselling author of *Perfect Little Flaws***

HUNTERLORE

DANA CLAIRE

CamCat
Books

CamCat Publishing, LLC
Fort Collins, Colorado 80524
camcatpublishing.com

Hardcover ISBN 9780744309683
Paperback ISBN 9780744309775
eBook ISBN 9780744309799
Audiobook ISBN 9780744309836

Library of Congress Control Number: 2024935285

Book and cover design by Maryann Appel
Cover artwork by Den-Belitsky, Paseven, Pialhovik, Ra2 Studio

5   3   1   2   4

To Katherine Bountry,
whose unwavering belief in this series
has breathed new life into it.
Your passion for *Hunterland* and *Hunterlore*
has deeply touched my heart.

Thank you.

1

OLIVIA

There are terrors in the night that have nothing to do with monsters, and I was determined to become one. But first, apparently, I needed to learn to defend myself.

I shifted my weight on the hard wooden bench we'd pushed against the wall, along with the rest of the furniture, to give Liam and Nikki space to spar in the center of the room. The basement had been meticulously transformed from a storage area into a small gym and studio apartment that played home to our Hunterland learning center, for all things monster related.

"Whoa!" My little sister Pepper covered her mouth, bouncing on the edge of the seat beside me as Liam ducked Nikki's wild punch. Nikki staggered when her fist met air instead of bone but smirked anyway.

Our simple, small-town Wisconsin lives had changed a few months ago when Liam Hunter, his sister, Jacqueline, and their father, Jack Hunter, showed up to investigate a string of suspicious suicides in my high school. Well, there was also that bit about a vampire nest and my mother turning into a vengeful spirit. That had thrown us for an even bigger loop.

While the Hunter family helped sort it all out, Liam discovered my sister and I had some magical abilities of our own, and Pepper and I had been fast-tracked to join them as hunters of things that go bump in the night.

Which brought us here. Doc, Hunterland's appointed leader and our current instructor, thought watching Liam and Nikki fight would make a good introduction to training. But each punch made me wonder if I'd withstand even a few seconds of a battle with either of them, despite my newfound healer abilities. All three of us were seniors in high school, but they felt years older than me, and watching them bob and weave only added to that experience gap.

Liam ducked again, and Nikki snarled as she regained her footing. Even when she missed, she did it with sex appeal, whereas I'd likely resemble a newborn baby deer discovering its legs. Nikki's body language shifted from slinky feline to prowling lioness, and I saw the monster hunter within, brimming with the ferocity I knew I needed to find for myself if I planned to survive this new life I'd stumbled into.

"Wow, look at them go." Pepper elbowed me in the side. "They look good out there."

Or they looked like two ex-lovers trying to show each other up, which for all intents and purposes they were. And of course, right after the twins showed up, Liam started to pull away. Instead of the budding romance I had thought we had started last month, now we felt like strangers passing each other in the halls of our shared living quarters. I asked for time to get to know each other, start with a friendship, with the assumption we'd end up being more. But his response was silence and distance. My ego was too fragile to actually ask what in the hell changed. So here we were, acting as if nothing had happened and the last several months between us meant diddly-squat.

My stomach clenched as Nikki flipped her perfect, lithe body on the exercise mats. Liam wasn't mine, and probably never would be at this point, but seeing the kind of girl he'd chosen in the past made me want to crawl into an oversized set of sweats and eat ice cream until I puked.

Nikki kicked Liam in the ribs and muttered something that sounded like "Sorry, love" in her annoyingly sexy British accent.

Pepper snorted. Her blue hair flopped over one eye as she leaned in. "That's gotta hurt."

I squirmed, unsure if she meant Nikki's powerful blow to Liam's kidney or the powerhouse-couple image the pair projected. As Pepper liked to point out every time I made doe eyes in the presence of our lead hunter, I'd been the one to push Liam into the friend zone first, so I had no cause to turn around and throw a jealous fit now that his old girlfriend had shown up.

Still, only a month ago . . . he'd been right there, sleeping next to me every other night, the two of us healing wounds we didn't want to talk about with anyone else after we'd both lost our mothers in the worst possible ways. But maybe that was why I'd feared letting him in as more than an ally, someone who understood my odd abilities and who related to family trauma caused by the supernatural. If I'd let that relationship continue without a friendship first, I'd have risked Liam's nomadic, closed-off lifestyle tearing us in two.

The air, already cloyed with sweat, thickened with the heavy scent of melted butter as Jazzy, Nikki's equally beautiful but less obnoxious twin, plopped next to Pepper on the black painted bench. Her slender fingers were wrapped around a large, red bowl filled with freshly popped popcorn. She motioned for us to help ourselves to the snack.

Pepper dove right into the buttery bowl. Jazzy smiled with bubble-gum pink lips, exposing her bright teeth. She bobbed her chin in the direction of Liam and Nikki. "This is when the two of them are actually fun to be around. Hold on to your knickers, it's about to get very entertaining. Nikki always says a good spar is just as satisfying as sex."

I groaned loudly, and Liam looked up at the sound. Nikki took advantage, landing a quick jab to his chiseled jaw. His blue eyes sliced into me as if it were my fault she'd clipped him. Grimacing, he rounded back on her.

Her lips curled into an impish grin, and she threw her perfect curls over her shoulder. "I'm going easy on you, mate. It's been so long since you've teamed up with real hunters, you seem a tad rusty." She purred—yes, purred—the last few words.

Ugh, what is she even doing here?

Of course, I knew the answer. Her and Jazzy's uncle, Doc—our current houseguest—had asked for their help in training my sister and me. But why couldn't Doc do it himself? I'd thought hunters worked in smaller packs—the lonesome road of a supernatural assassin traveling on society's knife edge. Why had so many congregated in my house? The vampire nest and vengeful spirits that had started this mess were gone.

I didn't have those answers yet. But I couldn't help but feel that with nothing to fight, the Hunterland gang were restless predators—and as a newbie, I was still prey.

Liam sidestepped to the right, evading a roundhouse kick so high, I wondered if Nikki could take flight. Her uncle, who was basically a supercomputer database of monster-hunting knowledge and lore, had mentioned she possessed a supernatural ability. Whatever it was, it probably trumped my power of premonition and status as resident healer. Just one more thing she had that I didn't.

Including Liam Hunter's attention.

Okay, yeah, pity party for one here. I didn't say I was above sulking, did I?

"Are you sure you're taking it easy on me?" Sarcasm soaked Liam's words. "From the way you're panting, I'd guess you're either in heat or out of shape."

Liam's dig didn't faze Nikki's performance. Her leg kicked out and swiped Liam's, sending him to the ground. She drove her fist toward his gut, but Liam rolled and scissored a leg around her neck, pinning her.

Within seconds she tapped out, and not a moment too soon. My throat had dried, and my angst was elevated to gag-reflex level.

Liam extended his hand, and Nikki accepted, rising with his assistance. His full lips were drawn upward. He rarely allowed peeks behind his hardened badass exterior, but when he did, that smile was so beautiful, it landed a gut punch to the heart.

I stood to excuse myself and end the torment, but the thunder of barreling boots on the stairs made me pause.

"Liam." Doc appeared, his wide-eyed gaze landing on each of us as he descended, fixing upon Liam last. He adjusted the maroon turban that matched his sweater. "There you are. You're needed. We have a situation."

My eyes trailed above him to my father, who followed. He stood dressed in full police uniform—odd considering this was his day off.

"What's going on?" My gaze darted back and forth between Doc and my father.

Dad's tired eyes found mine beneath lowered lashes. "We have a murder case. A *Hunterland* murder case."

2

OLIVIA

Liam pulled off his soaked, practically transparent shirt and dabbed his forehead. His well-defined abdominal muscles danced on display as he breathed in and out, curling my stomach. Okay, so I couldn't have him. Didn't mean I couldn't look anymore—even if it wasn't the right time to ogle at all that taut skin, no matter how it glistened, covered in sweat. My undisciplined eyes made me a glutton for punishment.

Liam strode toward my dad with his head held high. "What happened?" His brows scrunched.

"Five bodies turned up in the woods about fifteen miles from here. My boys are calling it an animal attack—limbs missing, torsos torn to shreds."

I shivered, while Dad raked a hand through his dark, newly thinning hair.

Finding out your dead wife ended up a vengeful ghost willing to kill her own family just to stay a spirit could age you quickly.

My father had encountered plenty of death, but supernatural murder took extra getting used to. It was likely why he had asked Doc to act as a live-in Hunterland tutor. And probably why he'd agreed to let Liam and his sister, Jac, stay when their dad asked. Agent Hunter didn't want to expose them to the hunt for their now-werewolf mother, Veronica Hunter.

"And you think otherwise?" Liam slicked back the wet strands of his dark hair. The muscles in his chest rippled with each movement as a single line of sweat traced along his pecs.

Dad nodded at him, Adam's apple bobbing. "The victims are all missing their . . . their h-hearts." He whisper-choked on the last word and gulped like it was hard to swallow.

I understood. I hadn't fully come to terms with knowing monsters were real either.

"Shape-shifters?" Pepper looked at Doc for confirmation. She'd taken to his hunter lessons over the past month way better than any standard school curriculum. Claws and fangs, human-heart diets, minds possessed by spirits, bodies sucked dry till they were skin and bones, dark legends coming to life. She excelled in those subjects. With him, that punk rebel act dissolved, and she was a regular teacher's pet.

"You'd be right, Poppet." Doc finger-combed his salt-and-pepper beard. "Most likely werewolves, with the full moon last night." He raised a brow at Liam.

Liam hung his T-shirt around his neck, holding on to the ends with his elbows hugged in tight as he paced the room. "Be thankful the body count wasn't higher. Five's nothing." Liam's cool composure had me throwing him a deep frown. I'd learned over the last several months that his style was less coddling and more a quick thwap to the back of the head, or in my case, the heart. In some ways, I appreciated the honesty, but when it came to gore and guts, a little tact would have been nice.

I fidgeted from foot to foot, still struggling to comprehend the reality of yet another mythical creature. "So, they can only shift on full moons, right?" Since dabbling in crystals, energetic vibrations, and spirituality, I had an advanced knowledge of astrology and the effects of the moon, sun, and stars. What I lacked were werewolf facts. We hadn't technically covered them yet in our studies. Doc's recently wrapped lessons on spirits, occultists, and vampires had already tapped out my mental reserves.

"No, they can shift whenever they want." Jazzy handed Nikki the popcorn bowl and threw her loose brown curls up into a bun, making her look like a tamer, more sophisticated version of her sweaty, still-panting twin. "But they can't control the change under the full moon." Unlike her sister, she'd come to training in a cute top with jeans. The twins were tall—like, model tall. Whereas her cut-off shirt would have met the top of my pants, it barely covered Jazzy's bra. Clearly, she hadn't intended to spar, or a boob might've fallen out. She crossed her legs at the ankles and leaned back, addressing Pepper and me. "Whether they want to or not, when the man in the moon flashes his pearly smile, they have to shift."

Nikki handed the bowl to bright-eyed Pepper, who elaborated: "And the only way they can shift back when the moon is full is by eating a human heart."

Ew. I plopped back onto the bench next to my sister, tucking my legs underneath me. How any of this was possible blew my mind and grossed me out.

"What if they don't?" I asked. My sister filled her mouth with a handful of popcorn, speaking between chews. "Eat a heart, I mean?"

My stomach churned. How could she stuff her face with food while we were discussing chowing down on organs? Pepper had a steel stomach compared to mine, especially when it came to the paranormal.

Nikki shrugged. "Consuming a human heart is the only way for them to become human again. Until then, they stay in their animal form. Too long like that and they'll go crazy, like a rabid dog." The sympathy tingeing her voice surprised me.

"Great. Another unexplainable case to solve." Dad rubbed the back of his neck and turned to Liam. "I'm on my way to the crime scene. I could use your help."

Liam released his T-shirt from around his neck and tucked it into his mesh shorts.. He grabbed his hoodie and threw it over his head, threading his arms into the sleeves and pulling down the hem.

"Sounds good. Let me change into jeans and we'll go. Nikki, you're on this one with me. Grab your gear."

Her green eyes sparkled like he'd crowned her homecoming queen. I really wanted to punch that look off her face, but I hardly knew how. And it wasn't like I could protest Liam's choice in partner. Really, what could I even say? I'd proved I knew nothing by asking the stupid werewolf question. I'd be a hindrance to the investigation. Sucky, but true.

"I'll be outside in the cruiser, waiting." Dad dipped his chin to the rest of us and headed upstairs.

I couldn't help but notice the heavy hunch to his shoulders the past several days. Monster hunting had taken a toll on him. I still wasn't sure he had processed our mother's transformation, let alone our need to destroy her.

"What about the rest of us?" Jazzy reached across me to grab another handful of popcorn from the bowl on Pepper's lap. If they didn't stop going over me, I was going to smack one of them.

"It's not necessary for us all to be there." Liam's eyes caught mine.

Warmth crept up my neck as a blush heated my cheeks. What he really meant was he didn't want *me* to be there.

"And we don't want Sheriff Davis's officers questioning why he's bringing teenagers to a closed crime scene," Liam added for good measure. "Nikki and I will look strange enough. We don't need an underage convoy."

"We'll go after they leave, then." Jazzy grabbed the popcorn back from Pepper, dismissing Liam's excuse with the same effortlessness she applied to scooping up her next handful. "I thought we were supposed to be training the Davis girls, not sheltering them. How can they learn about our world if we don't let them in?"

Liam cursed behind his hand, rubbing his face. "It's not safe."

Jazzy set the bowl on the floor and crossed her arms. "Nothing we do is safe." Her expression added an unspoken *duh* at the end. "They aren't made of glass. What's wrong with you?" Her lips thinned into a tight line as her eyes pleaded with her uncle to intervene. Doc shook his head, silently declining to get involved.

"She's not going. She's not properly trained." Liam gestured to me with all the authority of a drill sergeant.

I'd just readied a rebuttal when Jazzy speared Liam with a scowl. "Are you serious right now, mate? Are you so afraid for her safety that you won't even let her use her gifts?"

I tensed, fists clenched at my sides. They were talking like I was invisible. But my protests stuck on my tongue. What would I even say? I wanted to be involved, but going to a crime scene with bloody bodies wasn't all that appealing.

Having the choice to go? Now that sounded good. I'd much rather say no than be told I couldn't do something. I guessed in that way Pepper and I were alike.

Instead of answering Jazzy, Liam pivoted, heading to the stairs. I gaped at his back. Nikki breathed down his neck as she followed. She had watched the whole exchange in smug silence, probably pleased to have him all to herself on the mission.

"Liam Noah Hunter," Jazzy said, her syrupy sweet voice going hard as rock candy. "Do you want me to use my ability right now? Maybe that's how we can start training the girls, since you won't let them witness a crime scene. The fact you haven't allowed it speaks volumes. You're unfocused, and I am done waiting for you to wake up."

Jac, Doc, and Nikki all sucked in a breath. Pepper and I exchanged confused glances.

Liam spun around, his jaw twitching. He dropped his voice low. "You touch Olivia, and you'll have me to deal with."

Touch me? Sweat dampened my armpits. Suddenly, I wanted to be anywhere else but in that room. What was Jazzy's ability?

A roguish glint appeared in Jazzy's emerald eyes. "You don't scare me, mate." She stepped toward me, and I retreated. "Trust me." Her gaze softened, her eyes pleading with me to have faith in her.

"Olivia, don't." Liam's voice gave me pause. I was tired of his safeguarding. I deserved to be every bit a part of Hunterland as everyone else in this room, and I'd prove it. I steadied my legs, locking out my knees, and sucked in a breath.

Jazzy moved closer and I held my ground. She reached out and clutched my elbow. Her mouth moved, softly whispered words I couldn't understand escaping. Something in Latin, maybe. Heat permeated my veins like molten lava, and I screamed as if I'd really gone up in flames. Spots dotted my vision, until a burst of light morphed into colors and images.

I'd trusted Jazzy. She'd seemed nice. Maybe I was wrong. Maybe she was just as conniving as her sister. Maybe I'd put faith into the wrong hunter.

An earthy scent rife with stimulating pheromones enveloped me right before darkness crept in on both sides.

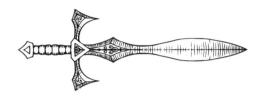

3

LIAM

Olivia's eyes fluttered shut, and her legs gave out. I dove as she crumbled, catching her head two inches from the ground. Soft puffs of air expelled from her parted lips. I glared up at Jazzy. She sported a "told you I would" smirk, her hands in the air in mock surrender.

How could she do this to Olivia? She was new to Hunterland, to hunters, to lore, to abilities. It was one thing to warn her monsters existed everywhere in this world, but it was a whole other thing to expose her to the people who hid in the shadows, killing the supernatural legends. We were our own type of horror. Jazzy had given Olivia no time to prepare, no time to understand, no explanation. I hated to imagine the spike of fear brought on by Jazzy's sudden spell. Olivia was probably still scared as hell, wherever she'd gone inside her head. *Dammit!*

"I will not forget this," I growled. One arm under Olivia's neck and the other under her knees, I carried her to the couch, setting her in my lap and cupping her face. "Olivia, can you hear me?" My thumb brushed across her warm cheek, our first touch in weeks. "Olivia, wake up."

My gaze traced her features. I couldn't deny it—Olivia was beautiful.. Subtle, delicate features that didn't need makeup to enhance, with hazel eyes that tightened your chest and a smile that stopped the world from turning. Too good for a guy like me.

Olivia blinked several times and then jolted as if startled to see me. She sucked in a deep breath and rubbed her eyes. "I . . . I had another vision." Her groggy voice sounded far away.

Some people called Olivia's kind seers, but in Hunterland we called it the power of premonition. Those with the ability helped level the playing field against the monsters.

"Yeah, I know." I sighed. "It's okay. It's Jazzy's ability. She's what we call an amp." I kept my voice steady to assuage Olivia's confusion. But once she got her bearings, I'd let Jazzy have it for inducing a prediction without proper warning. What was she thinking?

"What the hell is an amp?" Pepper said as she took a seat next to us. She placed her hand on Olivia's leg and gave a supportive squeeze. In the last couple of weeks, I'd witnessed a change in the Davis sisters' dynamic. Pepper didn't pick fights as much, and every once in a while she'd show real sisterly support.

Olivia pushed herself upright but didn't move off me. Not that I'd let her. Call it selfish, but I was using this moment to be close to her, and I wasn't ready to let go. Her hands rested on her thighs as she searched our faces for the answer.

"What did you see?" Doc asked. I had forgotten he was even there. Clearly, his niece's irresponsible actions hadn't upset him enough to scold her. I searched the room for someone who agreed with me, but when my eyes landed on Nikki, she had fixed her disapproving scowl on me, not her sister. Anyone who observed the way Nikki pursed her lips in Olivia's direction might believe she was jealous, but I knew better. She was scared. Scared that my leadership abilities had become impeded by a reason she deemed unworthy.

"I'm not sure what I saw exactly. It was an empty log cabin. Well, empty of people anyway." Olivia squinted. "This is going to sound weird."

I rubbed soothing circles on her back. "Go ahead. Nothing will sound out of the ordinary to us." I offered her a small smile. "Monster hunters, remember?"

In the last couple weeks, Olivia and I hadn't exchanged many words, simply because I didn't know which ones to use. She asked for friendship, to take things slowly.

I would have been fine with that. But then the twins showed up and reality crashed down, muddying my feelings. Their presence was a fierce reminder of my future, one lacking a home or stability. Instead of facing the reality, I chose to ignore it and Olivia.

So, when the girl I'd fallen for leaned into my side and accepted my warmth, the minute release of tension was a welcome change from the ice-cold temperatures between us. Like I said, I wasn't ready to end the moment.

Olivia looked at the ceiling. "It had to be a kitchen because there was an island, a stove, and a fridge but no furniture except one chair in the middle of an open space. Someone had coiled up a thick rope next to its legs, beside a roll of duct tape. The chair legs looked cemented into the ground." She bit her lower lip, leaving a tempting fine gloss along its curve.

What I wouldn't give to kiss her again.

"I don't know how, though. The curtains were partially drawn, so I could only see slivers of the room well." She paused. "There was an overhead light above the seat, though, dangling like they do in interrogation rooms in movies." She laughed nervously.

"Sounds like a good time," Nikki snarked. I ignored her and glanced up at Doc. Olivia's visions had proven extremely accurate when it came to settings.

He dipped his chin, a silent indication he had been thinking the same thing. "Let's get you to work on a sketch, Poppet. Maybe we can decipher the place better that way. Your visions of landscapes and locations are normally spot on, and if Jazzy better prepares you for her amp powers"—he shot Jazzy a pointed glare, *finally*—"you'll be able to hone your ability. We'll try again tomorrow."

"Okay," Olivia said, her hesitation evident.

I tucked a loose strand of Olivia's brown hair behind her ear and cupped her neck. "Are you okay? You're not hurt, right?"

She shook her head and seemed to regret it, fingertips moving to her temple. "I'm fine, just a little woozy." She paused, her gaze traveling to mine, then continued, "Thank you for catching me." The smile that graced her lips didn't extend to her eyes, but I'd take it. I knew we'd have to talk eventually, but I wasn't ready, so I did what I did best: held on to ignorance and flouted any other feelings along with Olivia.

Doc clapped his hands. "Okay, everyone, let's get ready. We are all going to the crime scene."

"The hell we are," I snapped.

"Liam, a word." Doc motioned for the others to get moving. "We will meet you upstairs."

Olivia slipped off my lap. The loss of her touch immediately chilled me. No matter my fumbling indecision, this girl had invaded my heart, and I couldn't get rid of her.

I wanted us to be together, but I'd realized that with me, Olivia would forever be in harm's way, and I wasn't about to be the reason she died. The horror of my mom's tragic end had kept me awake at night for years.

Still did, if I was being honest. I wasn't about to add to that dread. Nor would I be the reason I lost another woman I cared for.

The girls headed toward the stairs, Pepper excitedly talking about Jazzy's powers and wanting to learn more.

Once Doc and I were alone, he removed his reading glasses and placed them on the mahogany desk tucked against the righthand wall of the small gym. He leaned his hip against the edge. "William, I know you care about Olivia, but your eagerness to safeguard her is exactly what will get her killed."

"Excuse me?" I had thought he'd wanted to talk about the hunt, but this was about me? *My* conduct?

Doc remained calm. "I've never seen you like this." He exhaled. "And as your closest thing to an uncle, I'm thrilled you found someone." I attempted to object, but he held his finger up. "But you cannot protect her and be a supernatural hunter at the same time. It puts the lives of the humans you're tasked with saving in jeopardy."

Without thinking, I snapped back, "She doesn't belong in our world." My hands curled at my sides.

Doc shook his head like a disappointed parent. "If that were true, she wouldn't have abilities. She not only belongs in our world, but she's needed in it as well. If you can't help her, then stay away from her. You'll only hinder her growth."

I barely heard him over the thudding in my ears. Did they all think *I* was the one putting her in danger?

Anger festered in my gut. "What are you going to do about it?" I crossed my arms, challenging him. Did I sound like a child? Sure. Did I care?

Hell no. Olivia's safety was all that mattered.

Doc's demeanor remained intact, but his tone turned authoritative. "Send you back to London. We could use a representative at the Hunterland Library to help Elizabeth."

Beth was Doc's sister, Jazzy and Nikki's mum. At first, she'd planned to accompany the twins to Wisconsin, but since Doc had left, she'd remained our only representative at Hunterland's research center. It functioned as an open meeting place, sometimes even refuge, for our online community.

"It's your choice on how you handle things from here. You can either be the one to guide the Davis sisters to greatness or be the reason they fail.

My jaw ached from clamping my teeth on my last thread of control. "You may run Hunterland's resources, but with Dad gone, I run the hunts. You don't have the authority. You want everyone on this one? Fine. But just remember, in the future, it's my call."

With that, I left him and my fury behind.

As soon as my sister, Jac, got back from the store, the six of us piled into the Bronco while Doc rode in the sheriff's police car. Nikki jumped in the front seat like old times. Jac shook her head while Olivia's jaw developed a twitch. Navigating Nikki and the rest of our crew could be a full-time job on top of my own inner turmoil. *This should be fun.*

Olivia, Jazzy, and Pepper slid into the backseat, while my sister sat among our weapons in what Dad called a jump seat near the trunk door. It looked like the ones designated for flight attendants in airplanes. It had come in handy more than once. The thought of him immediately made my heart sink.

He'd left on his own hunt—to kill our mother turned monster. When he inevitably found her, she'd be dead and this time it would be final. I didn't blame him. I just wished he didn't have to go at it alone. My mother had abandoned us the second she didn't end her own life, trading in her humanity for the enemy.

I gulped, pushing the ache down deep inside. I couldn't handle abandonment and betrayal issues joining all my other stresses. My reopened wounds would have to wait.

Pepper leaned into the gap between the two front seats, resting her forearms on the center console. "So, tell me more about werewolves. Can we identify them when they're human?"

I pulled into the right lane, following Sheriff Davis's cruiser. "Their bodies run hot. They have intense strength and speed. Loud noises hurt their ears. And when angered their eyes will shift, sometimes their teeth and claws too." I slowed as we turned off the highway and pulled onto backroads, approaching the site. "But other than that, it's not that easy to tell an unshifted werewolf from another human. They aren't like drooling vampires who can't venture out during the day."

Nikki twisted in her seat. "You can always try and get them to touch silver if you're suspicious. It'll burn them. And it's kinda fun when they squeal." Her smile bled into her voice. Nikki was one of the best hunters I knew, but somewhat twisted. Because of the way she'd lost her father, she enjoyed killing monsters a little too much.

"No way. That is so—"

"What the hell is that?" Nikki yanked Pepper's arm forward and thrust it into my line of sight. "Liam, are you serious?"

I clenched my jaw. I didn't need to see the watch to know what she was squawking about. Last month, after a crazy vamp tried to run Pepper over in the school parking lot, I'd made Jac give Olivia and Pepper a set of the heart-rate-tracking and GPS watches our family wore to keep tabs on one another. Giving them to anyone other than Jac, Dad, and me went against our family code, and Nikki knew it.

"You never gave us watches!" Nikki shouted, throwing Pepper's arm backward with more force than necessary. Pepper landed hard in the middle seat with a small yelp.

"Hey, watch yourself." Olivia lunged over the center console, using my headrest for leverage. "I don't care how tough you are. Don't man-handle my sister. She didn't do anything to you."

My lips twitched, fighting back a smile. Olivia might appear mousey, but mess with her sister and she'd bare her tiger teeth in the face of any danger, including a British badass.

Nikki didn't even register Olivia's threat. She'd just noticed Olivia's wrist. "You have one, too?" Nikki glared a hole in my cheek. "Wow, never thought I'd see the day." She let out a low whistle, then slammed her back against the seat, arms crossed.

"Shut up, Nikki." My hands tightened around the wheel. Sure, commissioning those watches screamed "I care about the Davis sisters," maybe a little too much, but that was my business, not Nikki's.

"You won't let her come on hunts, you're paranoid about her safety, and you gave her a tracking watch. You've either gone entirely soft, mate, or you've lost your damn mind." She tossed a thumb at the backseat. "But whatever it is, get over it. We don't live lives that allow for this . . ."

I glared at her, daring her to finish that sentence.

She scowled right back, daring me to say she was wrong. "Just get over it already! We don't have that luxury." She turned to stare out the window, closing herself off from the rest of the car.

No one said another word, and when we parked at the crime scene, everyone clambered out of the vehicle as if their pants were full of fire ants.

Sheriff Davis waved from the ditch beside the road. "It's over here. I had the other officers clear the area. There's just two of my most trusted down there. We'll have to move the bodies soon. The coroner's already on the way." Sheriff Davis motioned for us to follow him into the nearby thickets.

I pushed my shoulders back and followed the Sheriff and Doc through a narrow opening in the trees. The deer path was a mere sliver of a trail, only slightly expanded by the sporadic human traffic it had endured throughout the day. The compacted dirt beneath our feet bore the imprints of previous travelers, their footfalls leaving a faint mark of passage. We ducked under branches, climbed over fallen trees, and looked out for random roots.

"Watch your step." I turned around to the girls and pointed to the fallen brush in our path.

The girls all wore scowls. Only Pepper seemed unaffected by my various alleged offenses over the past hour. I ground my teeth and silently wished for a solo hunt.

All around us, small creatures stirred and scattered. The leaves crackled under their feet as they scuttled away. Light shifted between the thick branches, casting shadows in our path.

"It's a couple yards that way." Sheriff Davis indicated to the right. I could already see a crimson lacquer seeping across the ground and the mangled limbs of the dead.

Just then, the trees swayed, and in the distance, I saw a flash of dark gray. I shot my arm out, stopping the girls in their tracks. Putting a finger to my lips to shush them, I closed my eyes and concentrated. One of the benefits of being Hunterland's founding family was access to a serum coded to our DNA, gifted to my family generations ago by one of the first occultists. When injected into our bloodstream, it heightened our awareness, including our sense of hearing. I was no vampire, but I'd give any bat using echolocation a run for its money.

I sucked in a breath and concentrated. Nails clawing against bark. Hissing. Growling. Five hundred feet southeast, give or take a yard.

I opened my eyes and pulled my handgun from its holster at the small of my back. This was it. The one reason I didn't want untrained hunters on the case. Werewolves. Now it was my responsibility to keep the girls alive or we'd all end up like the five bodies robbed of their hearts.

4

OLIVIA

Liam's arm darted out. A grimace tightened his features. I followed his line of vision but spotted nothing except trees and fog. Even the sun hid behind dark gray clouds, terrified of the monsters that lurked below.

"Run! Back to the car, now!" Liam's shoes kicked up the leaves that carpeted the forest floor as he took off into the woods, gun drawn and aimed in front of him. Within seconds, he'd vanished.

My heart leaped into my throat as Jazzy grabbed my arm. "Come on, love. You heard him. Now!"

"What? We're leaving?" I dug in my heels. Someone had to go with Liam.

"I buck orders as much as the next girl, but when Liam says run, we run." Jazzy dragged me to her side by the wrist. "On a hunt, he's in charge for a reason. And that's not ever up for debate."

"Uncle Harold, Sheriff Davis," Nikki yelled. She waved her hand, and Doc and Dad jogged over. As her sharp jaw hardened like a cut diamond, her ever-present snark faded into genuine concern, and my insides rolled.

"What's wrong?" Doc's eyes widened, scouring the forest for clues.

"Liam took off. Said to run back to the car. Do you think . . ."

Liam. He'd gone alone. Anything could happen to him. No one made any moves to give chase, though their concern showed in every tense set of shoulders. What were they waiting for?

"We have to help him," I shouted. Why were they all standing around?

Doc's eyes softened as they held mine. "He'll be fine, Poppet. Let's get you girls back to the car." He nodded to Nikki. "Do you have silver bullets in your gun?"

"We all do." Jac stepped in line beside me. I watched her eyes turn to thin slits with anger-darkened irises. I guessed she didn't want to leave her brother behind any more than I did.

"Good, get back to the car and protect Pepper and Olivia," Doc said. He motioned to my father. "Let's head after Liam in case it's a pack."

A pack? "Shouldn't you all go? Pepper and I will be fine at the car by ourselves." If it was a pack of werewolves, Liam needed all the help he could get. I'd ask later how many were usually in a pack, but I imagined a lot.

"Jazzy and Jac will go with you. Nikki, you're with us." Doc lifted his sweater and pulled a gun from his back, handing it to my father. "Use this. It has silver bullets. Remind me later—you need your own hunter kit." He turned to Jac, and she gave him a terse nod, wordlessly agreeing to put one together.

Nikki pulled a gun from an ankle holster and handed it to her uncle. "I have two. Take it." She grabbed a second gun from behind her back. "Let's bring Liam back in one piece."

Her words crushed my chest like a brick, making it hard to breath. If Nikki was concerned, then I was . . . The fear punched black across my vision. My legs wobbled. Any second now, I'd fall.

"Oh no, you don't." Jazzy wrapped her arm under mine. "Do you two ever talk about how you feel, or do you both just fret about each other in a devastatingly futile way?" She chuckled.

"They're stupid." Pepper threw her arm around my waist. "I got her." She leaned in, her breath hot at my ear. "Livy, get it together. He's going to be fine. It's Liam freaking Hunter. He's untouchable." Pepper winked. Her playfulness calmed me. Great, now my baby sister was my rock.

I nodded. A wordless response was all I could manage until I saw Liam in one piece again.

We retreated along the same path. Branches slapped at my clothes, little thorns clinging to my jacket as leaves crushed under my feet until we came to the clearing and the Bronco appeared.

I had hoped to find Liam leaned up against it sporting a cocky smile, but the car sat unattended. My shoulders slumped as fear wrapped itself around every limb. He had to be okay. I didn't know what I would do if he wasn't.

I rounded the rear of the car and stopped. My body froze. The thud of my pulse drummed in my ears, drowning out all other sounds. Yellow irises set above a gray muzzle on what I could only describe as a wolf the size of a bull singed me to the core. He snorted, puffing white, frosty ringlets of vapor out of his nostrils.

A scream caught in my throat, and I clasped my hand over my heart. The breath in my already tight chest seized, then clawed to be let out. I shut my eyes against a horrifying image of fangs tearing into my skin. *Please don't kill me,* I silently begged before peeling my lids back open. My skin puckered with goose bumps as the salt-and-pepper-furred werewolf sat back on its haunches, studying me. The breeze ruffled its fur, and its head jerked to the side as Pepper turned the corner. She gasped.

"What's the . . ." Jazzy followed with Jac, who almost barreled into me. Jac clasped her hands on my shoulder to steady herself, but Jazzy aimed her gun between the werewolf's illuminated irises.

"No, don't shoot." Pepper jumped in front of Jazzy's pistol, waving her hands wildly.

"Pepper, move," I screamed at the same time Jazzy yelled, "It's a werewolf." Jazzy's gaze darted between the bear-sized monster and Pepper.

"I know that." She rolled her eyes like we were the crazy ones. "Let me talk to him."

My fearless but likely stupid sister took a step toward the hulking killing machine. It scrutinized each of her movements intently. I grabbed Pepper's hand on instinct. Learning Pepper could speak to the supernatural in any form had been a shock to my system, but watching it was even more startling. Weeks ago I'd witnessed her communicate with a clan of drooling vampires, their speech like snarls and gurgles to the rest of us. Now, Hunterland needed her abilities, and there was nothing I could do to protect her from a future as a hunter. It's what she wanted. Dad and I had both accepted it. Didn't mean I had to like it. And didn't mean I'd let her do it alone.

Silence pressed in as we waited for her to relay her communication with the werewolf. Jazzy never lowered her gun, ready should the wolf make a wrong move. A fleeting comfort. He glanced at the weapon as if it were a toy, unbothered. All he seemed to care about was Pepper. His snout bobbed and shook as they silently spoke.

Pepper tilted her head. I had no idea what they were saying, but only a moment passed before my sister breathed the word *no*, tinged with sorrow. The wolf wagged its oversized muzzle, moisture spraying from its large nostrils. Pepper's eyes left the werewolf and found Jac. "He knows your family, personally."

Jac's mouth slackened. "What? How?" She scrunched her nose.

"He knows your . . ." Pepper's lashes lowered as she squeezed my hand. Whether it was for support or strength, I wasn't sure, but I squeezed back. Her voice shook. "He knows your mom. He's here on her orders. It's her pack who's investigating these unsanctioned killings."

Jac's eyes watered as her lips thinned into a flat line. Her hands trembled at her sides, but she said nothing.

Pepper turned back to the werewolf. Our hands let go as she knelt, one knee on the ground and the other bent, like she was approaching a skittish stray. "He says he isn't here to hurt anyone, just gather information. He wants to—"

A gunshot sounded. The werewolf lifted his head, looking beyond us. His jowls curled into a snarl. Moisture trickled from his canines like raindrops. A low growl vibrated. In a blink, he took off in the opposite direction, kicking up dirt in his wake.

I exhaled for what felt like the first time in minutes.

Liam and Nikki approached from within the distant trees, guns drawn, ready to fire. As they closed in, I could see sweat dripping from Liam's face. His tousled hair flopped over his forehead. Nikki had captured her long locks in a ponytail, the ends clinging to her damp neck.

"What in the actual fuck?" Liam hissed through his teeth as he reached the car. His eyes scanned us. "You all just decided to stand around staring at a werewolf? What were you trying to do, pet it?" His shock turned to fury that shook his voice while his gaze raked every inch of me, depositing trails of heat. I braced myself for a blowout as his lips parted, but a soft sob broke our eye contact. I followed his distracted gaze to Jac.

Liam went rigid as he took in her tears, pale complexion, and bloodshot eyes. Her whole body shivered.

"What happened, Jacqueline?" Liam secured his gun at his back and whisked her into a hug. "It's okay. You're okay. What happened? Tell me. You can tell me anything," he begged, whispering the last part.

"Mom," Jac croaked. "The werewolf knows Mom."

Liam's jaw dropped, and he blinked out into the trees.

A sisterly ache walloped my heart at the whimper behind her words. Jac was always so strong, so confident. I often forgot she was no older than Pepper—just a sophomore in high school. Her problems should be what to wear to homecoming, how to talk to a crush, maybe worrying about her grades, not hunting her own mother. I wanted to throw my arms around them both. I had never wanted to touch Liam more, to take away the pain brought on by every mention of his mother. His chin rested on Jac's head as he hushed her sobs, and his eyes found the group.

"What happened?" he asked, soft and wary.

I wet my dry lips and stepped forward. "As scary as that werewolf was up close, I'm not sure he was here to hurt us. Pepper spoke to him. He'd been ordered to investigate the five murdered bodies too. He said it wasn't his pack's doing."

Liam turned toward my sister. "He'd been ordered? Under whose authority?"

Pepper looked as uncomfortable as my jumbled insides. "The order came from your mom. She's his Alpha."

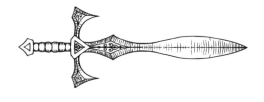

5

LIAM

Invisible hands choked my throat as Pepper's words sank into my bones. Mom was an Alpha werewolf? If Jac hadn't been in my arms, I might have pounded my fist into the driver's side of the Bronco. I needed to hit something, and the Bronco had been Mom's car.

I knew that would piss her off. Monster or not, that woman loved this vehicle. But to hear she'd not only chosen the life of a monster but opted to lead them boiled my blood so hot you could fry bacon on my forehead.

I inhaled a calming breath as Jac tilted her chin so her bloodshot eyes connected with mine. "How can Mom be an Alpha? Liam, how could she?"

Chills broke along my arms as I heard the desperation in my sister's voice. I understood the real questions beneath it. How could Mom desert her beliefs, her oath, her family? She'd become one of the animals we hunted. The deepest betrayal. Her choice forced us to track her down and use everything she'd taught us against her.

"She's a monster, Jac. They don't have hearts. They are driven by bloodlust and rage and animal instincts, not logic, not loyalty, and certainly not the selflessness *our* mom had. The Alpha she's become isn't her. It's just wearing her face."

Jac sniffled and rested her head back on my chest. I ran my hand down her hair, combing the blond locks at her back with my fingertips. "What else did he say?" I asked Pepper.

Pepper swallowed, then lifted her head. "His name is Fenton. He's your mom's second-in-command." She shifted, crunching leaves underfoot. "Your mom got word of the five eaten hearts in the woods, and she sent Fenton to investigate. Apparently, Veronica is the Alpha of a megapack, composed of seven smaller ones, all from the Midwest. The largest pack to ever exist. This is her territory, and she has a rule: no killing humans." She tucked a stray hair behind her ear. "They get their hearts another way. You started shooting so he never finished the rest. That's all I know."

Pepper's cheeks darkened from a chapped pink to flustered red, clashing against her vivid blue hair. I imagined her gift took a toll on her psyche. Weeks ago, she'd hidden her conversations with a certain vampire to spare my family's feelings, and today she was trying to soften the blow yet again. But what Pepper didn't understand was that I no longer looked at my mother as the woman who gave birth to me but as the woman who'd sealed her own death warrant because she couldn't do the right thing and end her life before it was too late. And because of that, my heart was made of Teflon, and nothing Pepper could say would permeate it.

"You did good, mate." Jazzy patted Pepper's back. "That's one hell of an ability you've got there. You stayed calm and in control. Not many in the field come by that quality naturally."

"Not bad." Nikki tousled Pepper's blue hair. "You're gonna make one hell of a hunter."

The twins were right. Pepper did good. No matter the pain it caused my sister and me. She'd put the mission first and stood in the face of a beast that could have ripped her arm off with one swipe of his claw. A lycanthrope that stood nearly six feet high, with the girth of a bear, and Pepper hadn't even flinched.

That was when it truly hit me. The Davis sisters *were* going to be hunters, and they needed to be trained. They both had abilities we could use in our world, abilities we needed to leverage against our supernatural enemies. And now that the stakes were higher, I'd take the help wherever I could get it.

I shook my head as another thought sank in, my gut twisting with understanding. Doc was also right. I had to choose. Hunterland or Olivia. My gaze sought the girl whose mere existence caused me to second-guess everything I'd ever known, and I knew what I had to do.

"The Davis sisters need advanced training. Their abilities are too precious to ignore. They need to hone their gifts, and it starts now." I gestured with my chin toward Jazzy. "You and Doc will work with Olivia on her visions. I want to know the location of that cabin, who's involved in the setup, and why it's significant. And I want to know yesterday."

"You got it," Jazzy said, her cat-like emerald eyes glittering with excitement.

"Nikki, I want you to work with Olivia. You'll not only train her how to fight, but how to survive our world. I want you two attached at the hip until you work your issues out and become a unit. I'll work with Pepper."

"What?" Olivia said as Nikki yelled, "No way!"

"Yes, way." I turned to Nikki, Jac still in my embrace. "You want me to get my shit together, right? You believe the Davis sisters are valuable assets to Hunterland?"

Nikki crossed her arms, her lips held tight as she nodded.

"Well, then, do your job. Your power will come in handy. She needs the kind of instruction I can't give her." There. Nikki had asked for the truth. She just got it out of me. I'd never be able to challenge Olivia the way she needed to be tested. I'd hold her back from her full potential, forever holding her safety higher than the mission. Doc knew it. Nikki knew it. And now, I did too.

Olivia's brow rose. "Wait. What's *her* ability?"

Nikki pulled out her hair band and shook her curls loose. "I have the power of probability," Nikki said through a wicked grin.

"What is that?" Pepper asked with a smile matching Nikki's. Sometimes her excitement for Hunterland scared me. She acted like we were movie stars fighting on the big screen rather than in real life-and-death battles.

Jazzy leaned back against the Bronco, squinting from the sun now poking through the clouds. "She can anticipate movements by processing equations at an accelerated speed."

"She what?" Pepper scrunched her nose, causing the bling in her nostril to glitter in the light.

"She sees the option with the highest possibility within seconds. She's one of Hunterland's best because she can predict where her adversary is headed by pure odds."

Nikki blew her a kiss. "Thanks, sis. I am pretty freaking awesome."

Jazzy rolled her eyes but smiled. "I can think of other words as well."

"So can I," I muttered, clearing my throat. "But right now, standing around here talking about Nikki isn't going to answer the question of who killed these campers. Let's go." I released Jac. She wiped a rogue tear from her cheek with her sleeve and stepped backward.

"Wait. Where's Dad and Doc?" Olivia turned in a circle.

"I told them to go protect the two police officers waiting at the crime scene. They'd never stand a chance against a werewolf. We'll call them from the car."

"What about the crime scene? Aren't we going back?" Pepper swung her thumb behind her like a hitchhiker.

"No. We're leaving." I turned to Nikki. "Jump seat. Jac takes the front."

Nikki didn't argue. She might be a tough act, but when it came to family, she understood. It was one of the reasons we tolerated each other so well. *Loss bonds loss.* That was something my father used to say after we'd thought my mother died. When you lose a family member to a hunt, you become part of an unspoken group of people. It's not a club anyone wants to join, but once you're in, you're family.

———

Later that night, I lay in bed staring at the ceiling and counting the footsteps outside my door. *Forty-two. Forty-three. Forty-four.* Given the weight of the feet hitting the hardwood, I knew it was Olivia. Over the past few months, she'd found her way into my bed. In the beginning, I'd thought I was the one comforting her. She'd snuggle up under my sheets with tears in her eyes. First, from the loss of her mother-turned-vengeful-spirit, then over the death of her best friend, Jessica, to a reckless vamp behind the wheel. I noticed though, that she'd come in on nights *I* needed *her* too. Like the night after I found out my mother was still alive. Like tonight, when I'd found out my mother was an Alpha leading a megapack. And normally, I would have welcomed her body pressed up against mine, calming me. But I'd made a choice this afternoon. A hard one. I'd chosen Hunterland's future. And by doing so, I'd also chosen Olivia's role in it. For her to excel as a hunter, I needed to let her go. Even if the pain of doing so cracked my chest in two.

I heard the twist of the knob and my stomach lurched. The soft call of my name stopped midturn as she realized what I had done. For the first time since living in the Davis home, I had bolted the door, silently saying goodbye to the first girl I'd ever loved and locking her not just out of my room but out of my heart.

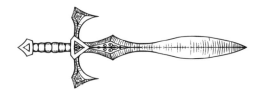

6

LIAM

My sister's screams tore through the Davis home. I jumped from the bed, grabbed my Glock, and ripped open my door only to run straight into Olivia in the hallway.

Wide-eyed, she steadied herself against her own bedroom door-jamb. I ran past her and into her room, gun raised.

Jac clamped her hands over her mouth, muffling her voice. Blond hair was tangled across her face, sticking to her tear-streaked cheeks.

"What's wrong?" My arm loosened, dangling my gun at my side. Olivia's body warmed my shirtless back, but she kept a safe distance. My muscles tensed, trying to rid themselves of adrenaline as concern washed over me.

My sister never had nightmares. But what else could this be? No man nor monster lurked in the room. She was alone.

Jac hugged her knees to her chest, and a lump formed in my throat. Her vulnerability pushed me forward. I moved into the room and knelt at the end of her blow-up mattress. Scared to touch her as if she were made of glass, I waited for some explanation, some reassurance that she was okay.

Tears slipped through her clenched eyelids. "Mom. I dreamt of Mom. I can't . . ." Her voice broke into sobs as she shook her head.

"Oh, Jac." The swelling in my throat threatened to choke me. Usually such a strong, resilient hunter, Jac made it easy to forget she was also a fourteen-year-old girl who'd lost her mother at the age of ten. And now, she was grieving all over again, pining for the woman who'd become a living beast.

"Jacqueline, it's okay to be sad." I swallowed. "It's even okay to be angry." Hot rage ate through my veins, though I didn't let the fire into my voice. Mom had not only died but she'd also turned our worst nightmare into a reality. I wanted to scream, punch something, anything to distract me from the torment. But this wasn't about me. I needed to be there for my sister.

Making a guttural sound, Jac ran her palms down her face. "I'm not sad . . . I'm broken. I can't . . . I just can't."

I pulled her in for a hug. Each of her sniffles constricted my heart, intensified my own grief. "Our mother died, Jac. She's not the person we remember. The transformation is complete. It's unchangeable." We both knew this, but part of me couldn't help but hope for the impossible. That we could get her back, somehow. I knew my sister and her optimism. Somewhere deep inside, she hoped the same, probably more intensely than me. That hope would be the death of her. Of us, if we weren't careful. "You have to let her go. We both do."

Olivia appeared at my side and motioned for me to move over. She knelt next to us.

"Can I lie with you?" Olivia asked Jac, her voice strong and comforting. "Sometimes when Pepper's upset, she feels better when I'm next to her. I could rub your back."

I knew how Pepper felt in those moments. Olivia had comforted me the same way.

Wiping away her tears, Jac nodded, lying back on the mattress. Olivia slid into her makeshift bed and stroked her hair.

"Do you want to talk about it?"

"No," Jac sniffled, and I felt my own throat clog with emotion.

Memories of Mom lying with a younger, crying Jac, sad because we were leaving her behind for a hunt, took form. Jac's biggest fear was my parents never coming back home after a mission. Mom would stroke her hair and sing her a Willie Nelson song. The faint sound of Mom's soft singing voice echoed in my mind.

Funny how a voice of cinnamon velvet could be so utterly cruel when wrapped inside a sharp memory. I swallowed down the conflicted emotions, watching Olivia take my mother's place in the image seared on my brain. Another woman I had to set free, superimposed on the first. The universe had a dark sense of humor.

"I'm going to sleep in your chair," I told Olivia, getting to my feet. "If you need me, wake me."

"Nonsense. Take my bed. I'll stay here on the floor with Jac."

The irony wasn't lost on me. I'd just pushed Olivia away from my bed, and she offered hers up without a second thought. If my heart could've sunk any deeper , it would have landed at my feet. "Okay."

I laid my gun down on Olivia's night table and slipped under her comforter. Propped up on two pillows, I watched the rhythm of Jac's and Olivia's inhales change beneath the sheet.

Jac's sunshine rays of blond hair spread over the edge of the mattress kept Mom on my mind, and as the low sounds of the girls' breathing began to lull me to sleep, Mom's face remained behind my closed lids and walked into my dreams.

Mom glanced at me from the driver's seat of the Bronco as we left the town of Rawlins behind and entered Wyoming's Red Desert, the two of us on a special mission.

I'd never felt cooler.

The Willie Nelson song she played on repeat while just the two of us were on a hunt rang clear. We bellowed our favorite part, both of us trying to outdo the other in volume.

On the road again
Goin' places that I've never been
Seein' things that I may never see again
And I can't wait to get on the road again

Mom laughed as the song ended, throwing me a wink like we were a regular family making memories. Not going off to kill or be killed.

As we rode through the desert, kicking up mahogany sand, the West seemed lawless. At fourteen, sitting in the passenger seat, a collection of all the junk food I wanted crammed in my lap before noon, I got to feel like an outlaw. Technically, I'd been one since birth, but the movie-worthy setting added a fantasy coating to the day.

"Think we'll see a chupacabra?" I asked around a mouthful of the triple-decker burger Mom had foolishly bet me I couldn't finish.

"Let's hope not." Mom cranked the AC. The cool air blew back in my face, a welcome breeze from the sun's heat beaming through the window. "Those are a monster you never *unsee*, if you get what I mean. They're even grosser than you when they eat."

"No idea what you mean." I stuffed a red licorice into the corner of my mouth between burger bites, letting it dangle.

Mom rolled her eyes to the car's ceiling. "Thank goodness I got a girl on the second try."

"Hey!" I said, licorice falling out of my open, outraged mouth.

Mom reached over to tickle my side. "So sensitive!"

"Stop! Uncle! Uncle!" I almost choked on my food, gasping for air through my laughter.

You wouldn't catch me giggling like a six-year-old in front of anybody else, but alone in a giddy bubble with Mom, I dropped the tough-guy act I'd been working on. It would become my mask after her death.

She returned both hands to the wheel, and I guzzled cardboard-tainted soda from the giant cup in the holder. "Why would a werewolf live out here alone in a little trailer? You think he got kicked out of a pack?"

Four days ago, a road-tripping family's van had been discovered broken down on the shoulder, only to be found without them in it by a patrolling trooper. The cop searched the surrounding area and found drag marks and blood trails leading to their heartless corpses in the brush behind the nearest mesa. And that's where we were headed now.

Dad had gotten the police report, and Mom noticed a mention of an abandoned trailer near the crime scene. The police had written it off in a single-line blip—too run-down and clean of blood to be relevant—but Mom didn't buy it. She dug through missing-person reports dating back five years and noticed they had something in common: the abandoned cars all turned up on the same road. Hunters didn't believe in coincidences. The reports alone were enough to prompt a closer look. But when Mom saw that three of the six latest victims were kids, she'd assigned herself the case. Thankfully, she'd invited me along for the ride.

"No, kiddo. Six victims. Six hearts. No single werewolf could eat that many before he shifted back."

"What if he's eating them as a human? What if that's why he got kicked out?"

Mom's lips quirked. "You've been watching too many serial-killer movies. Stick to the eighties and nineties classics."

I rolled my eyes. Mom had one movie genre—action—and two decades of film she chose to watch on repeat. At this point, I could recite every *Lethal Weapon* movie by heart. "Well, what's your theory, then?"

"I think it's a holding cell. The desert offers a lot of open space to roam when you shift, but not much in terms of prey to turn yourself back. With a full moon the other night, hearts were needed."

"So, they kidnap people close to the full moon and hold them out there to use later?"

She shrugged. "It's a theory. I'd say it's a small pack, but the leader's got experience. Maybe an old-timer trying to start fresh after leaving or losing their first pack."

Without warning, she went off road at a barely there trail distinguished by a faded sign that read, "Dilly's Gas n Go," and below that, "Service Station. Last garage for 300 miles."

I peeked over at the red arrow almost touching the F on the gas gauge and grabbed the map off the dash. "Uh, Mom, the site's not for another fifteen miles."

"I know. I'm working another theory on the way." She slowed; the windshield wipers struggled to fight the red dust caking the car.

I wrapped up my burger, casting a wary glance at the windswept brown-and-yellow structure ahead. Two pumps, a little store the size of a shed, and a one-car garage off to the side.

Not exactly inviting, but if you're a dad on a road trip and you forgot to fill up in Rawlins or your tire's going flat or your kids are whining for snacks . . .

I scrunched my forehead. "You think the family's car didn't break down on its own. You believe they stopped here first? The gas station is the baited trap."

Mom winked at me. "Now you're thinking like a hunter."

We rolled up to the one non-diesel pump, and already I felt eyes on us. Mom turned off the Bronco and started tying up her hair, casual as could be, so I ripped off a hunk of my Red Vine and tried to look like a dumb kid. A muscular guy sauntered out of the garage. He wiped his hands on a rag, like he'd been working hard in there despite it being empty, and tossed a full head of chestnut hair worthy of a Pantene commercial. He was younger and had far more teeth than I'd expected "Dilly" to have. If Mom was right about an old-timer running the pack, this wasn't him.

"If my hunch pans out, shoot to wing him, not to kill," Mom said through a sunny smile, ruffling my hair for show. "We need to locate the rest of the pack."

"Sure thing." I kicked my feet up on the dash and rolled down my window to rest an elbow on it.

Mom stepped out of the car and squinted at the ancient pump and its utter lack of a credit card slot or modern buttons.

"Howdy, ma'am," said Mr. Pantene, stuffing the rag in his back pocket. The name patch on his brown work shirt said Dave.

Eavesdropping, I chomped my Red Vine and pounded out a drumbeat on my raised knees.

Mom flashed the guy a polite grin.

"You know, this is a full-service station," he told her. "We don't make anybody pump their own gas, especially not a pretty thing like you."

Smile still in place, Mom rolled back her shoulders and rested her hands on her lower back, stretching so her cropped leather jacket peeled up to flash her 44 Magnum in the holster slung across her hips. She wore the gun out in the open, on a hunt or not, because it made your average sleazeball think twice before trying a pickup line or going to cop a feel.

"Old-fashioned service. Love it," she crooned, while Dave's dark eyes locked on the weapon.

He didn't pale or step back, but out in the desert, handguns couldn't be that uncommon. It didn't make him the wolf we were looking for. Still, I let a hand travel down my thigh to the butt of my own concealed weapon, already loaded with silver bullets.

"Yes, ma'am. Hospitality means more when you're in the middle of nowhere."

"Well, I guess I ought to take you up on it then."

Mom stepped aside for Dave to reach the pump. She leaned against the hood, legs stretched out long, and watched Dave finagle the clunky old contraption. His eyes trailed over Mom's frayed cut-off shorts, down toned calves to her dirty boots, and I ground my teeth. As if he'd heard, his gaze shifted up and connected with mine. He gave me a good-natured nod through the window, then got back to work. Did the wedding ring always go unnoticed?

"What brings you and your boy out here?" he asked Mom as the pump started with a low groan.

"Failing at camping. We have a spot not far, but the kid got hungry for grease instead of trail mix. You know growing boys." Mom smiled, more for my entertainment than Dave's, but he ate it up.

Dave's chuckle cut off, and he straightened, scratching his head. "You're already full-up ma'am."

Mom frowned, jutting out her lower lip more than usual. "That's so odd. I thought we were doing all right on gas, but the little arrow thingy said we were low. Think it's busted?"

Dave smiled wide at her fake oblivious-woman lingo. "I could have a look for ya. Free of charge. 'Course, if we need parts . . ."

"Oh, of course. Thank you. And let me pay you for that little bit of gas too, at least. Since it's not like the kid needs to buy any more snacks."

I had to wrangle my grin. Watching Mom work solo was always a special treat. No matter the character she played, she always underlaid it with a devil-may-care swagger people didn't notice until it was too late. She charmed with a well-veiled confidence, then struck like a viper. She was going for the kill now, reaching into her pocket where a trap lay in wait.

"Oh, no need, ma'am," said Dave.

"Nonsense," cooed Mom, pulling out a hefty handful of coins. "Consider it a tip, even though it's a poor one."

"Well, all right then," Dave drawled, and I held my breath watching him hold out his palm.

Most nickels don't have any silver in them, despite their color, but our family kept a collection of nickels minted during the Second World

War years, from 'forty-two to 'forty-five. Those were 35 percent silver, and they winked extra bright in the sun as they tumbled from Mom's hand into Dave's.

He hissed, trying to hide the pain. But the smell of his burning flesh as his fist clenched the coins couldn't be disguised. The lines crinkled around his eyes soon turned his smile into a grimace.

Mom drew her gun in a blink, but Dave chucked the coins at her face, and she shot blind, cheek turned instinctively aside. The Bronco's tire hissed, and the whole car tipped left as I shouldered my door open.

Dave ran behind the pump, blocking my shot as I raced around the hood, gun drawn. Mom pressed her back to her side of the pump, peeked around, and then pulled back as a shot rang out. A puff of dust three inches from my foot showed where Dave's bullet landed.

I reversed, jumping over the hood to crouch on the other side.

Mom caught my eye and gave me the signal to stay down with two waving fingers, then tapped them behind her shoulder to silently say, *Guard my back.*

I nodded, propping my gun on the hood to keep my aim steadier. I could see Dave's shadow lurking, awaiting an opening. When he next peeked his head out, he was flashing elongated, yellowed canines. Remembering Mom's instructions to wing him, I fired low on purpose, making him jerk back unharmed.

But Mom had loosened the gas pump from its holder, slinking around the other side of the machine. Wrapping her arm around at an awkward angle, she sprayed Dave with gas from behind. He let out a high scream of surprise, then choked on the fumes.

"Bitch!" Dave screamed between coughs. He staggered out from behind the pump, rubbing at his eyes and trying to shake the liquid from his hair. I fired, hitting his calf. When he dropped, Mom swooped in to clock him on the back of the head with the butt of her Magnum. He fell forward with a groan, dazed but conscious. Mom kept her barrel trained on his head and kicked him in the ribs to make sure he stayed down.

"Well, that was fun." She twisted her head. "Ready for a little more?"

I nodded. I knew what came next, so I holstered my weapon and rolled up my sleeves, giving Mom a look that I hoped looked cool and adult. "So, where are we gonna do this?"

Mom looked down at Dave, smile full of loathing. "Maybe in the trailer where he and his pack like to tie up families for slaughter."

"Better pop the tailgate then," I said.

"Sure, kiddo. But first, go grab us a spare tire and some of Davey's tools to help us fix our *other* problem." She gave Dave a pointed look. "After all, he likes to play mechanic. Pulling a spark plug here, ruining a serpentine belt there, making sure those cars roll to a stop in about . . . oh . . . fifteen miles? I say we return the favor. He isn't the only full-service shop in town."

I jogged toward the garage, a shot of retribution surging through my veins. This werewolf thought his pack's ruse was clever, but Mom, she made Sherlock Holmes look inept. She'd find out what she wanted by any means necessary. Davey never stood a chance. She'd just gotten warmed up.

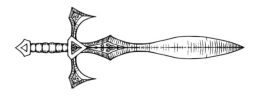

7

LIAM

A necessary evil, I thought, as Dave's blood made a Rorschach pattern of droplets across the trailer's floor. A matching pattern sprayed across the wall as Mom cocked back the hefty crescent wrench again.

She let out an exasperated sigh and straddled the rickety kitchen chair that matched the one we'd chained Dave to with silver-coated steel links.

His exposed arms were raw red and blistered from the constant burning that sent sweat trickling down his now-bleeding head. The blow would've cracked the skull of a human, but it only left Dave temporarily cross-eyed as he teetered on the edge of unconsciousness.

But his body healed so fast, he snapped back to reality quick enough to hear Mom say, "You can either tell me where the rest of your pack lives, or I can lure them here with your puppy-dog howls." Mom looked down at her watch, the one that matched Dad's, Jac's, and mine. "I'm sure your Alpha is wondering where you are by now."

She'd had her arms crossed over the chair back, wrench dangling from one hand. Now, she stood, twirling it once before she cracked it against his elbow, shattering the bone and sending chips of silver coating from the chains into his wounds. His blood *smoked*, and though he tried to keep his teeth clenched shut, a howl of agony bubbled up from his chest.

"I suppose *you'd* give up your family in a second, wouldn't you, hunter? You're not the most loyal kind. Your oath isn't to each other. It's to some deranged online society of zealots playing God." Dave leveled Mom with a look of hatred so depthless it raised the hairs on my arms. His eyes glowed as his pupils narrowed to slits.

That was real evil. Those animalistic eyes had looked at a terrified twelve-year-old girl a few days ago and felt nothing but hunger.

"See that's where you're wrong, pup," said Mom. "My family is small but mighty. How about yours?" She twirled the wrench again, then pushed the car battery we'd taken from his shop closer to his chair with her foot. "How many will come to your aid if I chain you up to an electric fence outside and let you cry to the moon?"

The wrench hit bone, shattering a kneecap. If Dave didn't give up a number before it healed, he'd have to feel that again.

I stood tall through his screams. Hands shoved deep in my pockets, I used Mom's stoic demeanor as my guide. She remained a rock. Neither pleasure nor regret for what she had to do showed in the straight line of her mouth and the firm, unflinching set of her brow.

Dave stifled his pain and spat on Mom's boots in answer. The sharp points of his elongating wolf teeth extended past his lips, glistening with spittle.

Her chest rose in a single, steady sigh. With a flick of her wrist, she brandished a silver knife.

"Numbers or location," she told Dave. "You give me one or the other, and it stops."

She plunged the knife into Dave's right shoulder and twisted. Yanked it out. Blood coated the blade.

"Tell me," she ordered, ignoring his heightened breathing, the low whimper in his throat.

The knife went into his gut, and I sucked in a breath. "Tell me." The squelch and the guttural sound Dave made kicked me right in the stomach, sending a ripple of nausea through my diaphragm.

I dropped my gaze as I gathered myself in two quick breaths. Or thought I did.

I wasn't sure if I'd made a sound or if my knee-jerk disgust showed on my face, but I realized Mom had clocked my discomfort the moment she drew the blade back out. Her iron façade flickered, and her sideways glance lingered.

She straightened, using the bloody knife to gesture over her shoulder.

"It's about to get loud in here, kiddo. Go check the perimeter; let me know if his pack's on their way."

A dismissal. An excuse to walk out.

I took it, whipping out my pistol with a nod that I hoped looked stern and collected, telling myself I'd do better next time. That one day, I'd handle it all with Mom's cool. One day, I'd be in her shoes and take the reins myself.

No matter the face the monsters wore, I'd remember the lives they'd taken to power me through it. We never came calling without cause. Dave and his buddies had murdered a girl barely older than Jac, a little boy just days past his fourth birthday party, and a teenager one year older than me. He could relive this moment every day for the rest of his life and still never make up for what he took.

The desert's nightly chill drove off the last of the nausea when it hit my cheeks. The sweat I worked up climbing the red mesa turned icy on my neck. By the time I sat on top of the flat rock platform with legs dangling over the sand and scree, the howling screams coming from the trailer didn't make me flinch.

Mom's low demands for answers rose and fell, cresting over her quarry's cries. And eventually, as I kept my eyes trained on the dark horizon, discerning tumbleweeds from potential oncoming threats,

Dave began to answer. I didn't catch every word, but enough to know he'd caved. A pack of six wolves. A location given in stops and starts.

I started clambering down the way I'd come. The shot rang out as I dropped to the ground. By the time I'd sauntered back in, Mom had already wiped her instruments clean and was scrubbing soap up to her elbows in the tiny sink filled with bottled water.

Dave was slumped in the chair, a silver bullet to the heart, among other injuries I didn't take time to assess.

"Nothing yet," I told her. "How far is the den?"

"A good way off. The leader's even smarter than I thought, keeping their killing zone far from home."

I grabbed her bag for her as she dried her arms. "Are we calling Dad?"

Mom laughed. "Only if you want to tell him good night." She flashed me a conspirator's grin. "I think you and I can handle five more were-wolves, don't you?"

I shrugged, a grin growing. "Sure. I could take all five myself."

"You wanna bet?"

"Oh yeah."

"The usual?" she asked as we made our way to the Bronco. "Keep in mind, you still owe me from earlier. You never finished that food."

I tugged open my door. "Double or nothing?"

She revved the engine. "You're on."

8

LIAM

I woke to the smell of coconut shampoo. Olivia's. I pressed my face into her pillow, savoring her scent before opening my eyes. When my lids lifted, the room was empty. I swung my legs out of bed, rose, and got dressed for school.

As I pulled my shirt over my head, I relived the realization of my dream. Hunters didn't believe in coincidences. If this was my mother's handiwork, I needed to tell someone. I'd start with Jazzy and see what she thought, then hope Olivia could conjure more of the vision. If Mom was nearby, maybe a sketch could give us a clue.

I found the Davis girls and my sister at the table eating breakfast, smiling and laughing. The rocks in my chest turned into dust. Jac's eyes were back to their clear and confident sky blue. All that remained of the night's troubles was a slight puffiness above her cheeks, but no one other than me would even notice. Pepper chowed down on pancakes and eggs, barely taking a breath in between bites. Doc sat in the living room watching the local news report about the campers murdered in the forest.

I spotted a yellow sticky note stuck to the middle of the fridge.

Gone to meet with the families of the deceased. Be back this afternoon.

Dad/Matt

Olivia moved past me toward the coffeepot. "You want some?" Her shoulder brushed mine ever so slightly. My heart stuttered, and my tongue stuck to the roof of my mouth. I grabbed her hand, intertwining our fingers.

Her breath caught at the unexpected touch. Hell, even I was surprised. Despite the promise to myself to steer clear, I found myself drawn back like a moth to flame.

The previous night, she'd supported my family. Even though I had locked my door, locked her out, she'd made sure to be there for us, to keep her bedroom open.

I leaned in. "Thank you," I whispered in her ear.

"Anytime," she said in a husky voice.

We both just stood there, neither one making a move to disengage.

A deep cough brought me back to reality. I dropped my arm, giving her hand a final squeeze before proceeding to the kitchen table to help Pepper eat the feast. Doc leaned against the door frame. "William, meet Matt at the precinct during your lunch period. He should be back by then. Since we didn't get much of a look yesterday, he wants you to view the crime scene photos and see if there's anything he and I missed last night. We don't have any leads, and every minute risks us losing traction."

"You got it." I pulled out a kitchen chair and sat.

"Olivia, let's try sketching this evening." Doc went to the coffeepot and refilled his mug.

"Sure." Olivia threw the word over her shoulder as she walked into the living room.

Doc joined me at the table. His strong hand clasped my shoulder. "I heard what you said to the girls yesterday. I'm glad you're on board."

I piled food onto my plate. "If they have abilities, it'd be foolish not to use them."

Doc squeezed my shoulder. "I'm proud of you."

After the four of us parted in the school hallways, I sought out the twins. Jazzy pushed Nikki's shoulder, laughing at a comment I'd missed. But her pink, painted lips tipped downward immediately when she spotted my approach.

"What's wrong?" Jazzy asked as Nikki turned and tilted her head, lips pursed. What the twins saw on my face I wasn't sure, but they sensed that something was off. When you know someone for most of your life, you can read them quicker than rolling news headlines, even when they might not want you to.

"Liam?" Nikki searched my body like I wore the answer on display.

I ran a hand through my hair and massaged my neck. "Jac had a bad night. She's . . ." I stopped, unable to say it out loud. Hurt. Broken. Scared. Angry. I dropped my hand against my thigh with a sharp, aggressive sound.

Nikki stepped forward and rested her palm on my chest, nodding. Though Nikki and I were never a couple, we had always been close friends. Nikki had sought me out one night to forget the pain of our shared reality, and sure, we might have slept together, but we were never anything more than each other's distraction. Deep down, she got me. And I got her too. But it had never been love, just loneliness and sadness creating a crater-sized hole in our hearts that needed filling.

"Our dad's death crushed us." She shared a look with her sister before turning back to me. "I don't know what we'd do if we found out he was alive again and one of them." She wrapped her arms around my neck and pulled me in for a hug. Not many people saw the softer side of Nikki, but Jazzy and I did, when she let us.

I returned the embrace, thankful for it. At that exact moment, Olivia rounded the corner of the hallway, moving through the crowd of students. My eyes found hers before they narrowed, shooting daggers at Nikki's back. She crossed her arms and I froze. Her red sweater was bunched at her waist, exposing her taut stomach. Feeling me tense, Nikki released and followed my stare.

Her resulting laugh rocked her back on her heels. "Not what it seems, little girl," she said. Although her condescension belied it, I knew she was trying to help.

Olivia jutted her chin out. "Do you get your kicks talking to people like that?"

"Like what?" Nikki snapped.

"Like they're below you. You realize those who live in glass houses shouldn't throw stones. And your London flat is all glass."

Jazzy sucked in a breath. Not many people stood up to Nikki, especially those who knew her strength.

Nikki's infamous smirk thinned as she charged Olivia, backing her up against a locker.

"Nikki," I warned, reaching for her. But she shrugged clear of my grasp. Students around us started to stare, but I stepped forward, a grimace firmly in place, and they scattered like cockroaches.

"Bloody hell, Nikki. Just stop," Jazzy added.

The first bell rang, and the students headed into their perspective classrooms. Thank God.

Nikki squared her shoulders and bristled, ignoring our scolding. "He's not yours, but even if he was, he'd still be family to us. And if he's hurting, if his sister's hurting, we are hurting. I'm not throwing our friendship in your face because your face doesn't matter to me." She pressed a finger to Olivia's chest. "Green doesn't look good on you, love. Get your shit together, or you'll never make it as a hunter."

"Nikki, enough." I tugged her back by the elbow. This time she let me, but she didn't stop running her mouth.

"A hunter doesn't have time for insecurities. Either get over yourself or get out." And with that, she shrugged out of my hold and stormed off. I shook my head while Jazzy frowned. The blood had drained from Olivia's face.

The healthy glow my thanks had put on her cheeks this morning was a distant memory. Disappointment pinched her brows as her gaze lifted to mine, and it nearly broke me.

"She may be a bitch to me, but she is very loyal to you and Hunter-land." Olivia shrugged. "I can't say that I don't admire that."

"She doesn't mean to be . . ."

"Yes, she does." Olivia waved me off. "It's fine. You don't owe me anything." She pivoted on her heels and left the way she'd come, but this time with slouched shoulders, a heavy head, and part of my heart.

Jazzy looped her arm through mine. "You can't control either of them, mate. You've got to let them find their way with each other."

"Like that's gonna happen."

"We're hunters. We put our lives on the line for the greater good, in more ways than one. They'll figure out their place in your life and each other's. It'll just take some time. And you'll have to give it to them." Jazzy gave me a squeeze. "Now, come on, handsome, let's talk about why you were really at my locker."

I walked Jazzy to her classroom. Olivia had the same schedule, but we took the longer route to avoid crossing her path. "When you help Olivia see the vision of the cabin, I need you to have her focus on the chair in the middle of the room. The setup is familiar to me." I lowered my voice as students passed us by.

Jazzy's fingers pressed into my arm. "What's familiar about it? There wasn't much to go on—just a chair in an empty kitchen."

I stopped and looked around. Stragglers picked up their pace as the warning bell rang, emptying the hall. I dragged Jazzy into a corner by her elbow. "Don't say anything to Doc, promise?" I asked, knowing this would sound almost like wishful thinking. And after Jac's rough night and my vivid dreams, this was the farthest thing from what I wanted. I just hoped Jazzy knew that.

"Olivia was only joking about an interrogation room, but that empty cabin screams kidnapping and torture. Someone's getting tied to that chair. The whole thing reminds me of one person, someone who used to find abandoned places in secluded areas for that sole purpose."

Jazzy's eyes darkened, then widened. "Wait, you know who would do this?"

The final bell rang and I nodded. "So do you."

"Who?" she breathed.

"My mother."

9

OLIVIA

I headed to the desk in the back of the classroom, still reeling from my encounter with Nikki. A huff of defeat slipped out as I dropped into my seat. I tossed my world history book on the desk and opened it to the page where we'd left off on Friday. My gaze drifted to the empty seat next to me, and my heart lurched for Jessica. I'd never glance over and catch her conspiratorial wink again. Or have her move into my personal space, only to steal a pen or paper—sometimes even my laptop—just so she could type me a smutty message and watch me blush.

After her death, Dustin and I had kept our old seating arrangements. Dustin sat behind me and Jessica to the right. As if in unspoken solidarity, no other students ever took her empty seat, leaving it as a shrine to her memory.

The second bell rang, and just before the teacher closed the door, Jazzy walked in. She mouthed, *Are you okay?*

A tight smile formed across my face as she approached. I didn't blame Jazzy for Nikki's ugly comments, but it was still hard to look at her and feel nothing, when they shared the same cat-like jade eyes, heart-shaped face, and perfect button nose.

Her warm hand rested on my shoulder and gave me a gentle squeeze before her eyes drifted to Dustin. "What's up, Papa Bear?" she crooned, using the nickname she'd crafted after Dustin defended her in the hallway from some idiot making fun of her accent.

A goofy grin lit Dustin's face as Jazzy slid into the chair across the aisle on my left. The breath I'd been holding, fearing she'd take Jessica's seat, escaped in a relieved exhale.

The twins didn't know the residual effects that my best friend's hit-and-run death had on me, and I wasn't about to go into detail about the crazed vampire who'd committed it or the unsettling proximity of the crime scene right outside the window where my English class met every day.

"I'll never stop loving the accent," Dustin said.

Jazzy blew him an appreciative kiss, and I could swear he swooned. Her short skirt and tight V-neck sweater would get anyone panting. I snorted out a laugh. Thankfully, neither of them noticed. Dustin didn't stand a chance. He and Jazzy played for different teams, as Jessica liked to say. He'd been friend-zoned from the start.

The final bell rang, and everyone hurried to their seats. I pulled out my notebook and opened it to my last page of scribbles, then grabbed my MacBook Air and arranged everything on my desk. A chair scraped against the cement floor, and I jumped, almost knocking over my computer.

I looked up to see a guy I didn't know settle next to me, in *Jessica's seat*. My eyes narrowed, staving off stinging tears brought on by the sharp pang that punched through my chest. He ran his hand through wavy, blond locks as he leaned back.

The big goofy smile that spread across his face said he'd misinterpreted my pointed glare.

"That was so rude of me. I just plopped down and didn't introduce myself. I literally ran here from the main office. First day and all." He blew out a breath.

Unwilling to engage with the chair thief, I went back to reorganizing my things.

"I'm Bradley Sanders. What a school you've got here! There're tiger prints everywhere. You guys take your mascot seriously." He slammed his books on his desk with a thud loud enough for the girl in front of him to turn around and pucker her brows. New Guy didn't even notice, just tugged materials from his backpack, humming all the while. When he finally looked up, it was in my direction. "So, what's your name, neighbor?"

This guy exuded a little too much pep for my liking first thing in the morning, especially after a Nikki encounter. Still, it would be rude not to respond. "Livy Davis."

His brow rose. "Having a bad day, Livy Davis?"

Of course, he was oblivious to the desecration he'd committed against my best friend's cherished seat. So how could I fault this guy on his first day? I relaxed my face and forced what I hope looked like a welcoming smile. "No. Sorry, it's . . . never mind. Welcome to Falkville Falls High."

"Thanks." He ducked his head and whispered, "Not a big conversationalist, are you?"

I shrugged, not willing to give an answer. At least not one that would make sense. *I used to be, before my life blew up in my face and I found out monsters were real* didn't have a same ring to it.

"Hmm. How about we fix that, then?" He tapped his fingers against the desk, drawing my eyes to his oversized hands.

Now I was the one raising my brow. "Fix what?"

"We can start small. I'll tell you something about me. Then you tell me something about you." I opened my mouth, but he held up a finger as if to say, *I'm not done.* "This way, after a couple of exchanges, we will be in a genuine conversation."

A small chuckle bubbled out of my mouth. "Does that work where you come from?"

He leaned into my personal space. "Does what work?"

"Humor?"

He tapped his bottom lip, then shot me a sweet smile. "Always."

I matched his grin with one of my own. "Good to know."

"I'll start. I like chocolate and sci-fi books, but chocolate more." Bradley waved his hand, letting me know it was my turn.

Why not! Maybe this was the distraction I needed from everything else going on in my life. "Coffee and crystals."

"Nice. I'm a tea fan myself but caffeinated, always caffeinated." He held up a paper cup. "And you'll have to tell me more about the crystals after class. I know nothing, except they look like rocks."

I smiled, remembering Jessica saying something very similar when I first introduced her to my crystal collection.

"Class, let's start off where . . ."

The teacher continued to instruct us, but my attention was focused on Bradley, who pretended to zip his mouth closed and concentrate on the front of the room. I couldn't help but widen my grin. He was nice to look at. Even Jessica would have approved, despite her lack of interest in guys. Lean like Liam but as wide as Dustin, Bradley dominated the room. But it was his air of confidence, a carefree vibe, that had glossy heads turning throughout class to steal peeks. His clothes hugged his body in all the right places, showing off his athletic build. A green sweater accentuated his emerald eyes, and if my heart hadn't already belonged to someone else, I might have had to dab some drool off my chin.

When the bell rang, I gathered my stuff.

"Can I walk you to your next class?" Bradley gently nudged my shoulder.

"She's all right, mate," Jazzy said with a voice as sharp as glass. Glancing back, I spotted Jazzy's frown—a grimace so deep it dimpled her chin.

Bradley twisted his lips. "Did you all have a bad day?"

I threw my head back and laughed. Possibly the first real one I'd had in weeks. But Jazzy didn't share my amusement. Her eyebrows folded inward, and her pink lips turned down.

"It's all right, Jaz. He's not going to bite." I threaded my arm through the stranger's, dragging him away. "Come on, new guy. Walk me to my locker, and then I'll walk you to your next class. I'm assuming you don't know your way around just yet?" I looked over my shoulder at a stunned Dustin and a glaring Jazzy. "See you guys at lunch."

Bradley chatted me up nonstop, barely taking breaths, from the moment we left class to the second we arrived at my locker. He told me about his three older brothers, his dad, and his move from the suburbs of Chicago to Falkville Falls.

While swapping my books, I spoke for the first time since class had ended and asked to see his schedule.

"So what's a guy do around here for fun on the weekends?" He handed me the paper printout from the office.

"It's winter, so not much." I scanned his schedule. I had gym next period and knew I could be late. I changed faster than any of the other girls in my class, affording me time to take Bradley to his next class— biology—without risking detention.

"Would you do me the honor of a Falkville Falls tour, then?"

I opened my mouth to respond, but a blast of heat filled the hallway as Liam stormed toward us, distracting me. "Who are you?" His eyes narrowed, the blue irises deepening until they practically blended into his pupils.

I breathed a sigh of frustration as he stopped just two feet from us.

"Hi, I'm Bradley Sanders." Bradley smiled and extended his hand. "And you are?"

Liam stared at it as if it were an alien object he didn't know how to use. When his eyes snapped up, he narrowed them. "None of your business." Liam crossed his arms and leaned his shoulder into the lockers.

"Strange name." Bradley's lips twitched as his gazed darted from Liam to me like he found this protective dance funny rather than awkward. I, on the other hand, shifted from foot to foot.

"She your girlfriend, man?" He held his hands up. "Not looking to cause any trouble. Didn't know she was spoken for when I asked her to hang out this weekend."

Liam turned to me, eyes wide.

I glared back before redirecting a smile toward Bradley. "I'd love to hang out with you this weekend." I pulled my shoulders back. "I could always use more friends," I added for good measure to make sure my intentions were clear.

Why not go out for some fun? I'd recently lost a friend; a new one would be nice, especially one who lived in a mundane world. He'd be a perfect distraction from the supernatural hell I had fallen into. Some days I felt like Alice spiraling down the rabbit hole, with all the new Hunterland lore I'd been learning from Doc tumbling around me. And after this weekend, coming face-to-face with a six-foot werewolf, I'd had my fill of paranormal encounters. Normal sounded good. And Bradley screamed normal.

Bradley tilted his head, his gaze again shifting between Liam and me. "Are you sure?"

I sighed. "Yes. I don't need his permission. He's just . . ." How did I even explain us? The easiest definition rolled off my tongue. ". . . protective. We're more like brother and sister. He lives with my family." I smiled. The least I could do was give him a little taste of his own medicine, seeing as he allowed Nikki to toss her weight around like a sumo wrestler.

In place of the scowl I'd hoped for, Liam's lips took on an arrogant tilt. "Yeah, just like brother and sister—the kind that sleep together." He pushed off the lockers and started to walk away. "See you at home, Sis. Nice meeting you, Hadley." He chuckled until he was out of sight.

My face fell as heat blasted my cheeks. *Sleep together. Seriously?* He made our shared moments of comfort sound like some cheap romp in the hay. I clenched my hands into fists. I wanted to strangle him and then . . .

Bradley smirked at Liam before addressing me. "You have very strange friends, Livy Davis." He shook his head. "But I'd love to learn more about them. Friday night?" He reached out and grabbed his schedule. "I think I'll be okay getting to my next class. I have an excellent sense of direction."

I laughed. "Oh yeah, you a Boy Scout or something?"

"Or something." He shrugged as if totally serious. "Add your number. I'll text you soon." He handed over his phone, the illuminated contact window awaiting my info.

I tapped in my digits and handed it back.

Moments later, my cell vibrated in my pocket as I headed to gym class. I took it out and swiped to the most recent text from an unknown number.

How many fake brothers do you have? I just want to be prepared when I pick you up on Friday. Should I wear protective gear?

A smile came unbidden as I saved Bradley's number in my phone. And for the first time since finding out monsters were real, the weight of Hunterland lessened, and I wondered if a real teenage life was still possible. Bradley would never be a love interest in the happy daydream I was concocting, but maybe, just maybe, he was my ticket back to Normal Town.

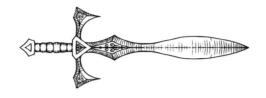

10

LIAM

I walked around Matt's office waiting for him to arrive back from interviewing the families of the deceased. He didn't have much on the walls, just a couple photos of the police officers he worked with, one with the mayor, and one of his wife and the girls. Other than two chairs in front of his desk, a bunch of filing cabinets, and an old-ass brown leather couch that you couldn't pay me to sit on, the room was pretty bare. I plopped down into one of the chairs and kicked my heels onto his desk as a folder landed in my lap.

"Make yourself at home."

I peered up to see a red-faced sheriff above me. Just to add salt on the wound, I smiled. "I've already made myself comfy in your house, thought I'd settle into your office too." I pointed to the school pictures of the girls in front of me in a bifold frame. "Would you like one of me and Jac to add to your collection?"

Matt smacked my legs off his desk, and I snickered.

"It'll be a cold day in hell before I have an eight-by-ten of you staring back at me every day."

I placed my hand over my heart. "You wound me with your words."

"I wish you were that easily wounded." Matt resettled the belt around his waist as he sat behind his mahogany desk. He rubbed his temples.

"Rough day?"

"I hate that part of my job. Meeting with the families, asking them questions you know they don't even have the brainpower to answer. Breaks my heart, watching them fall apart." He blew out a breath. "But I also know it's a necessity if we want to find their loved ones' killers."

"Normally, I'd agree, if this was a human transgression. But I doubt the families will be able to shed light on what happened in that forest." I pulled out the stack of crime scene photos and started to look through them. Two women and three men—all young, too young—stared back at me.

One was missing his jaw, while the rest just had claw marks across their faces. Blood and innards covered most of their bodies, especially their torsos. Some were missing limbs, while others were contorted in every direction, like bendable toy figurines.

"So, what did we find out about the campers?" I asked as I continued to scrutinize each photo.

"Everything is in the file you have there. We used their fingerprints to ID them. Thankfully, their hands were intact. Practically the only body part that went unscathed," he mumbled under his breath. "They were all college kids, sophomores, attending Lawrence University. None of them have had any priors. Come from good upbringings. Nothing unusual. They decided to take a couple days off from school and venture up this way for a trip. One of the men was actually training to become a park ranger."

I looked up. "Victims of werewolves very rarely have anything to do with their murders. Just wrong-place-wrong-time scenarios."

Matt leaned his head against the leather headrest of his worn-out chair. "Okay, if the victims can't tell us anything, what else can we get from the crime scene photos? I'm not used to the fatalities not having anything to do with their killers. Where do we even start? How do we get leads or suspects?"

I flipped through a couple more pictures. The cops took photos of everything, very detailed, exactly like a hunter would have. For that I was grateful we were working with someone as meticulous as Matt. But other than dead bodies, paw prints, claw marks, and bloodied leaves, dirt, and tree roots, there wasn't much in the way of evidence.

"Cases like these take time. It's the ones where the pack has a—" I stopped as my eyes landed on one of the pictures. The blood trail extended from the crime scene all the way to the forest edge along the narrow roadway. A bloodied matchbook sitting in a bed of leaves on the fringe of the forest sat in the upper right-hand corner of one of the printouts. So small I almost missed it.

"When you spoke to the families, did they mention that the campers stopped at a motel? Did your guys check the car navigation, the students' phones, and their email correspondence?" I handed Matt the photo. "Look at the top, in the corner. There's a bloodied match-book from the Apricot Inn."

"There weren't any addresses put into the navigation system. They knew where they were headed. Nothing to pull. We went through their phones and nothing but selfies and frivolous emails and texts. No motel reservation confirmations. My guys would have caught that." He rifled through his notes. "The families said that a couple of the kids didn't have Friday classes, so they told their parents they were going Thursday after school and staying through the weekend. Some of the relatives didn't even know about the trip."

I pulled out my phone and searched for the motel's address while Matt studied the image. "The Apricot Inn is thirty miles outside of Falkville Falls." I typed in Lawrence University. "That's odd."

"What is?" Matt's head snapped up.

"Coming from their college, it's way past their campsite location. Why would they drive beyond Falkville Falls to a motel for a night, then retrace their route? Wouldn't it make more sense to stay in between the two locations if they needed a rest stop?" I rubbed my chin. "And plus, real campers wouldn't go glamping before camping, especially if one of them was looking to become a park ranger. He'd want as much exposure to the outdoors as possible. It doesn't add up."

Matt picked up the office phone on his desk and pressed a button. "Can you call"—he looked down at the photo again—"the Apricot Inn and give them the names of our campers. Ask if any of them booked a night at their motel? Yeah. That's perfect. Thanks." Matt hung the phone up. "I'll have my guys check it out. You see anything else in that train wreck of a crime scene that might be helpful?"

I continued to look over the photos. Other than the matchbook, which could have been left by pretty much anyone who ever stopped on the side of the road or traveled through the forest, there wasn't much to go on. I stacked the photos back into the folder and handed it to Matt.

"All I can tell is that these students were killed by werewolves. They were easy prey for a wolf turned by the moon and just happened to be in the vicinity of a small clan. There's no trap here. My guess is, this was just a pack traveling through the area when they were forced to turn, and the college kids made it convenient to turn back. We're going to have to uncover every rock to find this one." I leaned back in my chair. "Have you found any word of similar killings in a thirty-mile radius? Maybe we could find a local pattern."

"No. Nothing comparable to this in Falkville Falls or the surrounding areas' history in recent years." Matt folded his hands on his desk. "Not to get into a touchy subject, but are we ever going to talk about the one clue we *do* have?"

The skin between my eyes pulled. "And what's that?"

Matt leaned forward. "The fact that my daughter had a conversation with a werewolf that is working the same case, and that particular supernatural reports to your mother."

My shoulders tensed, along with my jaw.

Matt held up his palms. "Listen, I never want to talk about my dead wife turned vengeful spirit either, but we don't have much to go on, and it's a little strange that a clan of werewolves are swearing they don't eat beating human hearts and they're investigating the same killings we are. You have to admit, most detectives would call this suspect."

I closed my eyes for a brief moment and composed myself. Matt had a point. He had to face his wife, the love of his life, as a monster. The least I could do was face the facts, even if my mother stood at the root of them.

"I have no idea why she would be investigating this. If what her second-in-command says is true, and this is her territory, then yes, an Alpha would have the right to find out who went against their wishes and deal with them." I forced myself to lean back in the chair and slow my breathing. "The good news is they probably didn't discover the bloodied matchbook. So, let's hope this is an actual clue and not someone who threw it out their window when they were driving by, and we get a lead that's not being tracked down by them."

Before Matt could respond, his office phone rang. He pressed the speaker button so I could hear. "Yes. What did you find out?"

"Nothing good. No one under the five college students' names checked into that motel. In fact, the motel owner was the one who answered the phone, and she said only three rooms have been occupied all month."

Matt slumped in his chair. "Ask her for the list of names and let's run them. See if anything comes up."

"You got it, boss."

I looked down at my watch. Only five minutes before lunch ended. "I've got to get back to school." I stood and headed for the door. Defeat weighed on my shoulders.

"Liam," Matt said, causing me to turn.

The creases around Matt's eyes and mouth reminded me of my father's right before he was about to say something unfavorable.

"I think we should put out a BOLO on your mother."

"What?" My brows jumped. "Are you nuts?"

Matt stood. "Obviously we wouldn't file it under her name since she's deceased in the system. But I think there might be someone with her description, a Jane Doe, who might have information on the investigation. We will keep it vague in the report."

I marched up to Matt's desk. "Let me tell you something about my mother. If she's here," I waved my arm around the room, "we will never know. She's a goddamn ghost. The only one who can catch her, who even stands a flying chance, is my father."

"Then maybe we should bring him home."

A burning sensation hit the back of my throat, hearing the one word I knew we'd never have. "This isn't our home, Matt." The anger in my voice seeped through my words. "Doc already called him, and he said he was working on something in Chicago and that if it didn't pan out he'd head back this way." I sighed. "The only reason we saw Fenton, her second-in-command, is because she wanted us to. Don't be naïve and believe for one minute my mother's motives align with ours."

Without waiting for a response, I opened the door and slammed it behind me. If my mother was roaming Falkville Falls, then we had a worse problem than five deaths. We would all be at risk and more lives would eventually be lost. *Matt better hope he's wrong.*

11

OLIVIA

By the end of the day, my exhaustion had caught up to me. And to think it was only Monday. I couldn't hide the yawning as I rested my head against the Bronco's window. My breath fogged the glass, blurring the suburban houses passing by. I used my sweater to wipe the moisture away and repositioned myself facing forward.

Liam caught my eye in the rearview mirror. "You're working with Jazzy tonight. She's coming over around six. So, get your schoolwork done, eat, and then go down to the basement. She and Doc will be waiting. Your goal is to pinpoint the cabin and get a better description of the kitchen."

"Okay, sure." I wanted to salute him but didn't think that'd win me any awards in a car filled with the Liam fan club.

Liam hadn't said more than two words to me in any of our shared classes after he returned from my father's office. When I asked him how it went, he just grunted a noncommittal response.

Now he was barking at me like a lieutenant to his soldier. I could've dealt with his demands if he'd also offered up his lighthearted side like he did the twins, Jac, and Pepper. But Liam built barriers like the Great

Wall of China when it came to me. I only wished I had a bulldozer to knock them down.

Liam glanced at me in the rearview. "Are you mad at me because I scared your new boyfriend, Hadley, away?"

I threw the back of his head an irritated glare, hoping he could somehow feel it.

"Boyfriend?" Pepper squeaked. Her gaze volleyed from Liam to me.

Jac twisted in the passenger seat and stared at me like I had ten windigo heads. "Who's Hadley?"

"He's not my boyfriend," I mumbled, shaking my head. "He's a new friend, and his name is Bradley."

"Same thing." The tilt of Liam's lips reflected in the rearview mirror. *Great. Glad he's entertained.*

"She has a date with him Friday night," Liam added.

Damn him and his supersonic-serum hearing. We hadn't mentioned the date until Liam had been a hallway away.

"And you don't care?" Pepper chirped at Liam, gripping on to the back of Jac's headrest with wide eyes.

"Pepper!" I tried to act unaffected by her question, biting the inside of my cheek while my heart went wild in my rib cage, awaiting his answer.

The wicked glint in his eyes depleted, dissolving his humor and subduing his voice to something more genuine. "Olivia deserves people outside this insane world we dumped on you both." He locked eyes with Pepper through the same mirror where I caught his gentle grin. "I think it's good she has someone like *Bradley* in her life, all teasing aside."

Pepper ate up his support, sighing like a swooning damsel, while I was fairly certain my heart had lodged itself into my throat so tightly, it'd stopped pumping.

My sister leaned forward. "That's so sweet." Then she smacked me on the arm, hard. "You're an idiot."

Sweet and salty Pepper.

I guess her new fickleness was better than her previous penchant for only salt, but honestly, could Liam do no wrong in her eyes?

I ignored her and went back to fogging the window when Jac asked, "Is that what you want?" She sounded almost hurt, like making new friends was an affront. "You want more friends in your life? Do you even know anything about him?"

I crossed my legs, as if somehow it would help block the onslaught of questions. "He seems nice and doesn't know anyone here." I played with the amethyst stone I had made into a ring. It absorbed negative energy, but it couldn't soak up the sting of losing your best friend. But the hole in my heart needed filling, and maybe helping Bradley adjust to Falkville Falls High School the way Jessica had taken me under her wing in first grade would ease my pain. "It felt like the right thing to do."

Jac turned back in her seat, muttering mostly to herself, "You'll miss movie night."

My heart sank. I hadn't thought about that. "Why don't I ask him to join us then?" No one spoke, leaving me to fidget with my fingers. "Ya know, because it's not a date. Then you guys could get to know him too, and he'd have more friends than just me."

"Whatever," mumbled Pepper. She leaned into the car door, putting obvious space between us.

"Yeah, sure," Jac forced out as if the word were serrated.

"I think that's a great idea," Liam added. "Plus, the twins will be helping Doc move into their place that night, so Bradley will have less of a crowd to please. An intimate setting." Liam waggled his brows.

Lovely.

After I finished my homework in my room, I headed down to the basement to meet Jazzy and Doc.

"Your move." Doc leaned back in his chair, his pointer finger tapping his chin.

"You guys play chess?" Made sense; their hunter styles were both more strategy than muscle.

"We sure do, Poppet. Chess is a great exercise for the mind." Doc tapped his temple. "Keeps an old man like me sharp."

Jazzy laughed. "You'll always be young at heart, Uncle Harold. That's why you're my favorite uncle."

"I'm your only uncle."

"Even if you weren't, you'd still be my favorite." Jazzy winked.

Doc blushed as red as his turban.

He *was* easy to love. Hell, even Pepper had warmed to him in record time, and she never liked anyone right away. Well, anyone except Liam Hunter.

I peered over Jazzy's shoulder. The skin between my brows crinkled when I realized the carved wooden pieces depicted mythical, fanged creatures. The incisors, meticulously sculpted into the mouths of the figures, varied in length and shape depending on the piece. The kings had curved saber-tooth fangs, while the bishops sported slender, pointed vampirical numbers. The knights had mammoth tusks, and the rooks flaunted mouthfuls of robust modern predator fangs, roaring like lions. The pieces were finished with a rich, dark stain that enhanced the wood's natural grain, adding depth to the overall design. I'd never seen something so beautiful yet frightful. But when my eyes landed on the queen, I paused. A human among the monsters.

"What's the queen supposed to be?" I asked, picking up the only figurine without sharp teeth.

"Ah, one of many Hunterland mysteries." Doc combed his fingers through his speckled beard. "According to Hunterland lore, it has something to do with our beginning. A piece of the puzzle to our creation." Doc held up the other queen. "She represents humanity in a world of evil. Lore tells us that Hunterland formed at the hands of those who feared monsters would eventually extinguish humankind if action weren't taken."

"Hunterland was started by a woman?"

Jazzy stared up at me with twinkling eyes. "Are you surprised?"

"Yes. Very." I'd never imagined Hunterland's beginning. Sure, I assumed it was born out of necessity, but no one ever spoke of the details. But to hear a woman had led the charge left me in awe, awash in pride.

Doc chuckled. "We don't know for sure, love, but that is the assumption. There're stories passed down by generations but nothing can be proven. Most likely an occultist, like our family, like you, but no one is really one hundred percent sure. Could have been anyone with foresight."

I understood having abilities meant I was a witch, or occultist as Doc called it, but it was still odd, hearing it out loud. To me, I was nothing more, nothing less than a normal teenager. These abilities still didn't feel like mine.

"How Hunterland came to be is a mystery to all hunters. The earliest entry in our database logs their hunt as if it's their hundredth, not first. The beginning was never recorded. But tales have been passed down, and these chess pieces are among many relics that depict a fanged army surrounded by a human woman. We believe she is the first of our people."

Jazzy pushed the board forward as if to call a stop. "In my eyes, she's some badass vigilante that birthed an inevitable institution. She's my unsung hero." She glanced back at me. "And she should be yours too." She rose from her chair. "I don't have any more moves left without my brilliant uncle winning. You ready to start drawing?" She indicated a small, round card table covered in colored pencils and large sketch pads next to the desk.

I have to be, don't I? No room for weakness or excuses in Hunterland. "I can't even make decent stick figures," I confessed as I followed her. "How am I going to draw a complete, intelligible picture from my mind?" If I drew a circle with two eyes and a half-moon mouth, I'd never live it down.

Jazzy shrugged. "I don't know much about your powers." She motioned to Doc. "But Uncle Harold's no Pablo Picasso, and his sketches can be as detailed as real life." Her slender fingers wrapped around my forearm. "But if you do draw a stick figure, I will die laughing. Either way, tonight will be a success." She batted her long eyelashes.

Doc released a small chuckle. "Let's hope for a little more than a doodle." He waved me over to the table. All three of us pulled out a chair and sat, and Doc handed me a box of colored pencils. "We need more than a sketch. The color of the house, the paint on the walls, anything you can see, you need to show us."

I stared at the blank page, more terrified than when I'd faced a werewolf, the vampire den last month, or even my mother's vengeful, murderous spirit. The future rested on my shoulders, but I didn't even know if I could envision the log cabin again.

Jazzy's hand wrapped around my wrist, drawing me out of my internal doubts. "You've got this."

I inhaled a calming breath and recited to myself, *I can do this.* Then I pulled out a piece of creedite, placing the hunk of rough crystals on the table.

"What's this?" Jazzy picked up the creedite and turned it in her palm. "It looks like an orange chunk of coral reef."

I chuckled. "Well, it's not. It's an energy stone known for its ability to attune one to elevated spiritual vibrations so that the holder may experience higher realms, channel messages, and enhance divine communication on all levels, helping to interpret messages from spirit guides."

Jazzy's eyes crossed. "It what?"

"I think it'll help my visions, allowing me to channel my ability at a higher level."

"Why didn't you just say that?" Jazzy pursed her lips like she wasn't convinced but nodded, nonetheless. "We'll take any help we can get." So would I. The pressure was starting to build. "Try not to overthink it. Just let me amp up your powers. Focus on what you envisioned. The kitchen, the chair, then look for more. Allow your eyes to search the whole scene as if you're there. Walk around in it. Reach your hand out and touch something. Breath in through your nose and try to smell your surroundings." I stared at her hand, upturned on the table awaiting mine, and she added, "Now that you know what it feels like, you won't faint. Close your eyes, take deep breaths, and go back to the place you saw."

I clutched the crystal in one hand, allowing the pointed edges to dig into my flesh, and reached out my other to Jazzy. Like microneedles tickling my skin, I felt Jazzy's powers invade my body as she wrapped her fingers around my wrist. My eyelids grew heavy and fell like a veil over my surroundings. Soft, melodic words in Latin brushed against my cheek as if she whispered them into my ears. Instantly, I was transported back to the log cabin. A gentle pressure built at my pulse point beneath Jazzy's fingertips. Everything went from blobs of paint to angles, points, and lines. Complete images formed out of the murk.

The once-vacant chair now became a chilling tableau, steeped in visceral horror. Upon its hard surface sat a man, his shirt saturated in a vivid tapestry of crimson. Dark, unruly strands of hair cascaded over his face, concealing his features. Binding him to the chair's wooden legs were thick ropes, cutting into his flesh.

As I turned, my heart racing with a mix of curiosity and trepidation, I came upon three figures. Shadows cloaked their faces, but each possessed a distinct silhouette. They huddled around the kitchen island, whispering conspiratorially. Their words, barely audible, danced on the edge of comprehension, an enigmatic puzzle I couldn't unravel.

Sunlight, filtering through the maroon drapes, infiltrated the room with glowing lines. Beyond the windowpane, the outline of trees swayed in an eerie harmony, a haunting backdrop to the unfolding scene before me. Yet, it was the floor that gripped my attention; a canvas of horror painted in shades of red.

Dana Claire

The worn-out hardwood bore witness to a malevolent tale written in blood droplets, leading an unsettling trail that snaked its way to the tormented man. The closer I got, the wider the scarlet tears expanded into ominous pools puddled at the man's feet. Was he dead, or did a flicker of life still linger, despite the crimson lake?

Jazzy said to walk around like I was actually in the room. I pictured my legs moving forward. I reached out, but nothing connected with my hands. Then I sucked in a breath. Bleach. I could smell cleaning supplies mixed in with a faint metallic scent. My fingers wiggled, trying again to touch something. The wall had no texture. The doorknob was an inert hunk of metal, impervious to my attempts to step outside and search for a mailbox number or a landmark on the driveway. The silhouettes' cloaks had no weight, nothing for my fingers to hook onto and draw them back. Like static on a radio, the voices and images fizzled and dissolved. I blinked my eyes open at the card table.

"I couldn't hold it." My heart sank into my stomach, triggering a nauseating shudder like I'd caught a nasty case of the flu and was about to vomit. I failed.

"That's okay. It's not a science, love. You did good." Doc picked up one of the pencils and offered it to me. "Now try and draw what you saw, every last detail. Use as many colors as you can, and while you sketch, tell us everything." He nodded to Jazzy. "She'll keep ahold of you to help."

I held the pencil in unsteady fingers, but once the tip hit the paper, my hand moved in a rhythm of its own, like a Ouija board. "I couldn't touch anything, like it was all made of mist."

"That's okay. What else?" Doc pushed.

I drew the background, everything I'd originally seen, first. The kitchen, the chair, the drapes. "The smells." I lifted my head, scrunching my nose. "They don't make sense."

Jazzy tapped my canvas. "Keep drawing while you talk."

"What about the smells don't make sense?" Doc pressed.

"It's run-down and rural, but no wood scent, no forest air or pine trees, no mold or must. Too clean, like antiseptic but cut with . . . metal maybe. I couldn't be sure."

My hand glided effortlessly across the pristine paper, seamlessly translating the vivid image that had taken root within the depths of my mind. Each deliberate stroke brought forth the chair and the figure slumped on it. His purposefully distressed jeans clung to his muscular thighs, while his baby blue, long-sleeved shirt hugged his well-defined chest, adorned with dark, arterial blood. His wild hair flowed, its texture appearing soft to the touch. His hands, wide and worn, were dotted with scars—as if this situation hadn't been his first run-in with violence. The tension etched upon his chiseled jawline evoked a sense of familiarity, reminding me . . .

My eyes fluttered open, and I gasped in astonishment, drawn to the detailed image that now adorned the expanse of my sketch pad. A surge of dread constricted my throat and stole my breath. Leaping from my chair, I pushed the round table aside. Fear clutched my lungs like a vice, invisible hands clawing at my throat. Tears streamed down my cheeks as I pointed my trembling finger at the drawing.

The man in the chair, drenched in his own lifeblood, was not an anonymous stranger.

It was Liam.

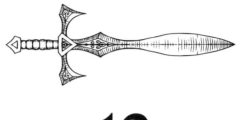

12

LIAM

I sat at the kitchen table, surrounded by books. An almost-empty pizza box rested on the adjacent chair, the lid open. The aromatic lure of fresh mozzarella and sauce lingered under my nose as I eyed the one remaining half-eaten piece staring back at me.

My phone buzzed, and Dad's name lit up on the screen.

"Hey, old man, where have you been?" I picked up the cold slice, but the soggy crust had me tossing it back into the box and closing the lid.

Dad chuckled. "Such a pleasant way to greet your father."

"Not pleasant, just accurate." I wiped the grease off my fingertips and onto my thigh. Dad and I had more of a partnership than father-son relationship. Although he'd like to pretend he'd ruled the roost since Mom's death, I'd pretty much felt like a solo act half the time. "So, you coming back to Falkville Falls?"

Dad called less and less often these days, which spoke volumes. Guilt had a funny way of messing with the mind. I imagined Dad harbored the same amount as me—if not more—for my mother turning into one of them.

"She's not there, Liam. I found her. She's in Chicago."

I sat upright. "But her second-in-command is here. He was at the crime scene."

"He may be, but she is not." He didn't lower his voice or sugarcoat it, and I was thankful for that, but it didn't ease the throb in my clenched jaw. "I've been trailing her for a week, learning her routine, seeing when she's most vulnerable." He paused, and his meaning sank into my bones. This was it. The end. Dad was preparing to make his move to kill Mom.

I glanced behind me to make sure my sister hadn't made her way back into the kitchen. "Do you want me to tell Jac? She's been a little . . ." I swallowed, forming a fist tight enough to snap my pencil. Jac had been off. Who could blame her? She always held it together, using logic rather than emotion to maintain her steady presence in our world. But now, with her feelings getting the best of her, I wasn't so sure she was stable enough to learn the truth.

"No." A dark laugh that didn't even sound like my father rang through the phone. I imagined him running his hands through his hair, pulling on the ends—something I caught myself doing when I felt stuck between a rock and a hard place. "Your sister is so much more like me than you. You're your mother's son."

"What's that supposed to mean?" My phone trembled against my ear from my hard grip. How could he say something like that? I was nothing like her. I'd never put my family through the horror she had.

"You both were born for this world. Your mother, whether she'd had hunter blood or not, would have found her way into Hunterland. Just like you."

"What are you saying? You're not a hunter? Jac's not a hunter? What the hell, Dad?" What *was* he saying? And why now?

"No. I'm not saying that at all. I love my life. I loved my wife, and I love my children. Hunterland gave me all of that. What I am saying, and something I've never told you before, is had I not been born into the world of Hunterland, I wouldn't have found it. It doesn't call to me the same way it does your mother or you. Being a hunter is what I do. I'm proud of that, but it's not who I am." My throat clogged, and I clenched my eyes. "I wouldn't change my life, not for one second, not even knowing what I have to do now. I hope you understand that."

Did I?

"I'll call when it's done, but in case you don't hear from me for a while, I love you, and for what it's worth, I am sorry."

He didn't wait for a response. The line went dead. What the hell just happened? It felt like my dad had slapped me.

The basement door flew open on a frantic Olivia. Her bloodshot eyes trapped mine.

"What? What happened?" I slid my chair back. The legs screeched against the tile floor. "Are you okay?" I stood, thoughts of my parents fading to black and white as I took in the worry lines slicing through every angle of Olivia's face.

She nervously bit her glossy lower lip, as if attempting to stifle a cry. Her brows furrowed. A sharp inhale preceded a short sob that reverberated through her trembling frame. Before I could inquire further, she rushed toward me, wrapped her arms tightly around my waist, and buried her tearstained cheek against my chest.

"It's you," she managed to utter between sniffles. "You're bleeding..." Her words hitched, consumed by her tears.

I encircled her with my arms, pulling her close until her heaving body found some semblance of calm. With my chin resting on her head, I whispered soothing words, a chant, a mantra, a promise that I had grown accustomed to uttering far too often lately between her and my sister. "It's okay. You're safe. I've got you. Just breathe."

I peered over her, straight into Jazzy's concerned eyes.

"She drew you." Jazzy rested her hand on her heart.

A joke about how handsome that drawing must be sat on the tip of my tongue, but Doc broke the silence first, his swift steps light on the stairs.

"You're captured and tied up." He braced Jazzy with a one-armed squeeze, swallowing hard. "And we can't tell if you're badly injured or dead."

"That's not exactly how I saw her tutoring going this evening," I muttered. "Can I see the drawing?"

Jazzy held up the paper while Olivia clung to me like a koala bear, her embrace unyielding and constricting my lungs. Guiding her gently, I walked us toward the sketch. Even though the outline of the person's head on the pad dipped to the floor, the undeniable resemblance was uncanny. Blood dripped from my face, leaving crimson trails that soaked into my shirt, staining it a vivid scarlet. Matching red puddles completed a macabre scene straight from a slasher or maybe Poe. I'd been in sticky situations before—a hunter rarely came out of a fight unscathed—but this looked like I might have lost the battle. For good.

"Visions aren't always accurate." Not a lie, but this one sure had details that were undeniable. Not that I wanted to admit that out loud. The blood trail alone looked nasty as hell. Staring at myself beaten to a bloody pulp didn't exactly give me warm fuzzies. But I was Liam Hunter; I wasn't going to flinch.

Jazzy shook her head. "Maybe. But I'm not sure how there's a sensible version where you aren't at least badly hurt. You mentioned this might have something to do with . . ." She paused, eyeing me.

I shook my head. "She's being handled as we speak. My dad just called." Jazzy knew what my somewhat coded answer meant. Dad had found my mother, and there'd be no future where my mother could take part in Olivia's vision.

Doc raised a brow but seemed to catch on when I shook my head.

Jazzy pulled the paper out of my hands and rolled it up small enough to stuff in her back pocket. "I'll take it home to Nikki tonight and see what she gets from it."

"Is there more than an image?" I kissed the top of Olivia's head. I hadn't meant to. It just happened. When it came to Olivia, a lot transpired without thought, as if my heart and brain couldn't get on the same page no matter how hard I tried.

Olivia didn't even seem to notice. She took a breath and pulled away, wiping her face a few times with the end of her sleeve. The smear of mascara streaked onto her cheeks like war paint, giving her eyes a wild look. I held on to her shoulders and lowered my forehead to hers. In a low voice, I asked, "Did you see anything else? Did you hear anything?"

"This is embarrassing." She sniffled, looking down at her shoes.

With my pointer finger, I lifted her chin. "Don't do that." She tried to look away, but I gently grabbed her face and brought it back to mine. "I'd never judge you for tears." A smile spread across my lips. "Especially when they're for me." I waggled my brows.

That seemed to sober her up. She smacked my chest. "Wow, your arrogance knows no bounds, Liam Hunter." Her nostrils flared. "I'm only upset because I can't see past that one scene, and I feel like I failed everyone."

Liar.

My lips rolled together as I fought to keep a smile off my face. Her fabrications were kinda cute. *Cute? Seriously?* This girl did things to me I'd take to the grave.

She shook her head. "I don't understand my abilities. I tried to hear, touch, see everything I could, but it was like running into a brick wall. Every attempt seemed to weaken the image, until it ended." Olivia dabbed at a final rogue tear with her sweater. "I'm sorry . . . I really did try." She stepped back. Heat bloomed across her cheeks in a shade of cotton-candy pink. "We need to do it again. Now. Let's go."

She pivoted, heading toward Jazzy, but I swiftly intervened, clasping her forearm. "Hey, hold on," I urged, my grip firm yet gentle as I pulled her back. "That's enough for one night. Let's give it some time. Okay?"

Her gaze lowered, fixating on my fingers entwined around her arm, before rising to meet my eyes, searching for answers. Maybe she questioned why I dared to bridge the distance I had created, or maybe she pondered the motives behind my interference. Either way, an array of questions settled into the creases of her face.

"You're too wound up to try again tonight." I pointed at her. "You can try again tomorrow if you're so hell-bent. But tonight, you rest."

"But what if—"

"Listen." I tugged on her arm, and she ventured back into my space. "I'm made of steel. I'll be fine. These visions help us evade bad futures. You've given us a starting point."

"Liam," Jazzy warned, knowing my words were as fictitious as big-foot. A vision that vague wouldn't help me evade anything, but I wasn't about to explain that to Olivia.

"Liam's right. We don't know exactly what this means. First things first. We get Nikki to look at this and provide us with probabilities." Doc hung his arm around Jazzy's shoulders. "You keep working with Olivia. She may eventually gain better access to her vision. The picture can get clearer. Sometimes we just need patience."

"See, silver lining," I said with false cheer.

Olivia sniffled, unconvinced.

Doc had always said visions weren't the be-all and end-all. I'd seen his predictions proven wrong firsthand. What concerned me most was Olivia's reaction, a full-on freak-out. Her erratic breathing and trembling body said she believed in this doomed fate. But I'd never let that happen. The only way I'd ever leave Olivia was to pursue the hunt, to keep the oath I took to Hunterland. Never in a body bag.

13

OLIVIA

I hadn't visited the local library in years, but that carpet-and-paper musk hit like I remembered. Just the right amount of comfort I needed after drawing Liam practically dead two days ago. Sleep hadn't found me in the last couple of evenings, and when it did, I'd woken up with night sweats. He said he'd be fine. But how could he be so sure?

Drive-through lattes in hand, Bradley and I bumped backpacks as we squeezed through the narrow entry scanner.

"Whoa, hot peppermint tea here." Despite his chiding, Bradley bonked our bags together again like we were battle turtles.

I choked on a sip of coffee and shushed him around a finger, having just been skewered by the eagle eye of a librarian who looked like she'd put up with enough today.

"Uh-oh." Bradley followed my gaze. "Eh, she doesn't look so bad. Back in my hometown, most librarians were reject nuns. Too angry to enter the cloth."

I swatted his bag. "They were not."

"I have the ruler marks to prove it." He rubbed his backside.

I clamped a hand over my mouth to stifle my loud "HA!"

The librarian arched her brow in a look that said, "Strike two," then returned to sorting a book cart behind the counter.

The occasional delighted squeal or tantrum whine from cavorting kids carried through the stacks while we wove our way to outlet-equipped tables by the far windows, but I supposed teenagers were held to higher standards.

As we sat, I took in the scenery, decorated with bright beanbags, construction-paper leaf cutouts, a paper mâché tree pillar, and stuffed jungle animals. I soaked it all in, absorbed in memories of coming here with a toddling Pepper. Memories that had nothing to do with Liam or monster hunters or near-death experiences. Bradley had seemed pumped when I suggested this place over the school library, where the prying Hunterland gang could easily search us out.

I couldn't even look at the Bronco anymore. Whether in my mind's eye or not, Liam was always leaning against the door, sliding over the hood, or twisting in the driver's seat to smirk at me, the wind in his hair. Hair that I now frequently imagined crusted with blood. Sitting cramped in the backseat with everybody and their powers that actually worked, feeling their knowing glances, had become torturous. That stupid vision ruined everything, including the little peace of mind I'd preserved these last few weeks. So when Bradley had chased me down the school's front steps and asked if I was down for a study session to knock out our latest English essays, I'd jumped at the chance, shooting Pepper a text that I had a different ride home.

"So, have you finished the book?"

"What do you mean?" I dragged myself back through the fog, guided by Bradley's voice.

He tapped his copy of *Frankenstein*, still wearing that open, childish smile. Nobody else in my life could smile like that. They'd seen too much. Or I should say, nobody *left* in my life. Jessica had smiled like that. She and Bradley lived in the moment. Right now, his biggest trouble was coming up with a thousand words and a thesis. I shook myself, but my grin felt strained. Even in English class, I couldn't escape talking about monsters.

"Not quite." I rubbed my forehead and clutched my warm coffee cup with my other hand. "Okay, I'm barely halfway, but I've got the SparkNotes."

He chuckled. "It's dense, huh?"

"Yeah, and so depressing. I can't read more than a few pages before I start stressing out."

"Yeah, it always sucks, watching the world kill something beautiful."

"Huh?" Curiosity snapped me fully into the moment.

"The monster. He starts out so pure. But because he *looks* like a walking corpse, no one can see that. They just see a monster. But he was a man first. Or . . . more like a boy. He didn't know anything, and the only thing people taught him was how to be ugly inside, to match their perception of his outside."

My jaw dangled. "Wow. Are you sure you need a study partner? It sounds like you've already got your paper written." Beautiful. He'd called a monster beautiful. Because, well, it wasn't real. It was fiction, and Bradley had no reason to ever question that like I had, from the moment I started reading, shuddering at the thought that reanimating a patchwork corpse might be plausible. If Liam read it, he'd probably start strategizing how to kill Victor Frankenstein's creation from the moment it took its first breath.

Bradley thumbed the pages of his book. "I just sympathize with the guy. My mom always found the good in people even if they didn't deserve it. She was a scientist, loved studying human behaviors. She never judged." He shrugged. "She knew what assumptions could do. I guess I'd like to think I follow in her footsteps in that way."

"That's so sweet." I squeezed his forearm. "I understand what you mean. I've been fighting an assumption of my own lately. Everyone keeps telling me I'm wrong." I let out a breath. "Maybe I am." I smiled. "Maybe this is exactly what I needed to hear."

He placed his hand over mine. "Glad I could help."

I nudged him with my shoulder. "Anyway, who could assume anything bad about you? You have, like, golden-retriever energy."

He stifled his laugh in the crook of his elbow, big frame shaking. "Thank you," he finally choked out. "I think."

"It's a good thing," I assured through a soft laugh.

"Some of my relatives are . . . rough around the edges, and people think what they wanna think. I get the impression the accusations make them act worse. Like they're leaning into the label . . . or something."

"I get it. I had a delinquent for a sister there for a little while. I don't know if I handled it well, but I always knew she did that stuff because she was hurting. Even if I'd just raked her over the coals, I'd go to war if anybody else made a comment about her, you know?"

Bradley's smiling cheeks touched his lower lashes. "Totally. I don't agree with everything my family does either, but I'd take a bullet for them. For anyone I loved."

"Exactly."

"So, you wanna teach this golden retriever some tricks? Like how to turn what I said about Frankenstein's monster into a proper thesis?"

I tapped my pencil on my scratch pad, where I'd started a rough outline of my essay yesterday. "Well . . . it sounds like you're saying the story is about prejudice."

"Yeah. I mean, Miss Hansen put that on the board as a theme, day one."

Well, damn, I needed to start paying better attention. Bradley didn't seem to notice my embarrassed flush. Still, even if I was stating the obvious, it felt good to talk about a monster like it couldn't hurt me. Maybe we could watch *Frankenstein* at movie night tomorrow. I almost said something, then snapped my teeth together. A bunch of my hunter friends watching a monster flick in front of my one normal friend? Total disaster. Jac would give a giddy rundown of her favorite weapons while Liam strategized his capture and kill plan in militaristic detail.

"Look at this line." Bradley flipped to a dog-eared page in his book. His finger traced the words as he read aloud. "'Accursed creator! Why did you form a monster so hideous that even YOU turned from me in disgust? God, in pity, made man beautiful and alluring, after his own image; but my form is a filthy type of yours, more horrid even from the very resemblance.' How could his creator abandon him knowing she did that to him? She's the one to blame."

"She?"

Bradley shook his head, his cheeks dotted pink. "He. Frankenstein. You know what I mean." He closed the book. "Even when the monster starts killing, you can't hate him, because his creator drove him to it and never taught him any better. Victor assumes the culprit is his monster all along, with no proof, even though he's essentially Victor's son. How's that for betrayal? I don't blame him for wanting revenge."

I frantically flipped back through my sparse chicken scratches. "Did revenge happen to be on Miss Hansen's list of themes, too? Because you could run with that." I tapped a finger on the page I wanted. "Oh yeah, I actually managed to get that one down. 'The dangers of revenge. How does the shift into revenge rob the monster of the humanity he craves?'"

Bradley rested his chin on a propped fist, staring unabashedly into my eyes. "Think she'll flunk me if my essay doesn't agree with that?"

"Nah. She likes opposing opinions. You just need to have proof, or she'll rip you apart."

Bradley opened his laptop. "Then I'm going to argue the monster's revenge was warranted. Victor's wasn't."

"Ah, so set it up as a compare and contrast. That'll work. But let me play devil's advocate?"

"Sure." He formed that open-mouthed, golden-retriever smile that made me imagine a big tongue lolling out the side. "But if I'm challenging the devil, shouldn't I have a fiddle?"

I laughed. "You know, Liam would . . ." I swallowed, slammed again by the nightmarish image of Liam crumpled in a chair. If that vision came to be, he might never blast his outlaw country tunes again. "He loves that song," I finished lamely. "I can't get into the twangy stuff."

"Ah well, I spent five years listening to music like that. Guess it got under my skin a little," said Bradley, grin slipping. "So, what's your question?"

"Why is the monster's vengeance justified? If some revenge is justifiable, then why isn't all of it? Where do you draw the line?"

Bradley leaned back, the line of his mouth serious now, thoughtful. "Because the monster is corrupted innocence, and Victor is the corruptor who can't handle the consequences of his actions. Revenge was the only way the monster could claim any power or any identity. Victor saw to that. By the end, it's the only way the monster can keep existing as a free person. Not that he was ever truly free."

I wasn't sure I agreed, but hey, I hadn't finished the book. What did I know?

Bradley swayed back into my space, arms on the table, and I saw marks in his palms where he'd dug his nails. I scrunched my brow but said nothing.

"So, now I've got my thesis"—he tapped my laptop—"Let's figure out yours."

We spent another hour in the library's solace. By the end of all the whispered chatter and ambient pencil scratching and keyboard clicking, I managed to get halfway back home in Bradley's car before the anxiety started knotting in my solar plexus again.

"We should do that more often. I clearly need help with my note-taking," I said over the radio.

Bradley turned the volume down and glanced my way. "Absolutely." His eyes widened. "Not about the note thing."

I laughed, and he joined in. God, it felt good to laugh.

"I mean, I had a good time," he clarified.

"Same time next week maybe?"

"Sure. And movie night's still on for Friday?"

"Yep!"

A minute of easy silence passed as we turned onto my road. "Hey, Olivia?"

"Hmm?"

"Thanks for making me feel welcome. It's been a long time since someone brought out my golden-retriever side."

I knew exactly how he felt. It had been a long time since someone brought the normal out of me too. I just wondered if my new world would one day swallow up the old and I'd never find it again.

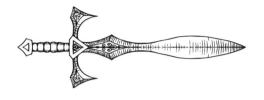

14

LIAM

Friday rolled around faster than I wanted. The only positive news this week came on Wednesday, when Nikki confirmed Olivia's drawing wasn't me. Didn't mean the situation wouldn't happen, but at least I should be safe. But now, here we were on my favorite night, and I had to spend it with Olivia's new buddy.

I understood why he drew her interest. Bradley didn't remind her of the new scary world she had been thrown into. He provided an escape. But it didn't make my blood boil any less, watching them at school laughing at each other's jokes or hanging on to each other's every word. Even though I'd given her up and there didn't seem to be anything romantic between them didn't mean it didn't bother me watching someone else make her smile.

Tonight, Jazzy and Nikki were helping Doc settle into their rented house in the heart of town. Beth, his sister, requested he go live with the twins during their stay in Falkville Falls, to provide the parental supervision she couldn't from Hunterland's library in London. Which meant this weekend I'd move down into Doc's bedroom, farther away from Olivia and the temptation of her body. It was easier this way, I told myself.

Now she wouldn't try to sneak in, and I wouldn't have to lock my door. We could go on pretending I wasn't avoiding her. Jac would move into the guest room that I had inhabited since moving into the Davis home, finally getting a bed and space of her own.

She deserved it. Fourteen was too old to be sleeping on a blow-up mattress.

Life as a hunter continued to be a moving target. It wasn't unusual for us to relocate from place to place, hunt to hunt. But somehow, since Jac and I had moved in with the Davis family, I experienced firsthand the comforts of stable living quarters. Even sleeping in the same bed every night had calmed me in ways I'd never thought possible. Moments at the Davis house felt like a dream, one I'd never told anyone I'd had before. One I'd never realized that my dad, based on what he'd said, might have shared.

Many times, I'd imagined Dad, Mom, Jac, and I living a mundane life in some four-bedroom home in the suburbs. Mom would have been an awesome detective, Dad a firefighter. Jac would have been in the marching band and probably president of some vegan healthy-living society. I might have played football or hockey, been a film production major when I went off to college.

But my family, from generation to generation, never had those opportunities. Instead, we had roles forced on us. The heads of the Hunterland community.

The only family gifted with the serum. The sole proprietors of the Hunterland estate and wealth. Whatever privileges you wanted to name, the one thing we didn't have was a choice.

A life where monsters didn't exist and our greatest troubles were minor, everyday complaints was nothing but a pipe dream. And now, as the kernels sizzled and popped, reality crashed on my head. Some ordinary Joe could give my girl something I never could: a future.

"How long does it take to make popcorn?" Jac asked as she entered the kitchen, dragging the bottoms of her pink sweatpants across the floor. They looked four inches too long . . . and familiar, with that rainbow stripe up the sides.

And then it hit me. Those were Mom's.

I averted my gaze as I poured the warm, buttery popcorn into a bowl. Jac would be embarrassed if she knew I'd noticed. Wearing them was one thing before we knew Veronica was a monster. Now, it said a whole lot more.

"Well, are you growing corn in here? Or is it ready?"

Jac's gaze followed mine to the overflowing container.

"Really, Liam. Were you going to bring it in the morning? We're starving."

"Depends. Is Bradley still yapping out there?"

Jac clucked her tongue. "And here I thought you didn't care. What did you say again?" Jac tapped her finger to her lips. "Oh, that's right. You said, 'Olivia should have normal friends.'"

"Whatever." I shoved the dish in her direction. "Be a doll and take that to the couch."

Jac curtsied before grabbing it. "Yes, Your Majesty."

I followed her in, taking the spot next to Pepper on the love seat.

"So, where'd you grow up?" Dustin asked Bradley as he retrieved his soda can from the coffee table.

"The suburbs of Chicago. I loved it there." Bradley dove into the popcorn bowl and stuffed his face.

"If you loved it so much, why are you here?" I extended my arm over the back of the couch.

"Liam," Olivia scolded.

I scrunched my brows in her direction. It was a perfectly normal question.

"No that's okay. It's a fair ask." Bradley patted Olivia's thigh. "Someone killed my mom, and it led my family here."

Olivia lifted her chin. "What?"

"Oh my God, that's awful." Jac covered her mouth.

"Why didn't you tell me that the other night in the library?" Olivia twisted in her seat to face Bradley. "That's why you were talking about her in the past tense. I didn't even realize it." She nibbled on her lower lip. "I am so sorry."

"I don't really talk about it much." Bradley shrugged. "Still hurts."

"We lost our mother too. We know how it feels," Pepper added.

"See, you're not alone." Olivia squeezed his leg before moving her hand back to her lap.

My eyes narrowed in on their touch and I ground my teeth so hard I feared they'd break.

"Yeah, man. Losing a parent is no fun." Dustin reached for the remote. "Sorry for your loss. You're in good company, though. We've all been there." I groaned audibly. Was this guy seriously trying to pull on our heartstrings with a dead mother act?

Pepper pinched my leg. "Liam!"

"Ow, what was that for?" I pushed Pepper's hand away and rubbed the afflicted spot. She normally sided with me. Where was her loyalty? Had I lost the Liam Hunter charm to Bradley the Bozo?

"Isn't it awful that Bradley lost his mother, to a murder no less?" Pepper's eyes widened, like she was trying to tell me I had to be nice now because he had a dead parent. Join the club. Everyone in this room had a dead parent. Even Dustin, whose dad died of a heart attack when he was in elementary school. He seemed to really like his stepfather, but he still knew the ache of that loss.

"How do you know she was murdered?" If this guy wanted drama, I'd bite, but he'd have to give up the details for his theatrics to work on me.

"Liam," Jac warned.

"What?" I glared at my sister. "He brought it up."

"Liam, is the interrogation necessary? I'm sure it's hard for Bradley to talk about." As Olivia twisted in her seat, her thigh pressed up against Bradley's, and I could feel a hot burn zip through my chest. "I'm sorry about him. He lost his mother too. I'm *sure*"—she stared at me with pointed accusation—"he didn't mean anything by his question."

"It's fine." Bradley waved off Olivia. "Actually, it's interesting you should ask." Bradley's lips twisted.

"I don't really think it's interesting at all." I crossed my leg over my shin and lay back into the cushions behind me. "But odd that you would think so." I waved my hand, enticing him to continue. "Well, how'd she die?"

My sister and Olivia groaned in unison.

Give a dog a bone, isn't that the saying?

"She was killed at work." Bradley eyed me up and down as if waiting for a reaction.

"Man, what did she do for a living?" Dustin laughed uncomfortably. He took another sip of his soda and let out a burp.

"Gross," Olivia complained, lip curled at Dustin.

Pepper and my sister leaned in, all anxious to hear Bradley's answer. But I was more eager to hear the lie. There was no way this story was legit. Unless she'd worked for the mob, why would she be killed at work?

"She was a procurement organ preservation specialist."

"A what?" Pepper asked while her hand mindlessly dove into the popcorn bowl she retrieved from Bradley.

"She worked for the hospital inspecting organs and finding them new homes."

"Fascinating," Jac whispered at the same time Pepper said, "Cool."

"Doesn't sound like a dangerous job to me." Unless . . . "Was she dealing in the black market?"

Bradley snickered. "Yeah, something like that. Anyway, she couldn't deliver product, and they killed her. Used her organs instead."

"Oh, Bradley." Olivia took his hand in hers and threaded their fingers. I had the sudden urge to jump off the couch and make Bradley meet his mother's fate. "I am so sorry. What about your dad?"

I clenched my fists in my lap until my knuckles went white with the struggle of restraint.

"He's here with me and my three brothers. Justice will one day be served." Bradley stared as if the words were meant for me. Or maybe he was trying to look intimidating, but whatever his intention, the only prickle on my skin surfaced in surprise. Bradley Sanders was a lot of things, but his story proved to be the one thing I'd never expected: honest.

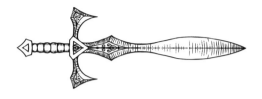

15

LIAM

Matt honked his horn for the third time, impatient as a fledgling vamp. The discovery of five more bodies earlier this morning had motivated the town sheriff to forgo his day off, and consequently, my ass had to follow. The new victims, five hikers, had been ripped to shreds, their chest cavities devoid of hearts, just like the campers. Matt had asked Nikki and I to join him down at the police station, where we would examine the fresh crime scene photos and compare them to the previous ones.

I swung open the basement door and called for Nikki. Her morning session with Olivia sounded more like a workout of the mouths. Each time I'd discreetly eavesdropped, I'd heard snide remarks and sarcastic jabs when I wanted to hear groans and thumps from productive sparring.

"There's been another killing. We've got to go. Matt's already on the street honking like his wheel's on fire. Hurry up!" I crammed the last bite of my egg sandwich into my mouth. Between munches, I added, "Olivia, Doc said he'll be here in an hour to go over some hunter lore with you. Be showered and ready." I wiped the ketchup lingering at the crook of mouth with my forearm. When no one answered, I shouted, "Nikki, let's get a move on!"

Nikki bounded up the steps, taking two at a time. "Keep your pants on." She gave me the once-over, batting her lashes. "Or not. I can think of better things we can do that don't involve a smelly precinct. Of course, you'll need to strip."

I shot her a condescending smirk, knowing she wasn't serious. "Not happening. Not even if you promised me all the sex in the world in a pool of ketchup. Now let's go."

Nikki's nose twisted. "Ew. Even your kinks are gross." She slipped her arms inside her peacoat. "Seriously, who likes ketchup as much as you do?"

"Just move." I ushered her out the door and walked toward the Bronco. The bitter chill in the air rivaled the frigid temperatures between Nikki and Olivia.

When I got in the car, I revved the engine and blasted the heat, warming my hands over the vents. Maybe one day we could have a hunt in Hawaii or San Diego. Somehow all the monsters lived in the snow-covered mountains and loved to come out and play during the off seasons. Would a little sunshine be too much to ask?

Nikki slammed her door with more force than necessary. She kicked up her heels on the dashboard and crossed her arms, sporting a full-on pout.

"I'm pretty sure the car doesn't deserve your wrath. Get your feet down." I swatted her legs, and she moved them. I'd take the small win. "What has a bee up your ass?"

She glared at me like I was supposed to know.

"What?" I asked, even more annoyed.

"Your girlfriend."

A small grin formed on my face, appreciating Olivia's uncanny ability to get under Nikki's skin. It felt like a long-overdue taste of her own medicine. Nikki had always been the type to stir up trouble, unaffected by the opinions of others. But ever since Olivia came into our lives, Nikki's cool had fled out the window, and I couldn't be more entertained.

"And right there." Nikki pointed at my mouth. "That's why I don't like her."

"I didn't even say anything." I tried suppressing my amusement with a cough as I put the car in reverse and pulled out of the driveway. Snow and ice lined the roads, reminding me of the salt barriers we'd laid out at the Davis house when it had been inhabited by a vengeful spirit. Again, hunting in warmer weather would be a nice change.

"Oh, no?" Nikki turned to face me. "The Liam I know would have denied she was your girlfriend. In fact, I'm pretty sure you would have made some sexist or derogatory comment about girls just for me teasing you about a significant other. But with Miss I Can Poorly Predict the Future, you get all moony and let that bollocks slide without a comment or argument otherwise."

"You are being ridiculous and theatrical. Ridiculous is par for the course." My brow rose. "Theatrical is kinda surprising. Isn't that what you claim Olivia is?" I taunted, hearing her this morning make the same jab toward Olivia.

"Eavesdropper!"

I threw her a sidelong glance that said, *Are you surprised?*

As I pulled onto the main highway, I noticed Matt's cruiser a couple cars in front of us. And he thought we'd be late. I'd probably beat the guy there.

"I'm not being theatrical. That girl has been a basket case since she drew you. And even when I gave logical reasoning it wasn't you, she fought me to the death over whether I was sure. She even brought it into our sparring sessions this week. I'd punch, and she'd retaliate with another scenario for how I could be wrong. It was draining. She ended up clocking me in the chin at one point because I lost concentration, what with her yapping on like a lapdog." Nikki rubbed at her jaw as if remembering the sneaky punch.

"Drawing someone you know beaten and battered would unsettle anyone." I flicked her thigh. "Even someone as tough as you."

Nikki groaned. "Whatever."

"You sure it's not me?"

"I'm pretty confident. The odds are in your favor." She tapped her lower lip. "It feels too civilized, calculated, very un-monster-like."

"There are monsters who act sophisticated."

She cocked a brow. "Really? You mean like Reginald, one of the Origins? Because that's what your girlfriend brought up." She slathered the word *girlfriend* with mockery, as if hoping to provoke a reaction, but she only succeeded in escalating her own frustration. Deep down, I secretly enjoyed it, even though I was fully aware of the bittersweet reality that such a relationship would forever remain an unattainable fantasy. And here I thought monsters would be the highlight of my believed fiction.

"Olivia might be right. I mean look what happened a couple months ago when Reginald got ahold of Pepper and used her to find my family."

"Did he hurt her?"

"Well, no. But he could have," I argued.

"Why would you think that? Did he act violent?"

"No."

"Then what would torturing Pepper have accomplished? His natural instinct is to use charm to manipulate his prey because that's what the more evolved vamps do. All our lore tells us that the Origins and those they made through their bloodline have a code of conduct. That drawing doesn't fit the mold. Plus, they cast shadows in the drawing, which means sunlight. If they were vamps, they would have burned."

I glared at Nikki. "Why didn't you just say that in the beginning?"

She shrugged. "This seemed more fun."

I groaned. "Okay, what about occultists?"

"What about them? Witches like my family are either hunters or unaware of their abilities, and bad witches only like to cause mischief and sudden death. There are no remnants in the image to suggest witches either. What would they torture you for, anyway?"

I thrummed my fingers on the steering wheel. "The Hunterland fortune?"

Nikki wrinkled her forehead. "Do you even know how to access that money? Because I could use a new pair of Jimmy Choos if you do."

My lips twisted. "Funny." I held up my finger. "I might not know, but Doc does, and so does my dad."

"Okay, then a witch would go after them. Plus, they don't have serum strength. Even if they were trained like Jazzy and me, we are no match for you, especially after a dose. They are human. And besides, witches have plenty of other ways to get rich. They certainly aren't going to torture a hunter for it." Nikki rubbed her hands together. "What else you got?"

"Werewolves?" I squinted.

"Because you know where all the best hearts live?"

"All right, you got jokes today, huh?" That *did* seem unlikely, but since we were in the middle of a werewolf case, it wasn't completely out of the question.

Nikki flipped her ponytail. "When am I not funny?"

"You don't really want me to answer that."

Nikki waved me off. "Back to the question. It could be, but why aren't there claw marks?"

My mind wandered to the last crime scene photos. "I don't know. But right about now, I'm ready for the unexpected, and that would certainly be unexpected."

Nikki tapped her bottom lip. "There's something else that adds to my probability stats."

"What?"

Nikki bent down and grabbed her purse. She unzipped the top and pulled out the drawing. My gaze darted from the road to the image. She pointed to the arms tied to the chair. "You're not wearing your hunter watch." She looked up at me. "Do you still take it off when you sleep?"

"Yeah," I admitted. Only Nikki knew why because, other than Olivia, only Nikki had made it into my bed enough times to notice.

"Nightmares?" She peeked over, the creases around her eyes showing she shared in the pain she knew they caused me. Her father's death had given her similar scars.

"Not as often, but yeah, I still relive my mom's murder." The watch had always picked up my increased heart rate and ended up waking Dad and Jac. It had happened so often none of us were getting any sleep. I'd started taking the watch off before bed to save my family from restless nights. Only Dad, Jac, and Nikki knew. But since living at the Davises' house, I hadn't had any night terrors.

"Keep it on from now on."

I nodded. "Did you tell Olivia about the watch?"

Nikki looked out the window away from me. "No." Her breath fogged the glass.

"Why?" When she didn't say anything, I tapped her forearm resting on the center console. "Nikki?"

When she turned back, her jaw tensed, a muscle popping in the lower left side. "Don't read into this too much, okay? I still don't like her."

"Okay?" I tilted my head waiting for Nikki to elaborate.

Nikki blew out a breath. "If she knew I was aware you didn't wear your watch at night, she'd probably get upset and think it's because we used to . . . ya know." Nikki shrugged.

I started to laugh, and Nikki shoved me hard. The wheel jiggled but I righted it quickly, still chuckling.

"Stop it right now or I'll . . ."

I mock-gasped. "Look at that, Nikki Patel does have a heart."

Nikki slapped my shoulder for good measure. "Whatever. Just don't read into it, okay? I still don't like your girlfriend."

For the first time, I actually wondered if that was true. I'd never known her to curb her responses to save another's feelings. There was hope for those two after all.

———————

We entered the precinct and headed straight for Matt, who stood next to three of his guys.

"I'm telling you, Sheriff, I think we have a rabid animal on the loose. We need to involve animal control. Maybe it's a mountain lion or black bears," the one I thought was named Officer Apple said. Back when we were investigating Falkville Falls High's hangings, this cop had brought a vamp case to the sheriff's attention. Only he'd had no idea a blood-sucker committed the killings. He'd chalked that one up to an animal too. How many times could they reason away brutal deaths with that lame excuse?

"Animal control has been alerted, and they are keeping an eye out. There's not much else they can do." The crinkles in Matt's forehead told me more than his words. He knew animal control stood no chance of stopping the beasts that plagued these forests, but it wasn't like he could tell his men that.

The officer removed his hat and held it to his chest. "What makes us all nervous is how close they're getting to the main roads." He lowered his voice. "People are talking about taking matters into their own hands. There's been hearsay the townsfolk have formed hunting groups. Should we enforce a curfew? Keep people in their homes at night? We have to do something."

"Office Apple, I hear your concerns. I think extra patrols after dark will suffice for now. We don't need the town in an uproar, panicking that they'll be eaten by a bunch of mountain lions or black bears." Matt squeezed his officer's shoulder.

"All right, boss." Officer Apple nodded.

Then, louder for the whole precinct to hear, Matt announced, "Business as usual. If you have townsfolk asking questions, you tell them this is an ongoing investigation, and when we know more, we will let them know. Until then, we will continue to keep the inhabitants of this fine town safe. But if they take matters into their own hands, we cannot guarantee that. They need to let us do our jobs. That is all."

The sheriff turned, seeing us at the entrance. "You two, my office." He pointed to his door.

Nikki and I walked through the arranged desk aisles to the back of the station. Eyes followed us, probably wondering why two teenage kids were here during all this commotion. A moment later, Matt followed, shutting the door behind him.

"This is a mess." He slapped his desk with two file folders as he plopped into his leather office chair. "We need to stop this before more people are killed."

Nikki and I sat in the two seats opposite Matt. I leaned back and crossed my leg over my thigh. "Agreed. That's why we are here."

Nikki reached out. "Can I see the crime scene pictures of the hikers?"

Matt handed over a folder. "Be my guest. To me, it looks just like what my guys are saying: another savage animal attack."

I could hear the frustration in Matt's voice. It was not easy being in charge knowing the impossible truth but unable to speak it or even fully accept it. Your instincts told you otherwise because of experience, and monsters were all new to Matt. His intuition and natural impulses fought to deny such claims, as any rational person would.

I watched Nikki flip through the photographs, coming back to one picture several times. "That's odd."

"What is?" I leaned over her shoulder for a peek and almost fell out of my chair.

"These." Nikki pointed to two of the five victims. Their bodies lay on top of each other a good six inches or more away from the other three bodies. Bloody as they appeared, more skin remained on their bones, whereas the other victims' flesh hung in tattered patches. "The same wolf killed these two. It committed less savagery because it went after two hearts instead of savoring one."

I grabbed the image out of her hand and perused it myself. She was right. Plus, these two bodies had been separated, or possibly corralled, from the group, cornered by one animal.

Matt pushed out of his chair, then walked around his desk to stand behind me. "How do you know?"

"The markings on the body," I answered. My eyes traced the claw marks. "The lines in their chests share similar patterns. It's a hunting style, a preferred kill method. Rare, if not impossible, that two wolves would share it."

I looked up at Matt's scrunched face, the expression pulled between confusion and disgust.

"It's like your signature. You usually write your name the same way, right?" I asked.

Matt shrugged a shoulder. "Well, yeah. I guess."

"You wouldn't go out of your way to write your name differently; your method comes from natural muscle memory. Same thing with killing. This pattern on both bodies is how this particular monster gets his hearts."

Nikki smacked my arm. "Not only that, but look at this . . ." She handed me another photo, then a second, and a third.

I grabbed the images with one hand and rubbed the spot she'd hit with the other. "You're so violent."

"Shut up and just look at them." She pointed to the specks of red on the foliage.

"That's a blood-spatter trail leading from the crime scene to the road," Matt explained. "What's strange about that?"

"That's not all. Look at the tracks in the dirt, in between the leaves." I traced my finger around the grooves.

Footprints. In the most recent crime scene, the paw indents changed yards away from the bodies meaning the werewolves shifted back after eating a heart, but the blood droplets continued in a steady line. I looked up, knowing Matt had no idea what both Nikki and I had noticed.

"One of the werewolves killed two bodies because they were bringing a heart back to another wolf. The blood specks are fat and circular. It's a drip pattern, not smears or high velocity spatter, from one heart being carried away from the scene." I pointed to the red splotches dotting the earth, then moved my fingers back to the images at the crime scene. "Here there's pawprints. Too many for me to be sure if there were four or five werewolves, but watch . . ." I flipped to the next picture. "They change to human footprints." I flipped to another picture. "All different sizes, and by my count, four sets, making that four werewolves. One heart eater is missing."

"I think the four of them are all men," Nikki added, looking from my boots to Matt's. "The sizes are too big and wide to be female."

"I agree." I handed the file back to Matt. "Give Nikki the first set of crime scene photos. The ones of the campers."

Matt stepped in front of my chair and leaned over his desk. He retrieved the second folder and handed it to Nikki. She breezed through it and then turned it over to me. It didn't take very long to see the same pattern.

"One of our bad guys is killing for another. I'm thinking there's a werewolf kid in all of this."

"What?" Matt's eyes widened. He removed his cap and rubbed his forearm against his forehead. "You think an innocent child is involved?"

"Not innocent." Nikki kicked her heels up onto Matt's desk and leaned back. "He or she is still a monster, but yeah, I think a child is involved too," she echoed. "The parent may be trying to make sure the kid doesn't get bloodthirsty, which is kinda wild because most monsters don't think like that. But it makes sense, in this case. I mean, werewolves are still human. The disease heightens their emotions, protectiveness included."

In our last case, we'd found out that vampires turned by Origins, the first vampires to exist, had more humanity than those farther away from the pure bloodline. "It could be similar to vampires. Maybe the werewolves that don't kill to obtain human hearts have more resolve than the beasts that kill for bloodlust."

Matt scratched his head. "What am I supposed to do with that? Do I start looking for four men and a kid? How does that help my investigation?" Matt plopped back in his chair.

"It's a pack, either a small one, or one part of a bigger pack. So yeah, the best thing we can do is start looking for four male adults and one child. Whether they live locally or are just visiting in town, I have no idea."

Matt pressed his fingers into his forehead, then grabbed the landline phone. "Officer Apple, please get me a list of all the children in the elementary school that do not have a mother listed as a legal guardian." He paused. "And while you're at it, check with the hotels and motels and see if a family of five have arrived recently in town, especially without a female adult." The deep baritone voice on the other line questioned his request. "I don't have to tell you why. I'm the sheriff. Just do it." Matt slammed the phone onto the receiver.

"Wait a minute." I jumped from my seat. "Motel. You just said *motel*. Have your guys call the Apricot Inn and ask them if one of the three rooms has four men and a kid or even just four men. They might be hiding the kid, so no one sees him or her."

"That's a great idea. Maybe we will get lucky." Matt picked up his office phone and started to bark out more orders.

Nikki pushed out of her seat and rubbed her hands together. "You ready?" She looked at me. The skin between her eyes crinkled.

As we exited the precinct, I grabbed her arm and swung her around to face me. "What are you thinking?" I arched my brow in a pointed stare. "You're doing that weird face-scrunch, nose-twitch thing you do when you have an unfavorable thought."

"You're not going to like it."

"Oh, I know I'm not." Impatience jolted my tongue. "Just spit it out."

"Do you think Pepper could tell if a human was a werewolf if she's in close proximity?"

My eyes widened. "What?"

Nikki stepped out of my grip and rubbed her palms down her face. "If Matt can figure out who the kid wolf is, maybe we can get Pepper in the same room to talk to them, see if she picks up anything."

"Are you nuts? You want to, on a hunch, put Pepper in front of possible werewolves? Olivia would never—"

Nikki held up her hand. "Stop right there. Olivia and you have one stupid commonality that needs to end now. Neither of you can dictate what another hunter wants and/or does. Pepper would do this. I know she would. She's weird, but fearless."

I gritted my teeth. Of course Pepper would. But the potential cost was what mattered. And that went beyond her safety. Pepper's ability scared me because sometimes I believed she sympathized with the monsters, that she thought they could be good—and that was more dangerous than all the monsters combined. That could lead to Hunterland's demise.

16

PEPPER

The wind blew strands of blue hair across my face as we stepped out of the grocery. I had heard whispers the entire time I perused the aisles but every time I'd turn to locate the source, only Doc, Jazzy, and Jac were there. Spirits loved to find me at the strangest moments. The shower. During an exam. Even while sleeping. But their whispers were distant echoes compared to when a vampire or werewolf spoke. Those voices rang clear as day. But this low vocal sound in the store didn't fit either bill, its words a *wa-wa* too loud to be a ghost but at the same time too murky to identify as a supernatural being—almost like he or she was being muffled.

"You think Liv and Nikki are okay together?" Jazzy asked, wrapping her purple scarf around her neck. "Actually, forget I asked about my sister. Do you think Liv is okay?"

The reason the three of us tagged along with Doc had less to do with needing food and more to do with Nikki and Livy holed up in the basement, sparring. Doc thought it'd be a good idea to let those two have alone time since Saturday's lesson was cut short when Liam and Nikki went to the precinct with Matt. The rest of us just wanted clear of the firing range of their perpetual wrath. Nikki and Livy needed more than alone time; they needed couples counseling.

"If by okay, you mean overbearing, protective, and wound too tight as usual, then yeah, I'm sure she's great." I rubbed my gloves together, breathing heat into them. The chill in the air seeped through my bones.

Jazzy and I loaded the bags from the cart into the trunk while Jac arranged them from the backseat and Doc started the car to warm it. Even though he'd moved out, he'd promised to keep our fridge stocked so we still ate like kings.

Before Doc arrived, all I knew were a couple homemade dishes Livy cooked up and the local restaurants. Dad hadn't been much of a chef and certainly wasn't home enough to practice.

Jazzy chuckled, taking the empty cart and motioning for me to follow her to the designated corral. I handed Jac my purse, Livy's protection charms clanking together as Jac tossed it into the backseat.

I was about to comment that my sister and Liam should just hook up already so maybe she'd chillax when Bradley Sanders materialized from behind a minivan.

"Pepper," he said, his hands shoved into his jean pockets, "is that you?"

I gave him a two-finger wave as he continued in our direction, his blond locks blowing in the breeze like a hair commercial.

"Bloody hell, this guy," Jazzy mumbled, pushing the trolley back into the cart return. Metal clanged as it locked into place.

"Aren't you cold?" I took inventory of his clothing—sneakers, jeans, and a long-sleeved T-shirt. Both Jazzy and I had on our puffy jackets, mine zipped up to my chin against the frigid air.

Bradley looked away as he rocked back on his heels. "Not really a jacket guy."

"Who says that?" Jazzy pursed her lips.

I elbowed Jazzy in the side.

"Your sister here?"

"She's home. But you should call her." I smiled.

"Or not," Jazzy mumbled.

I threaded my arm through Jazzy's, pulling her to my side. "I'm sure she'd love to hear from you. See you at school." I rushed off, dragging Jazzy with me to the car. "You don't have to be *so* rude. He's not a bad guy."

"I don't like him."

"I don't know why."

Can you hear me, kid?

My whole body stilled. The voice was no longer blocked.

Well, it's about time. Don't turn around. Just listen.

I closed my eyes. *You may want to unfreeze and blink. You're gonna give our little convo away.*

Deep breaths. I've got this. I wasn't sure if my little pep talk was for myself or the werewolf chirping in my ear, but I heard him chuckle anyway.

"Pepper, what's wrong with you?" Jazzy's hand landed on my shoulder as she shook me. "It's like you left earth for a second."

Tell her you need to use the restroom.

My eyes snapped open. "I have to pee," I blurted out, so loudly it got Jac's and Doc's attention.

"We're two minutes away from home, Poppet. Can it wait?" Doc asked as he shut the trunk that we forgot to close.

I started to dance, holding my crotch.

Well, that'll get them to believe you. Creative and disturbing to watch.

Shut up!

"Oh, dear heavens, just go," Doc said, exasperated. "We'll be in the car, waiting." He rounded to the driver's seat and slipped inside.

"I've gotta go too," Jac said as she shut the half-open back door. "Brrr. It's freezing." She interlaced her arm through mine. "We won't be long. Blast the heat, will ya." She threw the words over her shoulder as Jazzy took the front passenger seat.

Smooth, kid. Looks like you'll need to listen fast since we now have company. Guess the pee-pee dance didn't work.

I groaned.

"What's wrong with you?" Jac pulled me into her side as she blew a white puff into the air. "Do you feel okay? You're acting weirder than normal."

"Umm, yeah. I'm good. I just hate holding it."

The creases around Jac's eyes softened. "Me too, and Liam never stops to let me go. He always makes fun of my bladder size. It's not that small. I think I just metabolize fast. Plus, I eat a lot of vegetables, and they act like diuretics. I've had to go since we were in the frozen-food aisle."

I can't talk to you like this. We need to meet. Tomorrow. Same place you first saw me in wolf form. Don't bring your friends. They're annoying.

Panic shot through me. *Don't leave.* If we could find out why Fenton and Veronica were investigating, maybe Jac and Liam wouldn't be so sad about their mom. Maybe she was on our side. *Who are the werewolves killing in Falkville Falls? Why are you looking into it?*

I broke out of Jac's hold and spun in a stationary circle, desperately trying to find Fenton. He had to be nearby. My eyes darted in every direction. A woman with a stroller crossed my path. I dodged in front of her. Then two skateboarding teenagers nearly ran me over. I spun, avoiding a collision.

Finally, my gaze landed on a tall, broad-shouldered man, wearing a navy-blue hoodie that would barely block out the cold, walking away from me. His salt-and-pepper hair reminded me of the gray coat of the wolf we'd met in the woods.

See you soon, kid.

A Jeep wrangler with tinted windows pulled up, and he jumped in. He never turned around, but his hand came over his shoulder as he waved goodbye.

You. It's you. Wait!

I ran. My legs moved faster than ever before as I chased the car down, but I never came close. It sped away the second the guy got inside, tires squealing as they hightailed it out of the lot.

"Pepper, what the hell! Pepper." I heard Jac calling for me from behind.

"Damn it." I stomped my foot. "Damn it."

Jac caught up to me, out of breath. "What is going on with you?"

"We've got to go." Before I could turn around or even explain, Jazzy and Doc pulled up beside us.

Jazzy leaned out the open window, sheer disappointment filling the creases in her scrunched features. "Who spoke to you, love?"

"We'll talk about it at home. Get in," Doc ordered, his voice sterner than usual.

Jac shook her head as the puzzle pieces came together. "You can't hide stuff like this from us. We're on the same team. It doesn't take a genius to watch you run around like a madman talking to the air to know you're conversing with a supernatural. You're not the first we've seen with these powers." She pulled the door handle open but stilled. Over her shoulder she looked at me with sad eyes. "We're the good guys. You're supposed to trust us. Not them." And with that, she slipped inside.

I did trust them. But I also trusted my gut. I wished the other hunters understood that.

When we returned home, I followed Doc into the house and through the family room, where Nikki, Liam, and Livy were sitting, a movie on mute playing in the background. But instead of watching, they were arguing.

"You're so wrong," Livy said, her cheeks red as an apple.

"Yeah, like you'd ever side with me," Nikki grunted, clutching the throw blanket in her lap like it was Livy's neck.

"She's not agreeing with me because it's me." Liam smirked and Nikki flipped him the bird. He released a throaty chuckle. "She's agreeing with me because I am right." Liam threw a pillow at Nikki, who caught it in midair.

"What's going on in here?" Doc pointed to the open seat across from Livy, instructing me to sit and stay.

Jac and Jazzy brought the bags into the house from the car, as silent as they'd been on the drive home. Neither of them dared make eye contact with me. Okay, so they were pissed. I got it. I just wished people would give me the benefit of the doubt once in a while. Fenton trusted me, not the other hunters. If they wanted answers, they'd have to have faith in my abilities, but more important, they'd have to have faith in me.

"Nikki's just pissed because both Olivia and I think *Die Hard* is a Christmas movie and she disagrees," Liam answered like it was a real do-or-die situation. Stupid boy.

"Bloody hell." Doc rubbed the arc of his nose, adjusting his glasses before continuing. "That's why it sounded like a war zone in here?"

"It's a real controversy," Nikki added with a humph.

"I'll help bring the bags in," Liam said, standing.

Doc waved at him to stay seated. "No. I think you need to hear what happened at the grocery store with Pepper."

"Okay." Liam dragged the word out as he sat back down.

"What did you do? Did you tag a building?" Livy's eyes narrowed.

Months ago, that wouldn't have been too far-fetched. I ran with Billy Lyons and his crew, who'd defaced more than one structure, including five different schools. Little did we know our reckless exploits had inadvertently unleashed a vengeful spirit upon the state, targeting health teachers and nurses with its murderous plan.

Although my intentions had been rooted in unraveling the mystery and bringing justice, my family couldn't help but express their disapproval of my methods. I'd operated in secrecy, but in retrospect, those disagreements seemed trivial compared to the shocking revelation of my true abilities.

So, I could communicate with monsters—so what? The real concern lay in the fact that I not only spoke the revenants' language but also comprehended their beliefs. I had yet to encounter any malevolent creatures; rather, they seemed like souls misunderstood and unfairly judged. It made me wonder if maybe Hunterland had misconstrued the entire dynamic between hunters and monsters, overlooking the possibility of coexistence.

"Pepper," Livy scolded when I didn't confirm or deny.

I rolled my eyes. "No, I did not spray-paint any walls. Can you please get over that? It was more like a covert mission than vandalism anyway. I was just trying to figure out who was killing all the teachers. I don't know why you're not thanking me."

"Thanking you." Livy's voice escalated, her jaw ticking. "You nearly got yourself killed. Why would I—"

"She spoke to a revenant." Nikki crossed her arms over her chest and leaned back into the couch. "That's what happened at the store. You spoke to the undead. And let me guess, you tried to hide it?" She clucked her tongue.

I gritted my teeth. "The monster was not a revenant. He was alive, thank you very much." I tossed a half smirk in Nikki's direction, mocking her powers.

Liam stiffened. "A werewolf?"

"Yep." I popped the *p* for emphasis.

Nikki's sharp gaze swung toward me, and I swore she wanted to flay me with her glare.

"You did what?" Livy jumped up from her seat. "Was it the same one from the woods? What did he say? Are you hurt?" Her gaze traveled over my body.

"All right, Olivia, breathe, let's just hear Pepper out, okay?" Liam turned to Nikki. "And you're not helping. So, zip it." When his gaze reached me, he gave me a small smile. "Pepper, tell us what happened, and don't leave out any details."

Liam was usually the only one who got me. He had a knack for patience and actually listening, unlike my dumb sister, who constantly jumped down my throat. She swore things would be different now that she understood the crap I'd been through with our spirit mother. All those years of her haunting me with her ghostly problems and those annoying midnight conversations. Sure, at first, it was kinda cool to finally get to know Mamma, especially since I'd grown up without her. But then, after a year, it turned into a total nightmare. She'd clung to me like a stubborn barnacle, never leaving my side. And her anger? It consumed everything, infecting our relationship. She'd even taken it upon herself to off my history teacher when he'd acted all inappropriate with me. Talk about toxic, right?

By the time the Hunter family came barging into our home, I was beyond ready for Mamma's spirit to move the heck on.

But, nope, here we were again. Olivia had slipped right back into her old ways, playing the overbearing, suffocating substitute mother I never freaking asked for. Ugh, it was like I was trapped in some twisted, ghostly *Groundhog Day*.

I focused solely on Liam, tuning everyone else out. "Fenton tried to talk to me a couple times. But I couldn't understand him until we were in the parking lot, almost like there was a supernatural blockage. I've never not heard them before." I squinted, recalling the muddled foghorn voice chasing me around the store. "He must have stayed at a distance on purpose because his voice was so low, he sounded underwater."

Doc stroked his beard. "Do you have any black tourmaline on you?"

I twisted my nose. "What's that?"

Livy threw her head back and groaned at the ceiling. "I made her spirit-blocking charms attached to her purse."

I glared at my sister. "Why would you do that?"

"Why do you think? I'm trying to protect you, apparently from yourself as well as the supernaturals."

"I'm not afraid of them."

"Well, I am. Excuse me for wanting to keep my baby sister safe."

"Okay, Poppets, let's keep the course, shall we?" Doc waved. "Pepper, please proceed."

"Anyway, by the time we got outside, and I could hear him clearly, Jac was in my face about her small bladder, and he—"

"Her what?" Liam's brows crinkled.

I flicked my wrist. "Not relevant. She was talking too much, and Fenton said we should just meet tomorrow."

"Tomorrow?" Liam and Doc said at the same time Livy shouted, "Absolutely not."

"You suck," I snapped at Livy. "Could you drop the momma bear act? It's getting old." I crossed my arms over the frustration simmering in my chest. My sister promised she'd give me more freedom, but talk was cheap. Actions spoke volumes. And Livy proved again and again she couldn't loosen that stick wedged up her butt, no matter the situation.

Well, you know what? She can just screw off, for all I care.

The child in me wanted to stomp my feet but instead I held it together. "I'm going to meet him. I already told him I would." I'd go with or without them. Their choice.

Doc sighed.

"Going to meet who?" Jazzy walked into the living room chomping on a green apple. She plopped down on the couch next to her sister, who grabbed the fruit right from her hand and stole a bite.

"I'm calling Matt. We need to let him know," Doc said, leaving the room. I couldn't be sure, but I think he needed distance. From all of us.

"Fenton, my mother's second-in-command." Liam stood, his lips puckered like saying those words aloud disgusted him. Then they thinned out and tilted upward. "Looks like we've got a hunt to prepare for." Liam clapped his hands together.

A flicker of doubt sparked in my gut. A hunt? Was that what he thought this was? Whether his assessment was justified or not, I had yet to decide. But were we truly the hunters, or had the roles been reversed somehow, drawing us out to become the hunted? The distinction between the two had begun to blur. Perhaps those lines had never truly existed in the first place. The unsettling realization left me with a headache. I felt lost in a haze of uncertainty, where the boundaries of our existence as hunters and the supernatural creatures we pursued melded into an indistinguishable tangle.

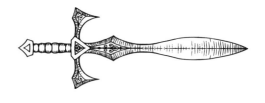

17

LIAM

I put away the last of my things as I settled into my new space. We moved so often, I changed beds, scenery, and room layouts without batting an eye, but something about having the whole remodeled basement to myself felt different. I had drawers, a closet, an armoire, even my own desk and training mat.

For the first time since I was little, I had a space to root down in and call mine.

My cell rang, and Matt's name popped up on the screen. I pressed speaker so I could hang up my leather jacket. "What's up? You on your way home?"

"Not yet. I've got a lead." Matt sounded drained. He'd been at the station all weekend. We'd barely seen him.

The second attack must've shaken him worse than the first. Multiple killings had that effect on people in our line of work. It meant we hadn't stopped the killers in time, and that made it personal. "If you can even call it that."

I grabbed my phone and held it to my ear. "Why doesn't this sound like good news?"

"It could be nothing, a wild goose chase." He sighed heavily. "The owner of the Apricot Inn mentioned three to six men staying in one of her occupied rooms."

My forehead wrinkled. "Three to six? Is this woman blind?" This lady sounded like she was seeing double.

"Like I said, it might be crap. But I want you to go check it out. If I send one of my officers, they won't know what to look for, or worse, they could end up becoming the next victims. At least you might notice something to tell us whether these are our killers. And you'll know how to defend yourself if by some off chance this is them."

I flung the hanger back into the closet and threaded my arms through the sleeves of my coat. At least we had Monday off for Presidents' Day weekend and school was closed. That gave me a chance to drive out there tonight and be back in time to get a good night's sleep for tomorrow's hunt for Fenton.

"I'll leave now." I grabbed my revolver and stuck it in the back of my pants. "I want to take Pepper with me. She might be able to hear them if they speak telepathically. Any objections?"

"None, as long as you promise to call for backup before approaching." He grunted. "And you keep her safe."

"I'd never let a thing happen to her."

"I didn't hear you promise you'd call for backup."

I held my free hand behind my back with crossed fingers. "You got it." If I found werewolves, I'd make Pepper wait in the car, but I'd kill them before returning. Hunters never ran in the face of danger. That risked other humans' lives, which went against our oath. Plus, I didn't need backup for three, or even six, lycanthropes. "What name's the room under?"

"Daryl Hamilton. We ran it and found nothing suspicious. It could be a fake."

"Got it. I'll keep you posted."

Pepper and I snuck out of the house before anyone noticed and jumped into the Bronco for the thirty-five-minute drive. We could be in and out, barring any complications, and back before ten. Easy peasy. The real problem was tomorrow. My number-one priority was to use Fenton for information and then kill him.

Dad would take care of Mom in Chicago, and then we'd go after her den together. Maybe Mom had ended up doing us a favor. Instead of going den to den, we'd get six at once. Couldn't be mad about those odds.

"I cannot believe my dad let me go with you on a hunt." Pepper bounced in her seat. "How exciting is this?" She rubbed her thighs. "God, Livy is gonna freak when she finds out. Can't believe we snuck out of the house." She twisted in her seat. "Do you think we'll actually get to talk to more werewolves?"

I shook my head. A hunter would say *kill*; Pepper said *talk*. Her powers encouraged her to see supernaturals with humanity, whereas we only saw them one way: killers. I worried about Pepper's future in Hunterland. Her priorities needed a reboot; but for tonight, I just needed her to listen. So, if she wanted to regard it as talking, I'd be fine with that.

We pulled into the almost-empty parking lot, rolling past three cars sporadically parked. I reached into the center console and pulled out a backup pistol filled with silver bullets, then handed it to Pepper. "It's loaded. If you think it's a werewolf, you point and pull the trigger. Aim for the heart and shoot to kill. But stay by my side unless I say run, understood?"

She nodded enthusiastically.

"Good. Keep the weapon hidden." I tossed her the keys. "If I tell you to run, you get back to the car and drive out of here. Don't stop until you get to the house. Got it?"

She nibbled on her thumbnail. "But I could—"

"No. You drive to your house and call Doc on your way to update him. He will send the twins for backup. Tell me you hear me, Pepper. I mean it."

"Fine," she groaned.

"Good. Now, let's go talk to the owner. I cannot wait to meet her." I chuckled to myself, imagining a tiny old woman with Coke-bottle glasses.

We opened the lobby door and bells jingled above our heads.

A woman in her late seventies, maybe early eighties, sat on a stool knitting a red-and-blue scarf. She watched a black-and-white show on her small TV, volume turned off. The place smelled like cedar and vanilla.

"Hey ya. Need a room?" She slid off her seat and put her yarn and needle down on the counter. "Just the two of ya?" She adjusted her purple glasses, blinking behind thick lenses—almost as owlish as I'd envisioned.

"Actually, we're looking for our friend's room. The name's Daryl Hamilton. Could you tell us his room number?" I leaned my forearms onto the counter, with Pepper loitering nearby.

Granny frowned. "Oh no ya don't. I told 'em boys to leave just an hour ago. Ain't no way I'm letting more of yas in that room. It only has two beds." She waved her pointer finger in my face, and I backed up. "I don't know what weird things you be doing, but this here is a clean, modest motel, and we won't have a scandal souring our good name. Ya hear?" She mumbled something under her breath about being too old for this business.

"Oh no, ma'am, we're actually here to bring them back to our house. We're not staying." I smiled, hoping for charming. I pulled Pepper into my side. "My sister here came to help with their little one."

The granny's white brow rose. "A young'un? Those are full-grown men. Are you telling me they snuck a child into room 108?"

"We'll be on our way." I swung Pepper around and pushed her straight out the door. "Come on. If she asked them to leave an hour ago, they might be gone."

"Aren't you worried she's gonna come after us?" Pepper looked up at me with a twisted nose.

I glanced over my shoulder at the main office and laughed. "No. By the time she catches up, we'll be driving home."

We hurried down the cement pathway, counting the numbers until we got to 108. The door stood slightly ajar.

"What the hell, Daryl?" a muffled voice asked. "That old witch is gonna come back here. We already wiped everything down. The others are waiting at the house. Let's go."

Whether these guys were common criminals or supernaturals, it didn't matter. No normal person wiped down their motel room before checking out. I drew my weapon and whispered to Pepper, "Car. Now!"

Pepper's eyes widened. She looked at the door, then me. "They heard you. One's escaping through the bathroom window. The Daryl guy stayed."

"Shit." Pepper heard them telepathically. I tossed my chin toward the Bronco. "Go. Now."

Pepper bit her lower lip, then surprisingly—thankfully—ran to the car. I kicked the door open and was met with a blade to the shoulder. My gun flew from my hands as the knife pinned my body against the adjacent wall.

Pain cut through the serum, spawning a guttural cry. "So, you like knives, huh?" With my free hand, I ripped the blade free of muscle and sinew.

The guy before me smiled, his claws and fangs on display. He was built like the Hulk, his brown hair brushing broad shoulders. Only his cable-knit sweater didn't scream monster.

"I like dead hunters better." He growled, curling his lips.

Most supernaturals knew a hunter when they saw one. A pretty good assumption when we didn't scream at their monstrous forms.

"Well, I like dead werewolves, so let's see who gets what they want first."

Daryl licked his lips, eyes trained on my beating heart. He lunged, but I moved faster, jumping over one of the queen-sized beds. Daryl swung around, but it was too late. I had already grabbed the silver knife from my boot sheath and flung it at Daryl's chest.

His hand whipped out so fast I almost missed it. His palm wrapped around the blade, stopping it an inch from his heart. A hiss slipped out of his mouth, and the smell of burning flesh assaulted my nostrils. He tossed the weapon at the window, scattering glass shards inside and outside the room.

Daryl came at me with full force and kicked me square in the chest with his boot. He was fast—real fast. Before I could buck up, his fist connected with my chin. Blood sprayed out of my mouth, but I rolled and avoided a body slam. I used momentum to stand and get back in the fight. He tried to swipe my legs out from under me, but I jumped. Anticipating my move, he grabbed the desk chair and slid it under my landing. My feet wobbled as they caught on wooden legs, and I stumbled to the ground.

The monster lunged forward, his full weight behind him, his claws inches from my skin. But I blocked him with my leather-clad forearm and pushed him back. He charged again, kicking me once in the side. My ribs cracked, but I didn't have time to worry about the injury. I managed to break a chair leg and use it to clock him in the kneecap, but it barely made him sway. With his other leg, he kicked me in the face, and just as the room blurred, shots were fired, and I blinked.

When my vision cleared, the werewolf was nowhere in sight, but Pepper stood over me, gun raised and arms shaking. I might have worried where her allegiance lay before, but at least now I knew: when push came to shove, Pepper wouldn't let me die. I guess that's all a hunter could ask for in the end.

18

OLIVIA

Yesterday, Jac moved out of my room and into the guest room, where Liam used to sleep. It had only been one night, but I already missed the sight of her blow-up bed on the floor, the sweet floral scents of her lotions, and the Willie Nelson tunes she'd belt out when she forgot I was around. I'd gotten used to sharing my space, and now that she was gone, the room felt ridiculously huge and empty.

Jac had a thirst for knowledge. She would spend hours examining my collection of stones, crystals, and gems, wanting to know all about their magical properties. My homemade balms fascinated her too. I'd caught her toying with them on past scars and using them to heal anything from paper cuts to scraped knees.

As I held the mixture I'd used on Liam the night before, when he came home with a bloodied shoulder and face and bruised ribs, I wondered if maybe my powers of prediction weren't reliable, but what about my healing abilities? Liam had already started to recover before he stormed off to bed, angrier than I'd ever seen him. From what Jac said, it was unusual that one werewolf got the upper hand on her brother. But since I was furious with him for taking Pepper on a hunt without telling me, I didn't give him much of a chance to speak, even if I couldn't voice my fears to my sister. I had promised to give her more freedom, though it killed me inside. And now with another hunt in front of us and Pepper at the helm, what could I really do but project my feelings onto Liam? I grabbed a new emollient I had whipped up, my latest creation, and shoved it into my purse. You never knew when a healing ointment could save the day.

"You ready?"

Jac stood in the bedroom doorway already dressed and equipped for our meet and greet with Fenton. Her blond hair was draped over her shoulders, bright against her black gear. It would've been hard to guess that this charming figure with pink lip gloss and rosy cheeks was a trained monster killer. She looked more like Bank Robber Barbie.

"I think I'm good." I reached into my stone collection, letting the right one call to me. When I pulled my hand back out, I opened my palm. In the center lay a tiger's eye.

"What's that one mean? It's pretty." Jac lifted up on her tippy toes to see.

I lowered it for her to regard the tapestry of rich golden hues. The mingling of warm amber and deep brown created patterns worthy of adorning a regal tiger.

"It's a powerful protection stone, known to boost your inner strength and willpower." Smooth to the touch, the stone boasted a lustrous sheen, like a polished gemstone plucked from a treasure trove. I grabbed an empty necklace chain and slipped it through the hole in the crystal. Almost all my precious gems could be turned into a necklace, bracelet, or ring. Contact with skin heightened their potency, so wearing them gave me the strongest vibrations.

"Perfect." She clapped her hands into a prayer position at her chest.

I grimaced at her wide smile as I latched the necklace clasp around my neck. "That doesn't feel like a good omen. You're making an already iffy situation sound more dangerous than I'd hoped."

Jac shrugged. "We don't hunt in plastic bubbles, so yeah, I think a protection stone that heightens your inner badass is perfect for any monster-hunting mission." She tossed me a leather satchel like the one she'd made for my dad a couple days earlier.

I caught it, and the weight almost threw me off balance. "What's inside?"

"All the fun stuff. Stakes, knives, salt, a gun, and a bottle of water." Her eyes widened. "Oh, and candy in case you need a little sugar rush. Liam adds that to everyone's kit, when he remembers." She stuck out her tongue like confection disgusted her. Considering her strict vegetable diet, it probably did.

I dug my hand inside and pulled out a package of red licorice. Jac's sudden intake of air made me look up. "What's wrong?"

She pointed at the candy in my hand. "That's what Liam used to take on hunts with our mom. They were kinda their special thing." She bit her lower lip.

I studied the Red Vine bag. "I don't know how to respond to that."

"Me neither," Jac said with a shrug.

"Hey, can I ask you something?"

"Sure."

"When Doc and Jazzy were playing chess the other day, they mentioned that a woman started Hunterland?" I tilted my head. "What do you know about it?"

Jac's lips twisted. "Not much. Only that she was a witch or something. Nothing's ever been documented on how we started. Why?" Her nose scrunched.

"Just curious. Don't you find it odd that no one seems to know how Hunterland started and by who?"

Jac shrugged. "You know what they say about curiosity. It killed the werecat." She curled her hand into a pretend claw. "Now, we better get going before my brother starts yelling for us."

Maybe she was right.

Maybe it didn't matter how Hunterland started. Or just maybe it would be the answer to all the unknown and someone doesn't want those secrets to be revealed. I placed the strap over my head and grabbed my phone.

Two unread messages appeared.

Thanks for inviting me to movie night. Let me know if you want to hang on Monday since we have the day off.

Bradley had sent that yesterday. I had been so preoccupied, I hadn't seen it. A couple hours later, he'd sent another.

Maybe we could watch the new Frankenstein movie, The Last Frankenstein.

Not wanting him to feel discarded, I wrote back fast. *I've never heard of that one, but rain check? Lunch Tuesday when we are all back?*

Without waiting for a response, I tucked the phone into my back pocket and followed Jac out the door.

Downstairs, Pepper rose to her feet, sporting a smile that could rival a certified lunatic's.

"What'd we miss?" I swiveled, looking around.

"This is Pepper's hunt, and considering how well she handled herself last night, I'm letting her choose who will go where." Liam reached for the two guns on the coffee table. He secured one at his back and the other into his ankle sheath as he said, "Pick two people to escort you to the meet and two people to stay at the car for backup."

Pepper allowed her eyes to roam the room, settling last on Liam. "You and Nikki can come meet Fenton with me, since you're the most skilled. Doc has the most experience, and . . ." She smiled at me. "My sister."

My heart went gooey. The previous night, when she got home from what I felt was a dangerous mission, I just listened as she bounced on my bed recapping the story. The only one I yelled at was Liam and that was in private. I guess my sister appreciated the way I handled the situation with her.

"Wanna go spar?" Jazzy hip bumped Jac, completely unfazed she wasn't selected.

"Sure." Jac and Jazzy headed down to the basement, while Dad's face burned red.

"You can patrol the highway entrance to the campgrounds. How's that?" Doc offered my father.

"Fine." Dad secured his weapon, then threaded his arms through his police jacket.

Nikki, my sister, and I squished into the backseat while Liam drove, and Doc sat shotgun. For a while, Liam and Doc talked shop. Apparently, Agent Hunter hadn't reported in since Monday night, when he'd called Liam with an update on Veronica. Everyone but Jac had been informed. Doc mentioned he was concerned, but Liam brushed it off.

"Dad's gone dark before. Not sure why you're worried." Liam made a right-hand turn.

"Fair enough. I'm sure if something was wrong he would have called." Doc twisted in his seat to face Pepper in the back. "Now, Poppet, Fenton's agenda is unclear, so let's try to get the information we need from him first before you give him a chance to make his request." Doc pointed at the turnoff Liam needed to take.

"How do you know he wants something?" Although Pepper's question was for Doc, she stared out the window, not a hundred percent focused on the conversation.

"Trust me. He wants something," Liam added.

"First, let's see if he has any leads on the killings or who attacked Liam last night. Then ask him why he's investigating it. I've never heard of a pack caring about dead humans. I'm interested in his response." Doc opened his sketch pad.

Was he having a vision? I craned my neck to see, but instead of drawing, he flipped through the book.

Nikki huffed. "When do we kill him?"

"Kill him?" Pepper shrieked, snapping out of her daze.

Doc scowled at his niece before addressing Pepper. "I know it's hard to hear, Poppet, but Fenton is a monster, and we will have to terminate him."

"How do you even know he's bad?" she stammered, her leg bouncing at my side. "He wasn't like the guy last night. Now *he* was evil."

"God, it's like she's working with them instead of us." Nikki groaned. "I knew you were weird, little Davis, but you do realize we're the good guys, right?"

"Shut up," I snapped.

"You shut up." Nikki shoved my shoulder with hers.

"Real mature," I muttered, scooting closer to my sister.

"Both of you shut up. Pepper was there when it mattered last night. Her loyalty is with us," Liam yelled, slamming on his brakes. He put the car in the park and threw open his door. Within a breath, he'd yanked open Nikki's door. "Out."

"What?" Her surprise mirrored my own. Was Liam tossing her out onto the side of the road? Not that I wouldn't be all for that, but wow!

Liam rounded the car and opened the tailgate to retrieve the longest gun I'd ever seen. "You can cut through the woods and stake out on higher ground."

"What the hell is that?" I swiveled to get a better view.

"Ooh, sniper rifle." Nikki rubbed her hands together and jumped out of the car. She reached for the long gun like a kid reaching for a teddy bear, smile and all. "Why didn't you just say that?" She smacked Liam's arm before grabbing her new toy.

Liam grinned, his signature cocky one that I loved and hated in equal measure. But to watch him toss it Nikki's way sent a roiling, sickly wave from my belly button to my throat. Not that I had any claim to those lips, but jealousy still got the best of me.

"Was more fun kicking your annoying butt out of the car. Remember, station yourself upwind, out of sight and earshot." Liam handed her what looked like a net of leaves, then rounded back to the front and slipped into the driver's seat. Not a minute later, we were back on the road.

"You don't have to kill him." Sadness coated Pepper's whisper. "He's not going to hurt anyone."

No one in the car responded, but my heart broke a little. Pepper didn't see the monsters the same way everyone else did. And I wasn't sure what to make of that. Was it a benefit or a curse?

19

OLIVIA

Liam parked on a dirt landing at the forest's edge, and we all exited the Bronco.

"Doc, you and Olivia stand by the car, but keep it running in case we need a fast escape." Mostly for me, he added, "Stay aware."

Doc acknowledged Liam's request with a dip of his chin, then went back to his drawings. He stopped on a page and studied it, while I studied him. What was he looking for?

Liam grabbed my bag and lifted it over my head, distracting me from Doc's odd behavior. He pulled out the gun Nikki had been training me with. "You remember how to use it?" He held it up, showing me again how to put one in the chamber, and then handed it over.

"Yeah." My voice trailed off. My eyes were fixated on Pepper. I wanted to reach out and hug her, to tell her to be careful and to listen to every word Liam said. But at the same time, I wanted her to know that I believed in her, that I trusted her, that I was proud of her for last night. For so long, I had acted like her mother, thinking that was what she needed. But now I'd finally realized that what she truly craved was a sister. Transitioning from one role to the other took some getting used to.

Pepper stared off into the trees, her body language completely relaxed.

The air rushed out of my lungs as I stood there, lost in a whirlwind of unsettling thoughts. What if Fenton attacked her? What if this entire encounter was nothing but an insidious ploy designed to ensnare his next meal?

Crippled by a potent mixture of panic and anxiety like a flurry of restless wings in my stomach, I hovered in frozen indecision. Nonetheless, in that crucial instant, like the heart-pounding second before a roller coaster dipped into a thrilling plunge, I drew in a steadying breath, summoning my wellspring of courage, determined to confront whatever lay ahead with unwavering resolve. After all, what other choice did I have?

A hand reached out and grabbed my shaky one. "I've got her."

Liam jolted me back to life like a defibrillator. If Fenton did try something, I knew Liam would put a silver bullet in his heart.

I nestled the gun between the waistband of my jeans and my black bodysuit, securing it the way Liam taught me, and nodded, trying to appear confident.

"I know you're mad at me . . ."

"No. I was just scared." I glanced at Pepper, then back to Liam. "She's pretty incredible, huh?"

Liam leaned in, cupping the back of my neck. "So are you."

I finally met his eyes, the lightest blue I'd ever seen them. My own reflected in his widened pupils. His gaze dropped to my lips, making the butterfly wings inside flutter for a whole new reason.

He pulled me in and kissed the top of my head. The skin tingled where his lips touched as if he'd branded me with a reminder of himself. He turned to Doc, who now had a pencil in his hand, sketching wildly. "Stop doodling and pay attention." Doc's head snapped up. "Do not leave her, for any reason. I don't care what you hear or think, you stay right by her side."

"We'll be fine," Doc concluded, then went right back to his sketch pad.

Pepper pushed Liam out of the way. "You don't get all the sappy moments. My turn." She wrapped her arms around me and whispered into my ear, "It's going to be okay. Fenton's not what they think he is. He won't hurt me. And if he tries, I have Liam-freaking-Hunter as my bodyguard. Hell, I saved *him* last night."

I sniffled, fighting back tears as I pulled out of her embrace. "When did you get so grown up, huh?" I mussed her blue hair. "Go on. Go get us the intel we need to put the bastards who killed those innocent campers and hikers in the ground."

Pepper saluted me. Her crooked grin all but made me laugh.

"Let's go." Liam waved to Pepper to follow him.

"Liam"—I rocked back on my heels as he turned around—"Pepper better not be the only one to come back in one piece. You hear me?"

Liam chuckled. "If I do die, I'm haunting your ass."

"Funny." I tightened the satchel strap at my shoulder, securing it in place. "I'll burn your bones, and you'll never stand a chance."

Liam smiled, a real one, a rare one. My heart fluttered in my chest, beating against my rib cage. "You better. A good hunter would never let me become a monster."

The double meaning hung in the air as he and my sister disappeared into the depths of the forest. There was a part of Liam that felt responsible for his mother's transformation. Not that I believed that at all. How could they have known she wouldn't end her own life, allowing herself to become the enemy? Still, I recognized the heavy burden Veronica's choice placed on her family. Even now, as her fate approached its inevitable conclusion, it had to be incredibly hard on all the Hunters.

Doc sucked in a breath. "Olivia," he wheezed, panic-stricken.

"What?" I twisted to meet his pale face.

He held up his sketch pad, but before I could piece together what he'd drawn, the click of a gun's safety froze my limbs.

"Bloody hell." Doc's words were a mere whisper. "Don't move."

Cold metal stung the side of my cheek, and I sipped in a pitiful breath.

"I'd take his advice, kiddo. Moving could be very bad for your health." The unfamiliar, syrupy-sweet voice held an edge that sent shivers up my spine. "Now why don't you enlighten me. Who are you? And even more important, who are you to my son?"

"Son?"

The woman chuckled. "Yes, the boy who just ogled you for the last three minutes, more concerned about your safety than the hunt. Because I don't know him very well anymore, now that he's practically a man, but I sure am interested in learning."

"Veronica," I breathed at the same time Doc said, "You don't want to hurt her."

"Nice to see you too, Harold. Interesting picture you drew. Guess your premonition was a little too late, but at least you sketched me to perfection. Dare I say I look good?"

I cringed. Doc had been envisioning Veronica for years now, but he could never figure out her location in the vision, so he'd hid it from the Hunter family.

I had stumbled upon the picture once and swore to him I'd keep his secret. The background must have popped into his head while we were driving, and he finally figured out the rest of his premonition. No wonder he was worried about Agent Hunter. He knew Veronica was still alive.

"What do you want?" Leaves crunched under Doc's feet.

"Stay right there, or I will kill the girl."

I bit the inside of my cheek, hoping to control my trembling lip. From everything I knew about Veronica, she meant what she said, a formidable woman who didn't throw out empty threats. Doc must have agreed, because his noisy movements stopped and all I heard was the whistle of my own breath through my shrinking airway.

"Toss all three of your weapons over there." Veronica pointed with her free hand to the spot she wanted, her fingers wandering into my peripheral vision.

I watched Doc remove the gun from his back.

"Slowly, Harold," Veronica warned.

He placed it on the ground, then kicked it farther away. Then he repeated the action with his ankle gun and his knife. When the enemy was someone you once trusted, you couldn't hide much. I hadn't even known Doc carried a blade. But Veronica did. She knew all the hunters' secrets. This wouldn't be good for any of us.

The gun left my cheek as Veronica rounded on me, still pointing the pistol at my head. "Can't say I was expecting this, but Liam's always been a bit of a wild card. He gets that from me. And here I thought I would just be observing, but you know what they say about curiosity." She stepped into my personal space and grabbed the gun in my waistband. "I'll be taking this. Thank you." She walked backward until she stood a couple arm's lengths away.

My mouth opened as she came into view. A cascade of golden curls framed a face dominated by the piercing blue eyes she'd given Jac and Liam. She moved with a feline fluidity that belied her newfound lupine nature. Her fitted jeans accentuated her sculpted thighs, while her white long-sleeved shirt clung to her chest, a vibrant contrast against the backdrop of a brown leather jacket reminiscent of Liam's signature one. Yet, it was the striking resemblance to Jac that left me slack-jawed. Anyone could've easily mistaken them for twins.

"What's your name?"

"Leave her alone." Doc's tone, calm and collected, opposed my wildly beating heart. How was he keeping it together? My insides were one tug away from unraveling.

She pouted her bottom lip. "Oh, you're no fun. I'm trying to get to know the girl my son's enamored with." Her eyes hardened as they moved to meet mine. "Answer the question."

What harm would come of her knowing my name, anyway? A resourceful woman like her could find out on her own, regardless. "Olivia Davis."

She swayed the gun around. "Olivia Davis, huh?" She tilted her head. "Are you a hunter?"

I pressed my lips together, refusing to answer.

She tsked. "Silence is just plain rude." She switched her mark and aimed the gun at Doc's head. "Three seconds to speak, Olivia Davis, or you can explain his death to Beth and the twins. Three. Two . . ."

"I guess. Okay?"

She repositioned the pistol back at me. Sweat dripped at the nape of my neck, pulse jumping. Sure, we'd been in tough spots before, but I'd never been on the receiving end of a loaded gun.

"You guess? How don't you know? It's really a yes-or-no question."

"I just started this hunter thing, okay? We've only been training for a couple months. But if I'm being honest, and since you have a gun pointed at my head and I have nothing to lose by telling the truth, I'm not all that experienced yet. So, I don't know if I have the proper title." My exhale blew my hair off my face.

She shook her head. "My son fell for a sorta hunter. Now that is baffling. And do you love him?"

I sucked in a breath that did little to tame the bubbling acid rising into my esophagus. Did I love Liam? Gun to my head, such a complicated question had such a simple answer, yet I couldn't bring my lips to move.

"Don't make me ask you again." Annoyance slipped into Veronica's timbre as she stepped into my space. The tip of the pistol touched my forehead, and I swallowed. "Well?"

I pulled my shoulders back and lifted my chin, the gun indenting my skin. Unflinching, I looked straight into the eyes of the woman who'd broken Liam's heart and answered.

"Yes."

20

PEPPER

The crunching and snapping of leaves and twigs under my feet announced our march into the forest, though Liam made no sound, driving us closer to where the five campers had been torn to shreds barely a week ago. No caution tape remained, but trampling police boots still disturbed the grass and surrounding foliage, leaving a clear path from the road to the crime scene. Blood still stained the rocks and leaves, a reminder of the atrocities committed here.

"I don't really get you and my sister. Like are you together? On a break? Do you make out still or—"

"Just keep walking." Liam surveyed the woods, searching.

The scent of pine swirled on the fresh winter air as a fog clung to my skin like the mist left by a hot shower. I kicked a rock, and it nailed a nearby tree trunk. "Do you like her?" Liam should know his audience. I didn't give up that easily.

"Pepper." He shaped my name around a rough warning, but I didn't care.

I continued to stare at the ground as I pressed. "You know, she has feelings for you, strong feelings."

Liam stopped and swung around, catching me when I tripped over a tree stump. "I am not having this conversation with you." He looked down at my feet. "And watch where you're walking," he bit out, as if he could sever the discussion and be rid of my pestering.

Tough luck. If he was going to be a giant tool bag, I was going to call him out on it. I crossed my arms, lips twisting.

"You can't deny the way you two act with each other. I mean, seriously, dude, what do you call that romantic hero goodbye you just gave her?" I made my voice a mocking, suave rasp.

Liam flushed. Point proven. One for Pepper. For a fearless hunter, Liam was a lame ass when it came to emotions and relationships.

"You're reading too much into it."

Now he was just a big fat liar. "Oh really. Would you pucker up to Dustin's noggin like that?" I pursed my lips against the unwanted vision I'd summoned. That would just be awkward.

Liam groaned. "You made your point. Happy?"

"No, actually." I kicked another stone. "Explain it to me. Why are you both so hot and cold with each other?"

"Pepper." This time he dipped my name in a pool of exasperation.

I blew out a pouf of air. "Olivia deserves more than some on again off again crap. I'm just saying, it'd be nice if someone fought for her. I thought maybe that could be you." I shrugged. "Maybe not. But I *had* hoped." Livy grew up way too fast. She'd never had someone dote on her. I kinda wanted that for my sister.

A branch snapped, and Liam's arm whipped out to halt my step. A haze settled over the trees, making it hard for my eyes to adjust to the movements in between the bark. Dark gray clouds covered the sun, leaving the breeze chilly. "What was that?"

"Well, at least you didn't bring the one with the small bladder." An older gentleman with a gray beard and spiky hair stepped forward. He had Agent Hunter's stature, tall and wide—graying hair too—but he was dressed like the Brawny paper towel guy, with a red-plaid shirt, distressed jeans, and brown boots. "She's too chatty." He leaned against a tree, positioning one foot against the trunk.

Liam aimed his gun at Fenton. "Don't move or I will kill you."

Fenton smiled, like the threat was funny. "Not really necessary, hunter." He pushed off the trunk with the heel of his boot. "Our interests are the same on this one. Kill the werewolves that killed the humans. Simple, really." He flicked his hand at the pointed weapon, treating it as he had Jazzy's gun in his wolf form, like it wasn't real. "Your Glock doesn't promote trust in our newfound partnership."

Liam kept the barrel steady. "The only relationship we have is Grim Reaper and the soul I'm sending to hell when this is all over."

"Suit yourself." Fenton shrugged, like the threat sounded empty. "I'd like to make a deal." Fenton crossed his arms at his chest; his biceps pulsed. "You have something we want, and we have something you want. How about an exchange?"

"I doubt you have anything that I would want," Liam hissed.

You've got a problem, a woman's clipped voice barked in my skull. *There's a sniper five hundred meters northeast of your location on higher ground. Hold your position.*

I knew she'd meant her warning for Fenton, but she had to know I'd be in range to overhear as well. Fenton shook his head, wordlessly asking me not to say anything. I bit my lower lip. Part of me wanted to tell Liam just to prove I was a reliable hunter, but my gut had different motives. I didn't want Nikki to shoot Fenton. I didn't believe he deserved to die. With my eyes, I tried to convey his secret female wolf friend would stay hidden. For now.

"Why don't we keep this conversation on the move?" Liam used the barrel of his gun to motion for Fenton to start walking.

"And let your little friend line up a better shot? No thanks. I think I'm good right here." Fenton backed up between two large oak trees, securing his safe location. "Are you interested in hearing who killed those campers and hikers or not?"

"Why do you even care? Why would a pack of werewolves investigate human deaths?"

Fenton smiled, exposing his sharp incisors. "You know, we aren't all bad."

"You keep telling yourself that."

Fenton's jaw ticked. "Your mother kicked out several rogue members of her pack when she found out their ringleader killed an innocent woman. We think they've come to Falkville Falls, and they're who murdered the five campers in the woods the night of the full moon and the hikers. We don't think their killing spree is over, either."

"Is one of their names Daryl?"

Fenton's bushy brows rose. "How do you know that name?"

My mouth dropped open. Did all werewolves know each other?

"Let's just say I met him last night. Lovely fella. Not chatty like you, but equally as ugly." Liam smirked.

Fenton stepped forward, worry lines creasing his forehead. "Did he know who you were? Did he know your name?"

Liam looked at me, lips pinched, then back to Fenton. "He knew I was a hunter but my name, no, I don't think so." He drew his shoulders back, gun arm flexing. "Why are they here? What's their plan?"

Fenton's lips pulled down, his lashes brushing his cheekbones. "You really can't put two and two together, hunter? Come on. You're a bright kid. Why do you think they're here?"

A pocket formed between Liam's eyebrows, a moment of confusion soon washed away by realization. He cursed. "Because of me. Or rather, specifically, my family, right?"

I guessed it before he said it, knowing that sometimes our relatives, good or bad, brought unwanted peril down on our heads. Mamma had done that for Livy and me. Life just sucked sometimes.

"They still see you as her son whether you share that view or not." Sympathy dropped Fenton's voice a decibel.

I placed my hand on Liam's shoulder. "It's not your fault."

"They're here in Falkville Falls because of my family. They're here for retribution against my Alpha werewolf mother. Ten people died because of it. How is this *not* my fault?" Liam growled, sparing a quick look in my direction. "If we weren't here . . ." The rest of Liam's words were drowned out by the voice of the female werewolf.

We need to go. Now. We'll have to get what we came for another way.

Fenton winked at me. "Been fun, kid. Looks like I gotta leave." He darted around the tree. Liam didn't hesitate. He pulled back on his trigger. The gun fired with a loud bang that jabbed my ears before I covered them. The bullet ricocheted off the tree, taking a chunk of bark with it, and missed Fenton's shoulder by inches.

Fenton chuckled as he dropped out of sight. Disembodied words drifted back to us. "Just so you know, the pup traveling with the rest of the guys isn't a child—he's your age. You find him; you'll find the rest."

Liam unloaded several more rounds, but Fenton dodged through the rustling vegetation, getting away clean.

A couple powerful shots from Nikki rang out in the distance.

"Stop," I shouted, running after Liam. Branches whipped against my cheeks, their sharp edges leaving stinging marks like razor cuts. Yet, the lashes of tiny sticks and pricks of thorns paled in comparison to the worry constricting my heart. An urgent need to stay close to Liam propelled me forward. "Just stop. He's not the bad guy." Hot tears streamed down my cheeks as I sucked in a shaky breath. I used my jacket sleeve to wipe them away.

Liam kept Fenton's pace, and I tried to follow, but a clumsy misstep on a tree root sent me hurtling toward the ground. Rocks split the knees of my jeans. The sharp sting of open wounds registered beneath my frantic fear. Gunshots rang out in the distance, making me flinch. Doubt clawed at me, Nikki's words needling me. If being a hunter meant killing without cause, then count me out. Maybe I had lost sight of which side I truly belonged to. Because, in that moment, as I squeezed my eyes shut, I silently rooted for Fenton's escape.

21

OLIVIA

Veronica's eyes widened, clearly taken aback. Hell, *I* hardly fathomed the weight of the word that had plowed through my lips—I loved Liam. I only wished I had mustered the courage to confess to him first. Now, with my survival seriously in question, I feared he would never know the truth.

Veronica chuckled. "Well, then my son deserves the best hunter. So, the next time you are asked, you'd better be able to answer that question without any doubt." Veronica backed up a couple steps and took a seat on a large rock behind her. She rested her forearm on her thigh, but kept the gun pointed in my direction. "You've got questions about the Hunterland community, right?" She waved her free hand. "So, ask."

"Veronica, let us go," Doc interrupted. "You've done nothing you can't take back yet. Let Olivia and I leave, and we won't come after you."

"Harold, do I look like I'm worried about you pursuing me? Now, keep your hands where I can see them, so I don't have to kill Olivia for your brave but foolish heroics." Red blotches crept up Doc's neck, dotting his cheeks pink, but he kept his hands up for Veronica to see. "Olivia, ignore him. Back to you. I asked my questions; it's only fair you ask yours. I'll give you three." She smirked, her apple-red cheeks lifting in a beauty-queen beam.

In this moment, the most effective course of action, and perhaps the only one available to me, was to stall until Liam returned. At the same time, the mere thought of him encountering his mother again filled me with palpable sympathetic pain. *The Alpha she's become isn't her,* he'd told Jac. *It's just wearing her face.*

I swallowed hard, forcing myself to stay focused on diverting a monster's attention. "How does no one know how Hunterland started?"

Blue eyes that looked so much like Liam's twinkled in response. "Now that's a good question," Veronica said with a wistful curve to her lips. "We do know. A witch by the name of Danica Davisa created Hunterland."

My jaw slackened. How did she know that when everyone else had claimed there were no records? "How is there no documentation about her?" I peeked over at Doc, whose eyes widened. "Did you know that?"

"Danica is a myth." Doc narrowed his gaze at Veronica.

"Oh, Harold. She is more than just tall tales. Don't mislead the girl."

I refocused on Veronica. "Why did Danica start Hunterland?"

"Her family was murdered by windigos. She wanted revenge."

Without thinking, I took a step closer. "She was an occultist, right?" Fervency lowered my tone. "Did she have natural abilities or use spells?"

A twitch of Veronica's lips told me she'd wanted me to ask that question. "She did have abilities, two in fact, and she used many spells. Most of our spells come from her."

I gasped. Even though it made sense, and Jazzy and Doc had said she was a witch, it still shocked me. The society we had been thrusted into was built by someone like me. That connection, that thread, drew me into the fold further than any other revelation. A comforting warmth spread through my core, purring at the confirmation that I truly belonged in this extraordinary world.

"What were they?"

"Sorry, kiddo, you've maxed out your questions." She glanced down at her watch. "And it's about time I leave." Veronica pushed off the rock. She closed her eyes for a flash, her lips moving as if muttering to herself. "Wait, please tell me. I'll . . ." What bargaining chip could I dangle that would be worth her indulging me? I played with the protection stone around my neck, the smooth edges familiar enough to put me at ease. "I'll give you another question. Ask me anything," I pleaded.

Veronica tilted her head. "Well, aren't you a surprising little thing . . ." Her voice trailed off as she observed my fingers latching onto my protection necklace. "Olivia Davis, do *you* have abilities?"

I nodded.

She threw her head back and cackled. "Of course, my son would find you." If I hadn't already known she was insane, she'd have proved it now. She raised her gun and aimed it at my chest, tightening her two-handed hold on the grip. "Let me guess. You have the powers of premonition and healing."

"How did you—"

Bang!

I never saw her pull the trigger, but the ring of the shot hot-wired every nerve ending. In a blink of adrenaline-spiked clarity, I saw the sunlight spark off the speeding bullet. Then came the impact. A hammer fist to the shoulder harder than anything Nikki had ever thrown my way. Searing pain erupted in my bone, radiating into my heart, as the bullet tore through my flesh, leaving behind a raw and jagged hole. It happened not once, but twice, as the projectile exited my back, finding its mark on the car behind me with a resounding metallic thud. A vignette fell over my vision, a symphony of black spots encroaching deeper, as I crumbled to the unforgiving ground. Doc rushed to my side, his arms enveloping me, cradling my head in a desperate attempt at solace and support.

"Let's call this a crash course. Shall we?" Veronica knelt in front of me.

"What did you do?" Doc's gaze darted between Veronica and me, burning with anger.

Without hesitation, he pressed his hands against my wound, applying firm and desperate pressure that sent a fresh starburst of agony up my neck. Blood seeped through his fingers, staining them crimson, as a primal scream tore from my lips, a desperate plea to dull the unbearable suffering.

"Keep your eyes on me, kiddo." Veronica gestured to her face with two fingers. "Learn how to heal yourself. That power *is* within you. The rest you'll figure out. Now that I know who you are, you'll see me again." Veronica stood and, without another word, took off into the foliage.

I blinked, but the blur on my vision worsened as I struggled to draw a breath, my lungs screaming. Each inhalation felt like a barrage of razor-sharp knives tearing into my chest, radiating horrific agony through every fiber of my being. Despite the overwhelming pain, my trembling hands—on instinct—moved to clutch my injured shoulder, the source of my torment.

Veronica had suggested I possessed the power to heal myself, but how? I lacked a knowledge of spells like Jazzy or the innate abilities of Nikki. Yet, a flicker of realization lightened my next breath.

I grasped Doc's hand in a weak grip. Ignoring my feeble attempts to communicate, Doc focused solely on relaying our location to the 911 operator.

Determined, I squeezed his hand with renewed resolve, desperately willing him to understand the urgency of my request. "Get my ointment . . ." I cursed as the exertion of speech sped up my heart rate and triggered an arterial spurt from my carotid that shot through Doc's middle and index fingers like a sputtering fountain. I'd already soaked my clothes and the ground below. ". . . from my bag."

"We need to get you to a hospital."

"Please," I gasped.

Doc put the phone on speaker and continued to talk to the operator as he searched through my things. He pulled out the small mason jar and twisted off the lid. "Now what?"

"Rub it over . . ." I had to catch my breath. My skin tingled like I had been bitten by a thousand poisonous snakes. ". . . the wound."

Doc tore away the remaining fabric that shielded my open flesh, exposing the raw injury beneath. As he applied the cooling gel onto my chest, I couldn't contain the anguished cry that erupted from my lips. Pain coursed through my veins like a merciless inferno, consuming my senses and leaving me breathless. Doc paused, his eyes meeting mine, but I was unable to articulate the desperate plea for him to continue. The monstrous pain seized every muscle, locking my jaw and deflating my spasming lungs. With clenched teeth and a silent prayer, I fixed my eyes on him, silently willing him to press on, to push through the torment and provide lifesaving relief.

"Fine. But if this doesn't work and all I end up doing is infecting it, you'll be the one to deal with William."

I bobbed my head. Liam would be puppy play compared to this pain. I'd take my chances.

My sister's voice pierced the chaos, calling out my name in urgent succession until she finally emerged into view. Right on her heels, Liam closed in, his expression dire. Worry etched unfamiliar lines in their faces, but the searing pain in my shoulder began to recede. A smile, wild and uncontainable, stretched across my face, reaching all the way to my cheeks.

"Olivia." Liam crashed at my side, forcefully displacing Doc. His hands roamed over my body, crimson staining his palms. He couldn't locate the bullet's entry point. "Where were you shot? What happened?"

An insane laugh erupted from my re-inflating chest as his words confirmed what I had already suspected—my skin had begun to heal.

Confusion mottled his brow. So, I explained.

"I met your mother."

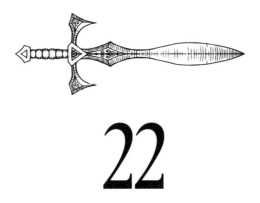

22

LIAM

Pacing outside Olivia's room, memory clashed with reason—*so much blood, too much, on her arms, her hair, her neck*—and the resulting fury heightened my lingering worry to raw terror of the unknown and my own inadequacies. Hunterland training steered clear of intense feelings. It focused on decisive action, compartmentalizing problems, and suppressing emotions—a necessity to survive as a hunter. But now, here I stood, anxiously awaiting Olivia's emergence from the shower like a crazed stalker, losing more of my sanity with each tick of the clock.

After our return to the house, we'd made a pact to keep Olivia's encounter with my werewolf mother a secret from Matt and Jac for obvious reasons. Olivia's gunshot wound had transformed into a star-shaped scar, inconspicuous to anyone who hadn't memorized every inch of her body, like I had. Jac remained oblivious to Mom's presence in town, and I had no intention of alerting her and causing unnecessary pain.

We needed a strategy, and that started with getting Dad back to Falkville Falls as quickly as possible. Except we had a problem. Every time we called him, it went straight to voicemail.

Not a great sign.

We'd burned Olivia's blood-stained clothes, I'd scrubbed away the traces of crimson from my own hands, and Pepper had lent her sister her outer sweater before heading home. To avoid contact with anyone at the Davis residence, we'd dropped Doc and Nikki at their rental house. Doc insisted on getting back right away. He'd wanted to speak to Beth and obtain certain documents from Hunterland's library in London regarding healer abilities. While Pepper, Nikki, and I were astonished by Olivia's seemingly miraculous recovery from a potentially fatal wound, Doc expressed more concern than shock. Sure, we knew she could heal cuts, bruises, and bumps, but a gunshot wound. Now, that was surprising.

Olivia dropped something in the shower, and the bang sent fresh anger surging through me as I replayed the moment I'd realized she was injured. It hadn't been the gunshot itself that stopped my pursuit of Fenton in the woods. With the chaos of Nikki's rifle and my own gunfire, it was difficult to discern one bullet from another. No, Olivia's agonizing screams had frozen every cell in my body, suspending me in place and compelling me to turn my back on a hunt. A feeling, so raw and unfamiliar, had coursed through my veins, readying me to unleash fury upon whoever had caused those cries.

I'd sprinted back toward the Bronco, ignoring the pain of exertion in my legs. Normal breaths proved impossible; I could only gulp down quick bursts of oxygen. Rage had propelled me forward. But when I'd arrived at the scene and spotted Olivia in a pool of her own blood, I'd collapsed to my knees—a future without her flashing before my eyes—and my heart had shattered into dust. The mere thought of laying her to rest . . . I couldn't even allow myself to go there now, knowing she'd pulled through.

Then, to learn that my werewolf mother had shot my . . . Damn it, what was Olivia to me? Friend? No chance. Girlfriend? We hadn't even had a proper conversation about our relationship to let me go there. The only word that resonated, capturing the essence of our connection, was *family*. Olivia had become family to me.

I dug my fingers into my temples as I muttered curses under my breath, the worn carpet beneath my feet a testament to my restlessness. I had harbored the desire to kill my mother before, but now, it intensified to bloodlust. I wanted to tear her limbs apart, feed them to a woodchipper, and strip her flesh from her bones for daring to harm Olivia.

"I'm fine, Liam."

My head snapped up to see Olivia standing in the open doorway with a towel wrapped around her head and a long T-shirt that said *Meowgical*. Ironic she'd selected the nightshirt she'd worn during our first kiss, when all I wanted to do was pull her close, wrap my arms around her, and seal my lips over hers.

"She shot you," I said, something I had been repeating to myself while trying to make sense of what happened. "She could have killed you." My rising anger made my nostrils flare, and for once, I didn't hold back. I closed the distance between us, firmly gripping Olivia as I pressed my forehead against hers. She smelled like soap and sunshine, a comforting contrast to the fury souring my every breath. The realization hit me hard—my mother had come close to robbing me of this, of Olivia, the only light to my darkness.

"She wasn't trying to kill me." Oliva's voice softened. For some unfathomable reason, Olivia hadn't placed any blame on my mother, which angered me even more.

My fingers pressed into her cotton tee. "What do you call shooting you? Where I'm from, bullets are used to kill, not as a friendly gesture in getting to know someone."

"I agree it was a little unorthodox." Olivia stepped out of my grasp. "But she wanted me to see that I could heal myself. In her own way, she thought she was helping."

No excuse would ever condone my mother's actions, but this reasoning was maddening. I spun, grabbing my head in frustration. "Are you listening to yourself? You think my monster mother shot you to try and help? Did you crack your skull too?" I hadn't meant to sound so harsh, but the words escaped of their own volition.

Olivia glared at me. "I know you don't want to hear this"—she bent over and towel dried her hair—"but she acted nothing like the monster you've made her out to be in your head. I'm not saying I like her or that what she did was okay. I've never experienced pain like that before, and I'd rather never again. But I truly believe she pushed me to understand my abilities better. No one has done that yet."

My mouth hung open for a second, stunned by her audacity. But my wrath quickly burned through it. "Oh, I'm sorry. Would you have preferred one of us shoot you instead?" I stacked my hands over my heart for a touch of theatrics. "My sincere apologies. I'm sure Nikki would be more than willing to accommodate your request."

"Very funny." She scrunched the ends of her hair in the towel again.

I dropped my arms, feeling the weight of my anger settle heavy between my shoulders as I resumed my restless pacing. Tension coiled within me, nibbling at my nerves as I listened to Olivia's infuriating defense of my mother's actions. The clash between my love for Olivia and my seething rage toward my mother escalated the inner maelstrom to new heights.

When Olivia flipped back upright, her lips turned down. "Don't look at me like that. I know it's not what you want to hear, and I'm not agreeing with Pepper on how to handle monsters. What I'm trying to say is, I think my interaction with her, although scary as hell, was exactly what I could've expected had she not been a monster. I think if your mom became my teacher after I joined Hunterland . . ." I couldn't tell if she was choosing her words carefully or waiting to see if I'd explode. ". . . she still would have shot me."

I pulled the ends of my hair, redirecting the tension so I could release my tongue from between my teeth. "I don't know if I want to lock you in a room and never let you out again or scream at the top of my lungs until I go deaf so I never have to hear you defend her again. I feel like I am losing my mind." I stomped over to her, but this time I didn't reach out and touch her. I was too afraid I'd shake the shit out of her. "This should have never happened." My voice rose like the wail of an untamable tempest. "She should be dead. D–E–A–D. Dead."

Olivia's gaze shot to mine before she glared at her mirror. The same mirror I'd shattered with my shotgun the first time we met because I saw her ghost-mother appear in front of it.

"You think I don't know what it's like to have a monster mother?" Her scowl deepened. "My mom tried to kill my sister." She held her fingers up and ticked off all the people her mother had hurt. "She knocked your dad unconscious, she choked out Doc, and she killed a teacher. I know how your heart is breaking right now. It's not easy hearing your mom's alive after you thought she was dead, but don't think for one second that I don't know how it feels." She slapped her hand to her heart. "I still feel it."

My pulse raced, and I was certain she could hear the choppy breaths forced from my lungs. "But you couldn't have stopped what happened to your mom, whereas I could have. I was there. She died because I couldn't save her. I'm the reason she's a monster, and it's my fault all of this is happening." My stomach lurched, and I glanced away, not wanting to see her expression. Olivia didn't know the story of my mother's death, just that it happened. Shame washed over me as pieces of that day trickled back.

"Tell me . . ." Olivia swallowed, her voice rough. "Tell me how she died."

I didn't want to relive that moment. I certainly didn't want to remember the details, the screams, the way my heart had lodged in my throat, the guilt that had eaten away at me after. But I also knew Olivia deserved the truth, and maybe if she heard it, she'd understand and see my mother the way I did.

"The threat of death hangs over every hunt, but when you're fourteen and the worst you've suffered is a broken bone or two, that threat floats higher in the atmosphere. You forget it. Out of sight, out of mind. You unconsciously let yourself believe you're invincible, and if you, a novice, can't be touched, then those hardened badasses you call your parents? They're immortal, right?"

Olivia offered me a small smile. "I think we all think our parents are indestructible. Until they're not. That's kinda part of being a kid." Olivia stepped closer and threaded her hand into mine. The warmth of her skin encouraged me to continue.

"Maybe. But I'm a hunter. I'm supposed to be trained to think differently." I ran my free hand through my hair and sighed. "I didn't see the danger descend closer that day, weighed down like the brimming rain clouds drawing too close and darkening our prospects as we packed. Like any other day, we handed weapons to each other over the scratchy duvet of a cheap motel. I didn't see any of it coming. Just another hunt."

The memory crashed into me like a wrecking ball to my brain.

Sliding a six-inch silver hunting knife in my lower back sheath, I caught Mom's eye as she loaded her big Clint Eastwood revolver. A 44 Magnum's kickback could put a cowboy on his ass, but Mom stayed rock steady whenever she came in blasting. She coddled that beast like a baby.

Jac, on the other hand, had a "girl gun" she was loading with silver 22's with all the care of an old lady packing her jewelry. She had Mom's hair and her dancer build, but the girl primped almost as much as Dad. He was putting his dense leather jacket on in the mirror, checking that every pocket had some new doodad or pointy object in it. He straightened his double hip holsters three times.

"All those gadgets, and you're still gonna lose the head count," I teased, shaking my head in feigned disappointment.

Dad brushed off the taunt with a cutting look through the mirror. "Your dad's used to me taking home that trophy, kiddo." Mom inspected her nails with a teasing smirk lifting her mouth. You'd think a mom would let her children win. I've been to a couple game nights at friends' houses where their parents fake losing. Mine on the other hand, would rather die than give up the rights to a victory.

"I meant me," I challenged, matching her grin. "And I expect a *real* trophy. Metaphors are for suckers."

Mom laughed. "That's cute, kiddo."

"I bet my TV channel choices for tomorrow on Mom," said Jac, smug as she finally holstered her gun and tossed her blond braid over one shoulder.

"I bet mine on me." I looked toward Dad.

"Leave me out of this," he said. "I don't even like TV."

"Liar. You're just scared to bet against Mom." I chuckled. "Chicken."

"She's scarier than you, kid."

"And that's exactly why I'm betting on me," said Mom. "I get the highest body count, and Liam gives up his serial-killer shows for a week. I get a number over ten, and I choose dinner for a week, and there won't be any vegetables"—she nodded to Jac—"or ketchup on the menu." She smirked at me.

"And when you lose?" I asked.

"My channel and dinner choices go to you."

"You're on! I'll have you watching *Hannibal* and eating ketchup in no time."

"Ew." Jac's nose twitched, while Mom and I shook on it.

I leaned over the bed. "You're going down." I gave her hand a strong pump.

I wish I'd hugged her instead. Silly as I know it was, my words still feel like a prophecy. Like I spoke it into being.

The first raindrops hit the windshield as Mom pulled out of the lot—she alone drove the Bronco. A gentle pitter-patter of round droplets clung to the window and blurred the view, leaving me with little to do but pester Jac.

"That peashooter's even tinier than you." I poked her holster, making her squirm. "What do you expect to do with that. Make 'em angry?"

"Aren't boys always saying size doesn't matter?" Jac snapped, face scrunched up in annoyance.

My comeback clogged up my throat, and my startled laugh came out strangled. "Dang, Jac came with the jokes today."

"Just what the heck do you know about crude stuff like that, young lady?" Dad asked from the passenger seat. He twisted and directed his accusing eyes at me, as if I were responsible.

"Liam started it. How am I in trouble?" Jac kicked my foot, and I messed her hair back. When she pushed my shoulder, I just chuckled.

"Don't dish it out if you can't take it, Liam." Mom eyed me in the rearview mirror with a mischievous glint.

"Oh, trust me, I can take any girly jab she throws at me. I'm just worried about her. I mean, werewolves are snacky, and she's bite sized."

"I'll show you a girly jab," Jac muttered under her breath, crossing her arms as she shifted her back to me to look out the window.

"You gotta get all this hostility out now, sis." I patted her shoulder and she swatted my hand. "Can't be swinging at me once we get to the den. I know it's, like, your first hunt and all, but don't worry, I'll show you how it's done."

"It is not my first hunt!"

"Ooh, that's right. I forgot you called that disaster with the vamp fledgling a real mission."

"Liam," Dad warned. *So protective.*

"Dad," I mimicked as the first peal of thunder rolled. "She's a Hunter. She should be able to handle a little joke."

Mom locked eyes with me for a second time, and I thought I was in for it until I saw the smile lines branching toward her temples. She winked at me in that confidential way of hers that made you feel special, like she saw your soul and liked its color. By the time our tires rolled up to the woodland cabin, the rain had taken up a pounding beat and churned the dirt drive to mud. The address came from the Hunterland message board—a tip from a supernatural enthusiast who suspected a dude in his college anthropology course was a werewolf and had accidentally uncovered a whole pack hiding out in a cabin owned by a known biker gang leader. It wasn't odd for packs to form street gangs, hiding the secret of their monthly bloodlust beneath the shroud of regular criminal activity.

Mom parked behind a copse lining the cabin's unruly grass, and the sky drenched us as we filed out. We drew our weapons as we jogged in V formation across the lawn. Dad took the porch steps first, using his big boot to decimate the basic front-door lock. The bang of our entry was met with silence, save for a tinny drip-drop of a roof leak hitting a bucket propped up on the brick foot of a cold fireplace.

I stuck with Jac, sweeping my gun across the threadbare living room—shag carpet and faded upholstery—and checking the one visible closet. Mom swept the galley kitchen, and Dad hurried upstairs.

Three rounds of "Clear!" echoed through the empty house. We reconvened around the sad salmon-pink couch.

Jac blew her sweeping bangs off her forehead in a lazy sigh, spinning her little gun around one finger inside the trigger guard—safety on. "If this is a werewolf hunt, I'm bored. Vamps are more fun."

"Hear that, friends?" said a voice from the doorway, making us all whirl. "The hunter cub thinks we're boring. Maybe we should play with her and give her a real good time."

He stood half behind the door Dad had knocked off the top hinge, body protected and a mouth full of elongated teeth grinning over the slanted edge. Patches of fur had sprouted at the base of his neck and around his pointed but still-fleshy ears. Jaundiced eyes flashed in the light of Mom's first fired round. Splinters flew off the door, and the half-morphed asshole staggered back with a cry, arm whipping around his back from the force of the Magnum shattering his shoulder bone.

I had the arrogance to think, *Dumbass. Gave up his position.*

Then the cabin rocked on its foundations. Bangs and crashes came from every direction, syncopated under a steady chorus of exhilarated howls. Windows shattered inward. Doors bashed against the walls. Boots thundered on the porch and squelched in the mud outside. And bodies with gleaming teeth and vicious black claws, ran, climbed, crawled, and leaped through every opening.

A trap.

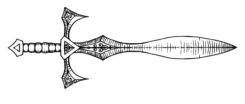

23

LIAM

We'd walked straight into a trap, the cage they'd laid, and now they were plugging the exits with their full numbers. A huge pack. Thirty at least. Felt like fifty. Hell, it could have been a hundred for all it mattered. We were out-fanged and out-clawed.

One bark from Dad and we all formed up behind the couch. One synchronized kick to the upholstered back and it toppled, tripping the nearest wave. Back together, we lit up the room, our guns' reports like thunderclaps. Growls became puppy whines and human screams of grief.

Reload.

A low wall of bodies caused the next approaching attackers' to stagger, giving me the seconds I needed to insert a new clip.

Not all the werewolves planned to fight with just tooth and nail. I saw hatchets, butterfly knives, a couple guns. Thank God for Kevlar.

When the first bullet hit my armored vest, I knocked over Jac as I fell.

Mom and Dad shifted position in a blink, towering over us. Human turrets. They targeted the armed wolves, dropping them quick.

"Bleeding?" Mom asked, voice more like a demand. Out of ammo, she pistol-whipped an oncoming woman, sending pieces of canine teeth flying, then opened the revolver chamber to toss out her casings and drop in more bullets.

"No," I said when my lungs remembered how to work. I jerked into a seated position, rammed my silver knife through a nearby kneecap, then shot the werewolf in the face when he bent over in agony.

"No." Jac shoved my butt off her leg. *Pop! Pop!* Her peashooter sounded like a toy, but it did its job. A drooling body thudded to the carpet, eyes going glossy as I stood over it.

"Higher ground," Dad directed.

We followed his lead, shifting around the fallen couch, guns blazing. As we crossed between it and the fireplace, Jac had to reload. Tongue poking between her lips in childish concentration—a reminder of her true age—she kept her head down like a rookie. Two rain-soaked mutts charged our flank, bright eyes locking on Jac's throat, and I had one bullet left, by my count.

I fired, hitting center mass on the frontrunner, then grabbed the pail of leaking roof water off the fireplace and swung. The clang of the bucket smacking the werewolf woman's head snapped Jac's eyes up, and she finished her off.

Reload.

Dad had reached the stairs, and he stood guard at their base, firing off shots while we all rushed past him to the second floor. The stairs led into a game room with a pool table and dartboard, bedroom doors branching off either side.

A flick of the light switch showed it was empty, and I turned back to see Mom grinning like a triumphant Valkyrie. With hip braced against the banister, she unloaded her entire chamber at the werewolves trying to give chase.

"Jac, see if there's a rain gutter or something we can use to get down from here," I said. I doubted the pack had any backup on the way—this had to be their full force—but I'd been trained by the best. Always have an exit strategy.

Then I squeezed between Mom and Dad, firing my fresh magazine and feeding off Mom's confidence. We were shooting fish in a barrel, and some of the werewolves were retreating deeper into the living room, less eager for fighting with the coppery scent of their friends' blood hanging in the air.

"Up to twelve." Mom nudged my arm as she reloaded.

Though I'd fired over twenty shots, my count was more like eight. Wolves didn't go down easy, even with silver. And aiming with a pistol was a bitch.

"Don't count your kills until they're confirmed," I countered.

"Where's the fun in that?" Mom asked.

I heard growls and whimpers below. Some of the pack was going full wolf. Why? To retreat? Or to boost their power? I guessed then, and know now, that a full-grown werewolf could leap as high as a second-story window. I needed to double-check, get a view of the lawn.

I turned toward Jac, heart cantering, just as the window shattered inward.

Jac screamed, dropping to her knees and throwing her arms over her head to block the stinging shards. A russet beast with hackles as long as knives leaped over the sill and landed with all four legs caging Jac. Its belly flattened her into a bow, trapping her gun. Dad called my sister's name, charging past me as I took aim. The wolf looked down, realizing the prey beneath it, and I fired a bullet between its ears. As it collapsed on top of Jac, Dad grabbed her hand, tugging her out. She sucked in a desperate breath as her head popped free of the fur.

"Jac, baby, are you all right?" Mom had turned, eyes wide with fear she rarely let show. Despite her grit, her killer aim, and the wit she seared onto every tough situation, she was still our mom. Back then at least.

Hell, we'd all turned when Jac screamed. She was the purest of us. The baby. The one heart not yet jaded.

We'd all, for just a second, forgotten. And it cost us everything.

I saw the hairy fucker grab her. Saw him take the last two stairs in one step. Saw his cheap anime tattoo on a bulging bicep revealed by a sleeveless vest. Saw the tufts of silver fur on his neck and the gleam of his teeth. Saw those black nails dig into Mom's shoulders and yank her against his chest, then force down her gun arm.

I raised my pistol, but my hands shook. The shot wasn't clean. I would hit her.

Mom threw back her head, cracking the werewolf's nose. Then she fired her downturned Magnum into his foot, trying to make him flinch, retreat, give me an opening, but he was a big sucker. He turned pain into fury, growling as he sank those elongated teeth into Mom's shoulder.

Jac was screaming again. High and wild. But this cry had a shape. In my shock, watching the spreading blood stain the neck of Mom's shirt beneath her jacket, the words didn't make sense at first. Then they snapped into too-sharp focus as adrenaline gave the world a hallucinogenic jolt. "Momma!" A child's word. A plea. Shrieked over and over. Because we all knew what it meant, that bite. Though I didn't admit it to myself just then.

I charged forward. Three more were on the stairs, and Mom was still alive. That was all that mattered. With a cry of mingled fury and anguish, Mom threw her weight against the wolf, knocking his head against the slanted wall of the staircase. His teeth released. She ripped her arm free of his grip, flipped the Magnum upside down as she aimed over her shoulder, and blew his brains all over the place.

I used the banister to kick out with both feet and knock the leading werewolf down the stairs. She tumbled, taking her buddies down with her. When they hit the living-room floor in a heap, Mom and I were both there. Three headshots. They were still ringing in my ears as Mom ran for an open window, yelling, "They're getting away!"

She took a shooter's stance by the window, firing out at the six or so wolves running full tilt toward the trees. But her injured shoulder made her hold her arm funny. The Magnum's kickback nearly shot the weapon out of her hands. That's when it really hit me. Mom couldn't fire her Magnum. Because she'd been bitten by a werewolf. The infection was already running through her veins. My limbs didn't want to work. I couldn't move to join her.

Instead, I watched in horrified silence as Dad jogged down the stairs with a wriggling, hysterical Jac over his shoulder. As he traversed the bodies, heading for the busted front door, Jac spotted Mom and reached out with both arms. Tears glossed her cheeks and clogged her throat so her sobs came out as coughs. Dad set her down, but when she tried to run to Mom, his arm barricaded her, tugging her against him like he almost feared Mom would bite her.

"Momma?" Jac gripped Dad's offending arm, as if asking Mom to make him let her go.

At her call, Mom turned around, tears in her eyes.

She let her Magnum dangle, her other hand pressed to her bleeding shoulder.

"We need to go, before they regroup out there," said Dad. He had gone the color of a corpse, his eyes bouncing from Mom's face to her wound. "We'll . . . we'll get that looked at."

Mom swallowed her tears, shaking her head. "No, Jackson." Her voice cracked. "You know I can't. There's nothing you can do for me now."

Dad set his jaw. "You don't know that!" Despite his outburst, he still held Jac back, and my heart bottomed out, leaving me cold all over. "We haven't looked into it that hard. There could be a way, if we act quickly."

"Mom, listen to him, please," I said, snapping out of my stupor and taking two steps toward her.

She threw up both hands to ward me off, and I jerked to a stop, all the wind knocked out of me by a blow that never made contact.

"No." She screwed her face up into the look that could make Dad's knees quake and used her "you will listen to me, mister" voice. "I can't go with you. Stay back. I need you to make me a hunter's promise and leave."

Jac looked up at Dad, expression slack with disbelief.

"I can't..." Dad squeezed his eyes shut, and I'd never seen him look so defeated.

"You will. Please, Jackson." Mom stood her ground even as her dripping tears made the blood on her neck run in pink rivulets. "Promise me you will take my children and leave." She sucked in a breath and with an exhale shouted, "Say it."

"A hunter's promise," said Dad, meeting her eye and charging the air with words I'm certain only they could hear.

"You too, Liam." The smile she turned on me was dipped in sorrow, making the corners quiver. "Show Jacqueline it's all right. Say it."

Protect Jacqueline. Now the unspoken words were for me. *Get her out of here.*

She'd heard the howls, just as I had. The mournful sounds brewed in the surrounding trees—a handful at first, then dozens.

At the next full moon, Mom would be the one howling. Of course, back then, I thought I knew her true intention. To fight until the end, take as many wolves with her as she could, and then end it if she found herself still standing. I'd thought that's what she wanted, and even though I wanted to pretend that spilling enough werewolf blood would somehow spare her, that I could kill my way to her salvation, I knew dragging this out would leave a worse scar on everyone's heart.

"A hunter's promise." I growled the words to kick-start my numbed throat.

"Liam? No," whimpered Jac.

"Yes, Jac. For Mom. Do it for Mom. You know it's the only way."

"I love you, sweetheart," said Mom, brightening her smile with whatever sliver of hope she had left. "This doesn't change that. You understand?"

Jac nodded slowly, her sobs returning full force. "A hunter's promise."

The howls were drawing nearer. From the north side. Soon, they'd surround the cabin. I wanted to let them come, take a few more out before we turned our backs on Mom. I drew my gun, but Dad wouldn't risk another loss.

With Jac propped on his hip like a giant three-year-old, he used his free hand to grab a hunk of my jacket and wrestle me out the front door just as the back one banged against the wall. I heard the wolves' claws on the wooden floor as I staggered down the porch steps. Heard their hungry yips and savage growls as Dad tossed Jac into the backseat. But I didn't close my eyes and submit to Dad's incessant tugging, ducking into the passenger seat, until Mom started screaming.

Those shrieks ripped through my head even when Dad slammed the door, crossed to the driver's side, and revved the engine. The engine that purred only for Mom. When Dad cranked the key, the Bronco roared, a gnashing, ugly sound that mingled with Mom's guttural cries of agony.

I couldn't open my eyes, couldn't bear what I might see through that busted front door. Not even when we barreled back down the dirt drive. Not when the wheels hit asphalt or minutes later when Jac's sobs turned into exhausted mewls of mourning. I didn't open them until Dad said, "We'll go back for her body and give her a proper hunter's burial."

I nodded, taking strength in the idea of getting a final goodbye.

But even that closure was robbed from me.

I was left to pick up the pieces of a shattered world, where nothing made sense. Lightning had struck our lives and done the impossible. An immortal had been slain.

24

OLIVIA

After Liam finished recounting his mother's heartbreaking story, he settled beside me on the bed on top of the covers. Unlike our previous nights together, as I drifted in and out of sleep, the mattress dipped, and I heard Liam's departure. I hadn't expected anything to change between us. I understood the pain he'd endured over his mother's death, the weight of the fear he might experience another similar loss. No matter what transpired between us, his past would always keep him at arm's length. The shared future I yearned for would remain forever out of reach. His mother's history had put everything into perspective. It didn't diminish the ache in my heart, but it did provide a certain cushioning, a sense of understanding. I couldn't bear the thought of putting Liam through such torment again. And now, as a hunter myself, I couldn't make him any promises about my own fate.

When I woke the next morning, I truly grasped the depth of my decision to join Hunterland and its cause for the first time. A wave of pride washed over me, filling a small portion of the void left by Liam. It didn't entirely alleviate the pain, but it brought a measure of solace, a bittersweet satisfaction.

"Why are you so quiet today?" Jac asked Liam as the four of us strolled up the school steps. She lowered her voice. "Are you still mad because Fenton got away?"

When we'd arrived home yesterday, Liam couldn't even look at Jac, so Pepper and I had told her the hunt went south and Fenton escaped without us learning much. Jac seemed to have accepted the stretched truth without any further questions. Until now.

"Leave it alone, Jac. I'm just tired. I slept maybe an hour last night." Liam stared at the snow-covered ground, never bothering to look up at his sister.

Overnight, a blanket of pristine white had transformed the school lot into a picturesque scene straight out of a storybook. The pavement shimmered under the morning sunlight, and white powder clung to the tree branches. Each step we took left imprints in the fresh snowfall, leaving a trail of footprints behind us as we entered through the doors.

The warm air was a welcome change from the crisp chill and frigid conversation.

"Well, why aren't you sleeping? Are you having nightmares again?" Jac continued. "You look like crap."

Pepper and I kept our mouths shut, stiff with awkwardness, but I agreed with Jac. From the moment Liam had stepped into the kitchen this morning to pour himself a cup of coffee, his crushing exhaustion was evident. The word "crap" couldn't capture the true extent of Liam's appearance. His once-neat Henley shirt bore deep wrinkles as if plucked from the bottom of the laundry hamper, reminiscent of a piece of abstract art. Dark circles like football paint marred his under eyes, resembling shadows deeper and darker than those of simple sleeplessness. He'd forgone his usual styling, and his cascade of perfect waves now looked like the tangled chaos of Pepper's own Cindy Lou Who bedhead.

"Is that why you had like three cups of black coffee this morning?" Jac pressed on, unwavering in her pursuit, like a determined journalist on the trail of her big-break story. I wished she would just let it go, but I wasn't about to say anything and draw more attention to his secrecy.

Liam rubbed his eyes but never commented.

"I'm surprised you're not twitching." She leaned in shoulder to shoulder and asked in hushed tones, "You took your serum again today, right?"

Liam's cheeks went the color of blood, and I swore I saw some steam emit from his flared nostrils. The fact his mother was roaming Falkville Falls, Fenton got away, and his father still hadn't turned up seemed to have eaten away at any patience he had left.

"Shut it, Jac. I mean it."

Pepper nudged my shoulder, her gum popping with a burst of artificial grape scent. I pushed her away. "Stop that." She tried to tell me something with her eyes, but she just managed to bug them out like one of those creepy Beanie Boos she used to collect. "You look nuts," I whispered.

"What are you two talking about?" Jac looked around at us.

Pepper's eyebrows folded inward to match her frown. I wanted to yell at her, but she'd already brought us under an unwanted spotlight. If Pepper kept this up, Jac was bound to get suspicious.

"Hey, man." Dustin slung his arm around Liam's shoulder, seamlessly joining our group in the bustling halls. His arrival provided a much-needed interruption that effortlessly diffused the tension like a breath of fresh air. A warm smile spread across my face in appreciation for Dustin's trusty, impeccable timing. "So, what did you guys get up to yesterday? I swear I was on the verge of boredom-induced insanity. This weather, though, am I right?" He shivered.

Liam grunted, and my sister pinched my arm.

"Will you stop it?" I swatted her away, but this time, I'd gotten her hint. She wanted me to take the attention off Liam. "We actually didn't do much. Just sat around watching true-crime shows." I glared at my sister to say, *Happy now?*

"Oh, which ones?" Bradley's voice snuck up behind me, and I jumped hard enough to drop my purse and bookbag. He grabbed my elbow to steady me. "Sorry about that." Bradley squatted and handed up my things. I readjusted the straps on my shoulder. "Thanks."

"I gotta get to class." Jac looped her arm through her brother's and dragged him away. "Come on. You can walk me." She might not have known the depths of Liam's present torment, but she knew his mood had soured. Leading him in the opposite direction rescued all of us from an uncomfortable situation. No way Liam had the patience to tolerate a chipper Bradley this morning.

As the two of them walked off, Bradley fixed an intense gaze on Liam. His jade eyes hardened like real gemstones. "Is that guy ever gonna give me a chance?"

I gently nudged his side to divert his gaze. "He's not used to making new friends."

"Shame. Was going to invite him out with my brothers and I next weekend."

Pepper threw her head back and laughed. "That would be a hard no. Liam does not do male bonding." My sister looked up to the left. "Or even female bonding. You'd have better luck asking Jazzy."

Bradley shrugged. "Too bad. I think they'd all get along."

"You clearly don't know Liam very well." Dustin patted Bradley's back.

"Oh, but I want to." He winked in my direction. "After all, everyone likes me. I've got golden retriever energy." My lips tipped upward. "See you in class." He took off down the hall.

"That's weird." My sister shook her head.

"What is?" I tilted my head.

Pepper's brows furrowed. "Uh, nothing. See you later." She shot down the hallway.

I watched as Bradley exchanged a couple words with a few girls from our class, then slipped into the adjacent classroom.

Maybe that's exactly what Liam needed, a friend outside of our world. I knew that's what helped me get through the hard times being part of Hunterland, having Dustin and now Bradley. I vowed in that very moment to work on helping Liam find balance. It was the least I could do.

25

PEPPER

I observed from around the corner of the hallway—feeling like a creeper—Dustin, Jazzy, Bradley, and Livy exiting first period together. While most of the gang headed in the opposite direction, Dustin saluted their little group and walked unknowingly my way. As he turned the corner, I stepped into his path.

"Whoa." Dustin skidded to a stop, nearly colliding with me. "What the hell? Why are you lurking in the shadows like a deviant?" His bushy eyebrows arched. "Are you back to tagging walls again?"

I rolled my eyes. Couldn't Livy and her friends let go of the past already? It had been months since I last sprayed graffiti on a building. "No, you big buffoon." I grabbed his arm and pulled him against the end of a line of lockers. "I need your help."

"Great. What did you get yourself into this time?" Dustin propped his hands on his hips. I couldn't decide if I wanted to laugh at him or give him a good smack. He always acted like he was my dad's age. Years ago he had labeled me the devil Davis and Livy the angel, and no amount of growing up seemed to change that. But I still needed his help, and I knew Dustin well enough to believe he wouldn't turn me down.

"You know I'm going to have to tell Liv whatever trouble you're into. I won't lie to her to cover for you."

"I'm not in trouble." A familiar annoyance crawled over my skin, twitching my slapping hand. Livy's friends and their constant suspicions! Jessica had always accused me of the same thing. They acted like I was a convict out on parole. "I. Need. Your. Help." I emphasized each word since he clearly didn't catch them the first time.

"Why?" Dustin leaned against the wall, and his broad shoulders blocked the world behind him. I often wondered why he played basketball instead of football with a frame like that. "The last time I said I'd help a Davis sister, I got involved in some seriously illegal stuff that could have ruined my chances of a career in law enforcement. Is it that kind of help?" He scowled with distrust.

A couple months earlier, Livy, Jessica, and Dustin had barely escaped felony charges for an illegal investigation involving the retention of personal information about nurses employed at our local hospital—stolen and provided by our old babysitter, who worked there. I could only imagine what he thought I wanted if he considered me the black sheep of the family.

Better get to the point, and fast.

"You're really good at research, and I'm not. I have this strange gut feeling, and I . . ." I cracked my knuckles, stalling for time. What if Dustin thought I had gone crazy? Or worse, what if he ended up tattling on me instead of helping?

"As long as it's not illegal, I'll help you. Research is my specialty."

I lifted up on my toes and threw my arms around Dustin's neck. "You are awesome." I released him and stepped back. A faint blush inched along his cheekbones. "Great. Let's go to the library."

"All right. Lead the way, little Davis. But after we do this, if I think Liv should know, I will tell her."

Fine by me. That was the whole point. "You got it." I pulled him out of the shadows, dragging him down the corridor.

Inside, Dustin walked to the back of the room and sat at one of the community computers while I hovered above him. The screen illuminated both our faces. "All right, what am I looking for?"

"What do you think of Bradley Sanders?"

Dustin peered up at me. "He's a little weird, possibly unbalanced." Dustin shrugged. "But his mom meddled in the black market and was murdered for it, so I suspect his childhood was different. He's pretty spirited to have gone through all that, though. Why? Are we here because of him?"

"Maybe. It's more concern over something I thought I heard." I bit the inside of my cheek, remembering the voice I'd heard as he walked away from us earlier today. Either there was a spirit following him or another supernatural, but I'd overheard something.

Dustin side-eyed me.

I slapped Dustin's shoulder. "Just help me and stop giving me weird looks. It's a gut feeling, okay?"

"Pepper." Dustin's tone held a warning I understood well. But thanks to Doc's Hunterland lore lessons, I'd started looking at things differently. Doc challenged us to listen twice as much as we spoke. He'd point to his ears and say, *We have two of these.* Then point to his mouth and say, *Only one of these. If you pay twice the attention to what people say, you'll learn their hidden truths. The devil is in the details and the spaces between.*

I shook my head. "Just humor me." I sighed. "What if his family is still part of the black market? If he's friends with Livy, she could wind up in a very dangerous position. Even if it's by accident."

"That's a really big stretch, Pepper." Dustin shot me puppy-dog eyes.

Maybe he was right, but it didn't mean I'd stop looking into it. I pointed at the keyboard. "Just do your super-duper detective investigation thingy that you do and look up his mother's death. Then we can find out more information about his brothers and father too. I don't know what we're looking for, but I might know when we find it."

Dustin placed his big mitts over the keyboard. "I really think you're overreacting. I mean if the guy's family is into some shady shit, we should be telling your father or Liam's dad, but . . ."

"Will you just do it? Please."

Dustin huffed, but instead of another protest, he tapped the keys.

After about an hour, Dustin found exactly what we had already known about the mother's death in Chicago. The murderer mutilated her something awful, ripping out all her organs perimortem and discarding what would never sell on the black market, leaving her for dead in her own clinical office. Statements from authorities claimed that a thorough investigation revealed she had illegally distributed organs and that one of her buyers killed her when a deal went south. Everything Bradley had alluded to on Friday was true. But we were missing something; we had to be.

"There has to be more," I mumbled.

Dustin continued typing, opening window after window in a string of articles and references. He'd read one, then flip back to the other to see if the data matched up. After the seventh window, he stopped, cursor hovering. "This might be something."

Leaning over Dustin was like sticking your head in a furnace.

"This says she was survived by her husband and *son*, singular. It only mentions Bradley." Dustin looked up at me. "That could mean the other three are Bradley's stepbrothers. Maybe his dad had a previous marriage. He said they were older, right?"

"Yeah." I nibbled my nail.

"Let's see if Bradley's dad remarried."

Dustin did an extensive search on Bradley's dad, Mark Sanders. No mention of a previous marriage or current marriage. Maybe I had this all wrong. Maybe the spirit or supernatural being wasn't after Bradley. Maybe the voice was something else entirely.

"Well, this is strange."

"What?" I leaned in and read the article pulled up on the computer.

Dana Claire

MYSTERIOUS DISAPPEARANCE OF CORPSE PUZZLES AUTHORITIES IN ILLINOIS STATE PARK

(Giant City State Park, Giant City, IL). *In a shocking development that has sent ripples of disbelief through the local community, a random killing in the picturesque mountains of an Illinois state park has taken a chilling twist. A local hiker stumbled upon a lifeless body while exploring a secluded trail. However, when authorities arrived at the scene, the corpse had mysteriously vanished, leaving investigators scratching their heads. The peculiar incident has raised questions about the nature of the crime and the identity of the individual involved.*

The discovery was made by Sarah Thompson, an avid hiker known for her love of nature and exploration. While venturing deep into the park's heart, she encountered a bloodied body lying motionless among the trees. In a horrific coincidence, she recognized the man as one Mark Sanders, a loyal patron of her coffee shop, the Bean on Main Street, Giant City.

Thompson contacted the authorities, who promptly dispatched a team to the area. However, upon arrival, the officials found no trace of the remains and no signs of a struggle. The vanishing act left investigators puzzled and eager to unravel the mysterious turn of events.

Forensic experts obtained DNA evidence from the crime scene, linking the vanished corpse to Sanders, confirming the validity of Thompson's claims. Later that day, however, Sanders was found alive and well, and has since denied being at the scene. His alibi has left investigators baffled. According to his account, he was miles from the crime scene during the estimated time of the incident.

Authorities have not released any additional statements or theories on the conundrum. In response to the perplexing events and the connection to his name, Mark Sanders and his family issued a brief statement expressing their bewilderment and requesting privacy during this trying time. "This whole situation is absolutely ridiculous. I have no idea how my DNA ended up on that trail," said Sanders. "I have never hiked, nor do I plan to hike in Giant City State Park. My connection with Miss Sarah Thompson is solely through her coffee shop. We have no relationship outside of that. I believe that she may have been suffering from dehydration and conjured up the whole scene in her head."

This perplexing incident in the Illinois State Park adds another layer to a long-standing mystery surrounding the area. Over the years, the park has gained a reputation for a disproportionate number of missing hikers and outdoors enthusiasts whose cases have gone unsolved. The vanishing corpse and the subsequent disappearance of evidence only serve to intensify the existing enigma surrounding the park.

While authorities remain tight-lipped about the ongoing investigation, the citizens eagerly await updates and hope for a resolution to this bizarre and bewildering occurrence. Until then, the mystery surrounding the vanished body, its connection to Sanders, and Thompson's shocking encounter continues to captivate the imaginations of all those seeking answers in this strange and perplexing case.

"That is strange," I muttered.

"You think Bradley's dad killed someone or something? Maybe it's linked to the organ black market his wife was associated with." Dustin continued to search, mouse clicking. "There's nothing else. No mention of him having any other sons or other marriages. According to everything we've found, Bradley doesn't seem to have any siblings." Dustin turned to me with a remorseful frown. "I don't think that's enough to call his family dangerous. But I can't say I regret skipping two periods to look this up. For now, let's keep a really close eye on him."

I agreed. The more I learned about Bradley and his family, the more certain I became that my sister was in harm's way. I'd lost my mother to a serial-killer spirit; I wasn't about to lose my sister to a vengeful black-market-mob ghost.

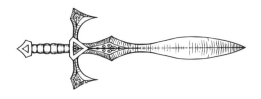

26

LIAM

I ran into Dustin at our lockers. We had the next class together and usually made our way there collectively. He pulled out his textbook and shoved it in his bag.

"We gotta talk, man." Dustin shut his locker and turned toward me. "Pepper thinks something's up with the new guy." Dustin looked left and right down the hallway and continued in a lower voice. "We skipped second and third period to see if his story about his family was true."

My ears perked up. Well, that was news to me. "What did you find out?"

"He wasn't lying. His mom was brutally murdered."

I'd never thought Bradley lied. In fact, I had been surprised by his honesty. Hunters were practically human lie detectors. We knew when something was fabricated. And although I thought Bradley might be a little eccentric, his story felt legit.

"That sucks." I finished filling my bag and zipped it up. No matter how badly I wanted to throttle Bradley, losing a parent in such a vicious way couldn't have been easy.

"But there's something else," Dustin leaned in and whispered, "I think his old man's involved too. Maybe his family came here to get out from under police scrutiny or maybe they're running from the people his mother screwed over. I don't know, man." His irises expanded, and I saw genuine fear swimming there. "What if they're here hiding from bad people who come looking for them and Liv gets caught up in it all?"

Now *that* got my attention. I shut my locker and turned to Dustin. "What makes you think his family is on the run? What if they just wanted to get away from the gossip that probably followed his mother's death?" I knew people who'd been on the run, always looking over their shoulder. Bradley Sanders didn't seem to fit that bill. Regardless, I'd do a deeper dive into their family history, because if Bradley's family was wrapped up in a criminal scandal, then Olivia could be in danger.

Dustin handed me a printout of their findings and I skimmed through it. I scratched my head. I knew Dustin loved crime investigations—the guy had a hard-on for anything police related—but this felt like a stretch. "I don't know." Hoisting my bag over my shoulder, I lounged against my locker.

"There's more. There are over a dozen unsolved killings in that part of the state park. But this was the only one that had no body at the scene." Dustin locked his door and shrugged. "Listen man, nothing against Bradley. I just don't think we should be leaving Liv alone with him. Not until we get to know him better at least." Dustin patted me on the back. Bradley walked by at that exact moment, his ear glued to his phone.

Maybe it *was* time I took a page out of Pepper's playbook. "I'll go talk to him. If there's something to be concerned about, I'll figure it out."

"If I hadn't already skipped two periods, I'd come with you. Let me know how it goes." Dustin gave me a two-fingered salute and took off down the hallway.

My upped serum dosage this morning—under threat of multiple werewolves' involvement in the area—turned out to be fortuitous. No one else could've overheard Bradley's conversation.

"Yeah, I heard you the first time." His murmur rang like a bell when I focused, surprising me with its bitter edge. "I'll produce results, but you better hold up your end of the deal."

"That didn't sound promising," I muttered under my breath.

Bradley turned around almost like he heard me. His lips stretched into a shit-eating grin. Not a moment later, he strutted out the front doors of the school. I watched from the window. Instead of going to his own car, he headed to the twins' rental. He bent down, as if examining their tires, then stood and continued to his own car.

What the hell?

His vehicle had its taillights facing me. So, when he slipped into the driver's seat, I threw open the school doors and snuck between automobiles to get to Jazzy and Nikki's sedan. When I leaned down, I noticed two of the tires were slashed. Did he do that? Did someone he knew do that? And why target the girls?

I ran to my car next, keeping one eye on Bradley, who seemed to be waiting, maybe for the car to heat up or maybe something more sinister. I inspected my tires. They were intact.

My head snapped up at a screeching sound. Bradley peeled out of his parking spot and headed toward the lot exit. I jumped into the Bronco, threw my bag on my seat, and let the engine roar. Bradley was up to something. Dustin was right; we couldn't leave him unattended with Olivia, or anyone else for that matter. There was too much at stake right now.

I followed him for over ten minutes before I called Doc.

He picked up on the first ring. "William, shouldn't you be in class?" *The Love Boat* played in the background. Doc loved that old classic TV show.

I ignored him. "Hey, you know that new kid at school that Olivia befriended?"

The TV volume lowered as papers ruffled. "Can't say I do, but go on."

"I think he just slashed your nieces' tires."

The background noise ceased to exist. "He what?!"

As monster hunters, we often overlooked everyday wickedness, always on the lookout for the worst of the worst. Fangs, claws, scales, poison, spells. Those were the deadly weapons used against us daily. So, when a normal crime like slicing tires occurred, we faltered. Questions most authorities asked weren't even on our radar. It took us twice the time to think like a human rather than a monster. But I'd had time with this puzzle.

"Jazzy hates him, and it's no secret, so it could just be payback for her attitude. He did come from a rough upbringing."

"So, you think it's a teenage prank?" Doc's flabbergasted tone made me suppress a chuckle. I bet if I'd called saying windigo claws had slashed that rubber, Doc wouldn't have even blinked. I could already picture him stroking his beard, puzzling over juvenile hoaxes.

"I don't think it's supernatural, but I do think it's crime related. Can you do me a favor? Get Matt involved. Look into the death of Bradley Sanders's mother in Chicago. I think there's more to it than Bradley admitted. Also, look into an incident involving Bradley's father at a state park. His DNA was left at the crime scene, but the whole thing is one mystery in a slew of murders there."

"All right. I'll start now. Are you at school?"

"No. I'm following him. I'll be back to pick the girls up before the last bell, but you'll need to get the twins' car fixed before they find out it was him, because if this is about Jazzy's sass, she'll show him a whole new level. And Nikki, she'll flay him alive."

"I'll have it done before they even know it happened. We don't have time for petty revenge antics. Matt and I have been looking through known associates of your mother and we cannot find anything on four men and a teenager. In fact, we now have more questions than when we started." Doc sighed. "Your mother is either planting information to throw us off or she's done one hell of a job hiding things." Doc paused. "Stay vigilant. Veronica's still out there, and her mission's not complete."

Didn't I know it! When it came to my mother, nothing was ever simple. Why would she start now?

"Have you heard from Dad?"

"No. But Beth has added an alert to the Hunterland online board. Every hunter in the Chicago area is out looking for him. We'll find him."

Bradley slowed down, forcing me to drop back. "I've got to go."

I ended the call. Once I handled Bradley, I'd join the hunt. We couldn't do this without my father, and I'd be damned before letting another hunter be in charge of his fate . . . or his life.

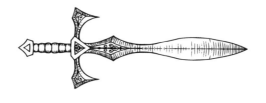

27

LIAM

As I pulled onto the shoulder and let the car behind me pass to form a bigger buffer, I wondered what I was about to walk into. Bradley didn't seem like a bad guy—not so bad anyway. His worst offense thus far was liking Olivia. But if his parents had been wrapped up in some illegal crime syndicate, well, that would change everything.

After a second car passed, I rolled back onto the highway. By the time I caught up, I saw the rear of Bradley's car parked at the edge of a gravel driveway with fresh tire tracks. Instead of alerting him or whomever he was meeting of my own arrival, I parked the Bronco in a rest area a couple hundred feet down the road and took off on foot.

I hid behind the trees until I got closer to the small house. Two unfamiliar cars stood parked on the grass. One a gutted black Jeep and the other an old, run-down station wagon with duct tape on the side windows.

Inch by inch, careful not to disturb the woodland below my feet, I crept closer. I gaped. Blood droplets trailed up the steps onto the rotted porch. Even before I dragged my hand over one of them, smearing the bright red blob between my fingers, I knew it was fresh. My gaze flicked to the forest surrounding the log cabin, then to the gravel driveway. Nothing about this place screamed livable—it was more like a place to hide dead bodies. Perfect for a horror film.

The porch light flickered, and the front door was swaying as if someone just passed through in a hurry.

What the hell has this idiot gotten himself into?

I tilted my head to the side, pricking up my ears. The serum ran through my veins, sharpening my senses. Birds whistled around me, the leaves shifted in the wind, but when I concentrated on the house, a faint thump sounded inside. Then a groan followed. Either Bradley had fallen victim or he'd inflicted violence.

Neither ideal. If Bradley was part of the mob, I'd kill him for even laying an eye on Olivia. But if this was his family's doing and Bradley was caught in the middle, I'd save his ass and beat the crap out of his father and older brothers for putting him in this position. Regardless, the last thing we needed right now, with werewolves on the loose, was some stupid, ordinary police case where Olivia ended up involved or, worse, endangered.

I wrapped my fingers around the door handle and pushed it open just enough to slip through, adrenaline buzzing and serum hardening my muscles to granite. I also had my Glock 45 strapped to my back. No matter what this moron had involved himself in, I'd get us out of it.

I stepped farther into the hallway. A light dangled at eye level, half pulled out of the ceiling. Peeling wallpaper lined the hallway, and I tiptoed across splintered hardwood. Yet, I couldn't smell old wallpaper glue or rotting wood. Instead, the odor of a sterile mixture like bleach and ammonia stung my nose, making my nostril hairs curl and my eyes water. Something didn't add up. Why would an abandoned cabin in the middle of nowhere be washed down with hospital-grade cleaners?

Voices from down the hallway alerted me to two men with Bradley on the other side of the wall. "She gave you fair warning. You knew exactly what you were getting into the second you chose your side."

Another thud and groan. "Do you think you should be forgiven? You made the wrong choice."

Was Bradley committing crimes too?

"I never had a choice. That was stolen from me. It's her fault. She brought me into this world, then abandoned me when I needed her most. *She* left me for dead. *She* gave me no other option. What did she expect?" Bradley's next swear was garbled like he had marbles stuffed in his cheeks.

A second voice, deeper and more commanding, interrupted. "She saved you from a horrible fate. Did everything in her power to keep you as safe as possible. And this is how you repay her? You've sentenced yourself to death. I don't even feel bad for you. None of us do. And yet here you are, still alive and bartering. I'd be nervous if I were you. Those who walk a fine line usually misstep."

Death? Bartering? I sucked in a breath. Whatever they were pissed about, it sounded like Bradley had stepped into quicksand. He might not be my favorite person, but it wasn't like I had planned on killing the guy. These guys sure as hell wanted his head, though.

Time to break this party up and save his ass.

I rounded the corner and jolted to a stop, paralyzed by the scene unfolding before me.

Two half-turned werewolves sliced their claws through Bradley's skin, holding him still like nails driven through a board. Saliva-coated fangs protruded from their mouths. A third salivating animal stood before Bradley like a displeased manager. I knew that spiky gray hair and matching stubble. Fenton. He threw a punch straight into Bradley's chin so hard the bone cracked. Blood sprayed across the floor and stained Fenton's flannel. He used the shirt to wipe the remnants off his knuckles with a satisfied smirk. I assessed the damage to Bradley and stopped short on his glowing yellow eyes, the pupils slitted rather than round and human.

You've got to be kidding me.

Bradley was a lycanthrope. How the hell had I missed that? How had the twins, Doc, *and* Jac missed it? We were all trained, and no one had a clue, which made me wonder how many times we had wandered into close proximity to a monster and not known. But, Pepper, she'd suspected something off about him. She might not have pinpointed what, but her instincts made her dig deeper. I wondered if she'd tapped into his supernatural side. Maybe she'd heard him internally speak and not even realized it. Or maybe her powers were stronger than we could even imagine.

I reached for my gun, realizing too late I had left the one with silver bullets in the car. The hunk of junk at my back would be of no use. I'd prepared for the wrong enemy. It wasn't like I could drag along my whole arsenal at all times. Hell, I'd end up carrying a luggage set.

If I could get back to the car . . .

I tried to reverse my steps in hopes of getting to the Bronco's stash of monster firearms, but the floor creaked. The element of surprise vanished before I had any defense. Now I had to rely on brute force. I just hoped that my serum strength would be enough.

"Let him go," I yelled as six eyes lifted to mine. Not sure why I chose those words. I'd end up having to kill Bradley too. But for now, he was the lesser evil.

Bradley's gaze darted from Fenton to me. "See, I told you he'd follow me. Now, let my pack go free. You got what you wanted. I delivered him to your doorstep, didn't I?"

My chest filled with hot rage, my blood rushing like the aftermath of a dam break. He'd baited me, led me straight into a trap to save his pathetic monster family's furry asses.

"Nice of you to join us, hunter." My mother's second-in-command spoke to me but never took his eyes off Bradley. Unconcerned and unsurprised.

He knew I was here the whole time. I crossed my arms at my chest. "See how nice I am when I send you to your maker. This won't end like our first meeting."

Fenton smiled but kept his sights set on a bleeding Bradley. "You're half right, kid. This time we'll get to the transaction part." He gripped Bradley's chin, pinching hard enough to make Bradley wince. "You may go. But don't think this is over. You've bought your freedom for a little while longer. She's not done with you, disloyal mutt." He jerked his head at his two feral buddies as he released his grip. "Let him go."

They retracted their claws, and blood rained around Bradley's feet. He righted himself, wiping the crimson smears off his mouth. When he looked over at me, his eyes narrowed. He spat a mixture of white froth and red sputum at my boots. Then, with lightning speed, he ran out of the house and never looked back.

Fan-fucking-tastic.

Fenton raised himself to his full height. "Don't be mad at him. It wasn't his idea to lure you here."

"Comforting," I snarked.

He turned to the two lackeys. "Follow him." He grabbed a towel on the counter behind him and wiped more of the sweat and blood off his face. "And when you find his pack, kill them like you should have, back in Chicago."

My jaw ticked. Sure, I'd end up killing Bradley and his werewolf family, but talk about betrayal. These creatures were monsters in every way, shape, and form. No loyalty, no trust, no oath to live by. Whenever the opportunity to put these foul beasts into their grave appeared, it left the taste of satisfaction on my tongue, and today I'd get to slay them with my bare hands.

But before I could act, the two flunkies shifted to obey the boss's orders. In a blink, their noses filled with small, translucent whiskers. Bones popped, rearranging themselves beneath stretched skin. A crackle like milk poured over rice cereal preceded a coat of striped hair sprouting through their pores. I think I gasped, but the tearing of their clothes drowned the sound. Tailbones elongated from their spines, bending into a broad arch. Mews like I'd never heard escaped their wolf-like jaws as pawed hands slapped onto the wooden floors. They stood over six feet tall and, by my guesstimate, eight feet long including the tail. Their shredded clothes fell around their new claws.

I held my breath. I'd never witnessed a shape-shifter's transformation before. My brain finally caught up to my eyes, as both forms darted out after Bradley.

Fenton looked over and sighed. "Sorry about this, kid."

The whack came out of nowhere.

The back of my head exploded in a pain so ferocious that bile crawled up my throat. When the second one hit, I crumpled to the ground, my jaw hitting the floor with enough force to blur my vision. Blood pooled around my mouth as everything faded to black.

28

OLIVIA

Jazzy and Nikki sat waiting on the stone wall outside school as Jac, Pepper, and I exited the building. The twins threw their heads back, roaring with laughter over some private joke. Seeing them together like that almost made me believe Nikki would be a fun friend. I missed Jessica, and although Jazzy and I had formed a close friendship, Nikki possessed more of my old friend's spirit. She always told me the truth, never sugarcoated life, and when I really needed to be challenged, she stood up to me. In fact, there were moments when, I daresay, Nikki had made me a better person. She sure as hell had made me a better monster hunter.

When we were training, I saw how much she wanted to help me. Then Liam would step into the room, and everything changed—like the space shifted and we entered a new reality. Her eyes would narrow at me, her lips pulled down. Liam triggered the ugly side of her. Or maybe he prompted memories she'd rather forget. I couldn't necessarily tell. Did she want him? Or did she just want me not to want him? I sighed internally. I was damned either way.

As we approached the twins, Jac's brows creased. She swiveled around. "Where's Liam?" She froze as she surveyed the empty spot beside their car and then scoured the lot. "Where's the Bronco?" The concern pitched up her voice.

We all did a sweep of our own. No Bronco.

Nikki jumped off her seat, pulled out her phone, and dialed. She held it to her ear and stared me down like I had something to do with Liam's disappearance. When no one answered, her eyes dove into mine with pointed accusation, and she called again. "What did you do?"

Heat bloomed across my cheeks as I watched her dial a third time. "Why the hell would this be my fault?" I gestured at the vacant spot. "I'm just as surprised as you are." Irritation pinched the back of my neck. Nikki always blamed me for anything Liam related.

She shot me a look before tucking her phone into her back pocket. I guessed four calls in a row met her femme fatale limit.

"No, you're not. You don't have my power." Nikki popped her hip, one hair-flip away from being cast in *Mean Girls*. "The chances of this happening outside of your influence are miniscule."

I ran my tongue over my teeth. "God, your precious power! How could I forget? You only ram it down my throat every time we train." I bit the inside of my cheek, a technique I had been using whenever I really wanted to punch her. "So, why don't you figure out where Liam is instead of blaming me? You know, actually use your power instead of just talking about it." I mirrored her hands-on-hips posture. "Well?"

"Okay, guys, let's just calm down." Jazzy stepped between us, blocking Nikki's burning stare. "There's got to be a reasonable explanation for his disappearance. He wouldn't just strand you girls here without cause."

"I can find him on the app." Jac grabbed her phone out of her purse, sounding hopeful. Her manicured nails tapped away at the screen.

My shoulder relaxed. Thank God, someone who actually had a solution rather than accusations. I was sick of playing Nikki's enemy number one.

"He's nowhere," Jac breathed, her hands shaking. "He's not registering on the app. He's not . . ."

"What does that mean?" Pepper leaned over her shoulder as if the screen would explain the nonexistent Liam dot that we'd always seen on our own phones.

I swallowed. Fear took root inside my throat, growing a softball-sized lump. Where the hell could he be?

Jac twisted to face Nikki. "Why wouldn't he be on the app? Even if he was hurt or kidnapped, jailed or dead . . ." Jac clapped her hand over her mouth as if she couldn't believe what she'd just said.

"He's not dead, love," Jazzy soothed her, gently pushing down Jac's trembling arm, a hand concealing the troubling screen.

"There's a good reason he's gone. I'm sure of it." I stepped forward and wrapped my fingers around Jac's shoulder with a squeeze. *Think, Olivia, think.* "When does he turn the watch off?" I already knew the answer. Never. He even showered with it on. I'd seen him in a towel and catalogued that bare glistening skin enough times to remember the watch around his wrist.

"Only at night," Jac answered, squinting like she was staring at the sun.

That's right. Liam removed it when he slept, but even then, I wasn't so sure he'd shut the power off. Not that I was about to say that out loud.

"But why would he be sleeping right now? And where?" Jac looked back at her phone like it could offer her up an answer.

"He's been having trouble getting rest, maybe he left for a nap." Jazzy tapped her lip. "Actually, he complained all morning about barely sleeping last night. I bet he went back to the Davises' house and forgot to set his alarm."

Jac swallowed. "That makes sense. He's been a grouch. When I pushed him about what was wrong earlier, he did say he was just tired. And he doesn't like to scare me if the watch picks up his nightmares and registers a blood-pressure spike." She wagged her head. "Yeah, you're probably right. He's home napping." With cheeks dotted with restored pink, she tucked her phone into the side pocket of her jacket, seemingly satisfied with that answer.

"Hey, girls." Dustin sidled up beside me, draping his arm over my shoulder. The twins plastered smiles across their faces, shooting their perfectly aligned teeth in his direction. Dustin looked around. "Where's Liam?"

"Probably at home sleeping." I glared up at my best friend. He'd broken his tension-diffusing streak.

Dustin scratched his head. "Huh?" His eyes wandered the lot before finding me again. "When did he leave? I saw him right after fifth period. He said he was going outside to talk to Bradley, and I haven't seen him since." Dustin tilted his head. "Actually, I haven't seen either of them since."

"Oh my God," Nikki lamented to the sky, gripping the top of her head. The creases around her mouth warned that she was about to tell me off, but then Jac sniffled, her lips wobbling. I feared tears would soon follow.

Jazzy grabbed her sister by the arm and yanked her back. "He probably went home. As for where Bradley is, who knows and who cares? We can all squeeze into our car. Let's go wake Liam up, order some food, and study together. I'll call and let Uncle Harold know the plan. Maybe he's even at the Davis house now." She tried to smile, but it lacked her usual spark. My stomach crawled into my throat. She felt, as we all did, that something was wrong.

"Is everything okay?" Dustin looked to me for confirmation.

It had become an art form, lying to Dustin. Some days I wanted to tell him about Hunterland, about us, but moments like these when I saw terror in everyone's eyes, I knew subjecting someone else I loved to this life was selfish.

I faked a chipper "Of course."

The crinkle in his brow told me he didn't believe me, but Dustin never asked too many questions. Part of me thought he knew we were all hiding a secret and believed we were just biding our time before we told him. The other part hoped for his total ignorance.

Jazzy pulled out her phone and dialed. "Hey, Uncle Harold." Jazzy threaded her arm through Jac's. "Are you at the Davis house? Oh yeah, great. Can you do me a favor and check on Liam? I think he's napping in his room, your old one." She paused. "Yeah sure. I'll hold." Jazzy motioned for us all to start walking to the rental.

Dustin followed at Nikki's side, chatting her up. I could tell she was making an effort to distract him—a hand brushing his shoulder here, her hip brushing against his leg there. That girl had mad skills when it came to seduction. Her sexuality knew no bounds. I envied her for that. I assessed my jeans, vans, and basic sweater. Not that I needed skintight clothing, but I'd never be able to pull off the painted-on attire she could.

Pepper leaned into my side, gripping my elbow to haul me back half a step. "Liv, we have a problem. Dad's with Doc at the station. They're looking into a cold case." She lowered her voice another decibel. "I just spoke to him before final bell. He asked me to tell Liam to drop us off and then meet him at the precinct after school, which means Doc isn't at our—"

"I know," I whispered back. "Jac's been on edge lately. The twins are worried about her. Jazzy's lying. I think Liam's in trouble."

At the sedan we all said our goodbyes to Dustin. I watched Jazzy and Nikki share a conspiratorial look. Jazzy used her eyes to motion to the back of the car, using some twin code I couldn't decipher.

"I just have to grab something." Jazzy popped the trunk. A moment later, she moved to Jac's side. Nikki walked behind Jazzy and grabbed something from her hand. My mouth barely formed a complete O before Nikki plunged a needle into Jac's neck. Jazzy caught her as she crumpled and shot Pepper and me a disapproving frown for shrieking.

"What the hell?" I whisper-yelled, looking over my shoulder and scanning the parking lot. Not a soul glanced over at us. Thank God. "What are you doing?"

Jazzy helped Nikki place Jac into the backseat of their sedan. Over her shoulder, she threw me an answer. "Sedating her."

"Yeah, I can see that." I clutched my chest. "But don't you think that's taking this a little too far? I mean she's completely knocked out."

"For good reason, mate." Jazzy soothed Jac's hair. "She's been unhinged lately about her mother and it's about to get worse. Jack is missing and now Liam. Earlier today, Liam followed Bradley out of the school parking lot after he saw him slash our tires. He called Uncle Harold and asked him to investigate Bradley's mom's death and his dad's involvement in a cold case."

"What?" I scratched my head.

"During that time, our uncle had our tires fixed, hoping we wouldn't find out and kill Bradley."

"Oh, I'm gonna kill him, all right." Nikki slipped into the seat next to Jac and cradled her like a rag doll. "I'm just not sure what weapon I'm going to use yet." She waved to Pepper to climb in.

"Where was Liam going?" Pepper dropped her bookbag on the backseat floorboard and scooched in next to a limp Jac.

"Uncle Harold has no idea. He spoke to him three hours ago." Jazzy swung around to meet my gaze. "But because of Liam's hunch, guess what they found when they dug into Bradley's dad's story?" She proffered the question like I should have a clue.

"What?" I threw up my hands. "I have no idea."

"His father was involved in a case linked to twelve other murders where the bodies were ripped to shreds, leaving Hunterland to assume it was—"

"Werewolves," Pepper breathed. Her hand clutched her chest. "Their hearts were missing, weren't they?"

I glanced down at her. "What are you talking about?"

Pepper tilted her head back, staring at the car ceiling, and groaned. "I thought I heard a spirit today around Bradley, but it must have been him. I was worried so I asked Dustin to help me research, and we found out that his father was involved in a murder case where the body went missing." She lowered her chin, then peeked out the door at Jazzy and me. "The only evidence at the crime scene was his blood. But I swear they didn't mention the other bodies were missing hearts or torn to shreds. At least it wasn't in the article we read."

Jazzy shook her head. "That's because the authorities kept that part out of the news. All the other bodies resembled the ones we found here in Falkville Falls. But Mark Sanders didn't become their next meal the night he was attacked."

My hand flew to my mouth. "He became one of them." My chest ached and my lungs burned from trying to keep my emotions at bay. Everything hurt.

She placed her hand on my bicep and squeezed. "I think your premonition was right all along. I think Liam's been kidnapped."

29

LIAM

I woke up with a throbbing headache like a fist pounding on the inside of my skull. Whatever they hit me with had rung me like a gong. I blinked in wild succession, clearing my vision so I could take inventory of my surroundings. There on the counter lay my hunter watch, tablet, and cell phone, each smashed to pieces. The Bronco hadn't been so hidden after all. I shook my head. Smart move on their part. Now the team couldn't locate and rescue me.

I assessed my body. Blood covered my jeans, soaked my shirt, and stuck to my face, sticky and wet. From a lousy fall and two hits over the head? This looked excessive—maybe arterial. I moved my shackled limbs, trying to break free of my restraints, but no amount of struggling loosened the ropes. Instead, a wildfire of pain spread from my ankles up my legs and from my wrists up my arms. Even my surprised inhalation left me wincing. Something wasn't right. I should have been able to break the arms off a simple chair, but for all my effort, the legs of my seat didn't even hop off the floor when I yanked my aching body upward. They'd sapped my energy—probably beat me up while I was knocked out.

My gaze darted around, and a familiar scene poked at my subconscious.

Son of a bitch.

Olivia's words echoed. *It looked like a kitchen because there was an island, a stove, and a fridge but no furniture, except one chair in the middle of an open space. Someone had coiled up a thick rope next to its legs, beside a stack of duct tape . . . The curtains were partially drawn . . .* There was an overhead light above the seat, though, dangling like they do in interrogation rooms in movies.

I tilted my chin upward and found myself staring directly into the bulb from her drawing. And wouldn't you know, my arms were tied with thick rope and secured with more duct-tape than the go-cart Jac made in fifth grade. In my weakened state, I'd never get out of this. Worse, the theory that had been banging in my head like a snare drum for weeks became cold, hard fact. I *knew.* Any lingering doubts dissolved in the harsh fluorescent light of what I recognized as an interrogation. I knew who'd brought me here.

My mother.

"She's not here." The gravelly voice from earlier spoke. He came from behind, rounding my chair. Fenton stayed a healthy distance away, but it didn't stop me from trying to jerk myself forward. Every nerve in my body yearned to destroy him, but his beating had burned through my serum. A strategy provided by my mother, no doubt.

"The chair's bolted into the ground. We took the liberty of tiring you out so the hunter juice would wear off faster. You're staying there indefinitely."

I spat red saliva at his feet. "Yeah, dumbass, I know. But thanks for the science lesson."

His gaze followed the mixture of spittle and blood, then lifted back up to mine, ignoring my wiseass response. "Since our meeting in the woods didn't go as planned, we hoped this little gathering could end our charade and get us what we want." He leaned back against the island.

"I don't give a rat's ass what you want. You'll never get anything from me. She'll never get anything from me. You might as well kill me now."

Fenton held his mask of indifference. "She talks about you and your sister, ya know. Often. Before you even John Wayne'd it into here to unwittingly defend another monster, I knew those footsteps belonged to you. Only her son could move like a ghost, almost inaudible. In fact, had I not intended Bradley to lead you here, I would have thought it was the wind. She said in many ways you are a better hunter than even her. That's a pretty high compliment coming from someone as skilled as your mother." He dipped his chin like he'd flattered me.

"She's a monster, not a hunter, and certainly not my mother," I growled. "And if she knows what's good for her, she'll keep our names out of her filthy mouth. She's as good as dead, or she will be when my father finds her."

Fenton huffed, shaking his head like a disappointed uncle. "Maybe he already found her and couldn't do the job. Maybe your father got cold feet when he realized she's not so evil after all."

My eyes narrowed until I was squinting between stinging red slits, peripherals blurring. "He'd never give up the chance to eradicate a monster, even if the monster *looked* like my mother."

Fenton leaned against the counter, studying me. "Did you have any idea Bradley was a werewolf?"

I growled. He knew damn well I'd had no idea.

"Did he act violent in school toward you or any of your friends?"

I shook my head. His lack of aggression at school wasn't the point. "You don't get it, do you?"

"Enlighten me." Fenton waved his hand.

"No, Bradley didn't do anything hostile for the couple of weeks he's been at school. And no, he doesn't appear to be a monster. But you're not grasping the most important part. It's not about the times a monster doesn't kill. It's about the times they do. He has it in him to butcher. He's steered by animalistic behavior and instinct, not logic, and every full moon tests his bloodlust. One day, he'll kill. A heart will pump too loudly when he's desperate, and he will rob that innocent human of life. And if someone like me doesn't put a stop to it, we are just as guilty as him. In fact, we are worse, because we're grounded by what's right and wrong. And if we weren't here to regulate that, humanity would never survive your kind. So yes, I will kill you, I will kill Bradley, and if my father doesn't, I will kill my mother."

Gray eyes stared back at me, then drifted to the window in a ponderous silence so long I didn't expect him to speak. "What if they didn't have bloodlust?" His scrutinizing gaze captured me again, as if breaking me down into pieces.

I jutted my chin out. "What? What are you talking about?"

"What if monsters, as you call them, didn't suffer from bloodlust?"

"It's not possible."

Fenton shrugged. "We think it could be. But we need your help to prove it."

"You're delusional. First of all, it's not true, and secondly, I'd never help your kind."

Fenton tilted his head. "If a werewolf is turned and they don't eat a live, beating human heart after infection, they do not possess bloodlust." He crossed his arms. "And what's more, we've even seen wolves who once killed for live, beating hearts turn to preserved organs and decrease their bloodthirst. It's fascinating."

Yeah, real fascinating. Fenton spoke as if these instances were experiments in some measly high school science project, not cold-blooded murder.

"Would you eradicate innocent werewolves that have never killed before?"

"There's no such thing!" I shouted, my voice hoarse.

"What if I told you your mother's never killed a human. Could you kill her then? Could you be her executioner knowing she's never murdered your kind?"

My lips twisted. Anger resurfaced. I had pondered Fenton's question since finding out my mother had turned into a monster. When it came down to it, could I kill her? I wanted the answer to be yes, a million times, yes. Part of me knew I could, but a sliver of doubt still ate at me, that I'd never be prepared to deal with the reality of putting a bullet into my mom's chest even if she had massacred a hundred humans. The thought that she had turned but never killed anyone for their heart messed with my head even more, and I refused to let Fenton get under my skin. I would kill her if presented the chance, because I didn't have a choice. A fact I had to remember no matter what lies Fenton spewed at me.

"Could you really see your mother for the first time in five years and still pull the trigger?" He pushed off the counter and took a couple steps toward me, then knelt, looking up at me. "I don't think you could. If you saw the way she still loves you, respects you." He shook his head. "You're still her son, her family. She's no different now than she was when she hunted by your side."

My mouth curled into a cruel grin. Fenton's words were the cold bucket of water I needed to snap back to reality. He couldn't be further from the truth. Those five years away meant I hadn't a clue who she was now, and she had no clue how deeply her death had changed me.

"Oh, she's different all right. She can pretend to love me. Hell, she can continue to pretend she's a hunter, for all I care. But don't think for one second, you know me. I doubt my mother told you much if you think I'd let her keep breathing after what she did to my family, Olivia included."

Fenton dipped his chin. "Shame you see it that way." His gaze lifted over my head as a female voice intervened.

"Oh, I told him enough, kiddo. But it's not him who needs to listen. It's you."

30

OLIVIA

As soon as I shut the bathroom door, I leaned back and gulped the stale air of the cramped room. Pepper's robe hanging from the door cushioned my head as I closed my eyes. What had happened to Liam? Where the hell had he gone?

And why wasn't Bradley answering his phone? Dustin saw Liam last, and he claimed Liam followed Bradley outside. Now, both were missing. No one believed that was a coincidence after finding out Bradley's father was most likely a werewolf. But nothing added up, no matter how many ways I tried to calculate it. Bradley had shown no signs of being anything but a teenager. Not that I had made him touch silver. Although, after this disaster, I might very well make that a stipulation of becoming my friend. Silver friendship bracelets for anyone interested in being a part of Livy Davis's life.

I splashed water onto my face and glanced at myself in the mirror, not recognizing the girl staring back. My quickened pulse left a flush high on my cheekbones, my hazel eyes had dulled to a cloudy gray, and chestnut tendrils clung to my sweat-damp face and neck. I was a hot mess. Dark bags sat under my lashes, a reminder none of us were sleeping well. It hadn't helped that Liam and I no longer found comfort in each other's arms at night, making drifting off far harder.

A gentle knock sounded at the door, and I whipped my head toward it.

"Olivia?"

I patted my face on the hand towel, hoping Doc would just go away.

"Olivia, the twins and I are going to stay here tonight, in case Jac wakes up. We think it's for the best."

I mustered the courage to speak. "Yeah. Okay."

"You need to take a breather. Do something to clear your head. You're trying too hard to force your abilities. It doesn't work that way."

From the second we arrived home, I'd made Jazzy squeeze my arm again and again, trying to elicit some sort of vision. But nothing happened, well, except swallowing down the bile brought up by every electrocution-like jolt. I was a failure, not to mention responsible for the entire mess. If I had managed to explore the rest of the vision, we could have avoided this or at least had enough information to find Liam now.

"Why don't you watch TV, work on your homework, or do laundry? Distract your thoughts. I think you need to calm down before we try again."

How could I calm down? Every second was a moment closer to losing him.

"Liam is a survivor," Doc said as if he knew what I was thinking. "You'd better believe he won't make a liar out of me for that."

The fading footsteps signaled Doc's departure. He was right. Liam was a survivor. I had to hold on to that belief or I'd crumble.

For the next couple of hours, I flitted around the house keeping busy. I did the dishes and the laundry, dusted and vacuumed the living room, cleaned up Pepper's room—even scrubbed the bathtub. By the time Nikki waltzed into my room, only one load of laundry stood between me and more anxious pacing. Maybe I could move on to cleaning the twins' house next.

"Watching you play Cinderella has been fun and all, but I'm thinking you need a different type of diversion. Let's spar."

"Go away." I refused to meet her eyes as I continued to fold Pepper's T-shirts with perfect corners and smoothed down the middle until no wrinkles remained.

"It wasn't really a suggestion. I do some of my best thinking—or not thinking—when fighting. Maybe you will too."

My head snapped up, and I glared at her. Nikki lounged against the door frame in pink yoga pants and a cropped athletic shirt, her expression smug.

"Unless you believe acting like a housemaid will speed up locating Liam." She lifted one of her perfectly trimmed brows, challenging me.

I sat on the edge of the bed, folding the remaining shirt on my lap and grinding my teeth. Of course she wanted to fight. What better way to make me bleed? She blamed me for Liam's disappearance because I was the one who allowed Bradley into all of our lives. But unbeknownst to her, my guilt was already beating me up. She didn't have to. It crushed me like a freight train to my chest.

"You're just looking to kick my butt because you think it's my fault he's missing." I huffed.

Nikki looked down at her nails. "Maybe. Or maybe I'm feeling charitable."

I rolled my eyes. "Yeah, because you're a regular philanthropist. How could I forget?"

Shutting the door behind her, she stalked into the room. She folded her arms across her chest as she stared down at me, probably seeing more than I wanted her to. "Take the help when someone offers it. You are not the only one hurting here. We all are." She kicked my bare foot with her sneaker. "Get dressed and meet me on the mat in five minutes. And if you're not down there by then, I'll come drag you by your pretty princess waves."

And with that, she sashayed out.

I quickly changed and met her in our makeshift gym. Maybe getting my ass handed to me would make me feel better. I mean, I couldn't feel any worse.

Nikki smiled when I entered. "Glad you could join me." She looked down at her watch. "And with one minute to spare. Impressive." She gathered her hair and wrapped a rubber band around it. Before she'd even threaded the last strand through, I swung a fist at her face, just like she'd taught me. It landed smack dab in the center. The crack of her nose reverberated up my forearm—music to my ears. I smirked as she stumbled backward, releasing her hair.

"What the . . .?" She covered her bleeding nose with her hand, staining the webs of her fingers.

"Surprising your opponent is sometimes the best weapon, right, Nik? Well, surprise!"

Nikki wiped her hands on her pants, smearing blood into the fabric, and sniffled. She pounced like a tiger—graceful, but built like a truck. A palm strike to my breastbone knocked me backward. I choked, battered lungs dispelling all my air in one grunt.

I tumbled, taking out everything on Liam's desk with me. Pens and pencils flew across the room. A desk lamp toppled to the ground, the bulb smashed to pieces. In the corner of my eye, I saw Liam's mom's cracked, leather-bound notebook among the papers that found their way to the floor. The binder that helped us uncover the serial killings a couple of months ago. Liam studied the darn thing like the Bible, swearing the answers to most mysteries lay inside. Article clippings and photos slipped out and scattered like trash rather than Liam's favorite possessions.

"You did that on purpose because it's his stuff," I growled. Maybe she did. Maybe she didn't. But right now, my anger had no outlet besides tearing into the British bombshell who'd helped bust up my life, and I'd see to it she got every last heated drop of backsplash when I erupted.

"So what if I did?" Nikki snarked. She didn't wait for me to find my footing; she stalked me like prey.

But instead of succumbing to her next blow, I aimed at her shin with the toe of my shoe, hoping to take her to the ground like she had me. A small stumble was my only gratification as she reached for my leg. I knocked her hands just enough to evade her grasp and rolled. I bucked up to a standing position but not fast enough. Her roundhouse kick to my kidney had me flying through the air, limbs flopping like a Muppet until I crashed into the cement floor on the other side of the blue tackle mat.

I gasped on impact, my elbow and hip bone screaming.

"What do you think happened to him, Liv?" She stalked forward, taunting me as I tried to catch my breath and sit up. I scooted back on my butt until I hit the cold wall behind me, but she kept coming. "Do you think he's injured, dead? Do you think Bradley's werewolf father has him? Do you think they ate his heart already? Maybe turned him into one of them? Maybe they're torturing him for information about his mother . . ."

I shot up and shoved her shoulders. She barely budged, but it was enough for me to round the table, fleeing her reach. If I could just—

Pain sliced my scalp as Nikki grabbed me by my hair and pulled me back. "Do you think he chased after your new lapdog because he cares so much about you? That because of you, we might have lost him? Forever?"

A sound between a cry and a groan slipped through my lips. "I don't know."

She tossed me to the ground, and I rolled, landing on my back. "Figure it out." She tapped her head. "Think. It's your power to see things. Think." Her voice rose, but without the usual snarl or venom. It peaked in a desperate shriek. Nikki was scared.

She slammed her heel down on my chest, digging in. A loud grunt vibrated in my throat, but it never made it past my lips. I stared at Nikki in complete shock. Even if I could speak, I would have no idea what to say to her.

"You told Liam that Veronica was the only one who ever pushed you hard enough. Well, here I am, pushing. Think, goddamn it, think." She pressed harder, eyes boring into mine.

Fight or flight took over. I wiggled my hands out from underneath me. In one quick motion, I wrapped my fingers around her ankle and twisted as hard as I could. Nikki lost her footing and crashed down next to me. I pushed myself up into a seat and rubbed my bruised chest, wheezing.

"It doesn't work like that," I shouted through coughs, wiping away streams of tears. "You can't force a vision out of me with violence. If nothing happened with Jazzy, what makes you think this will work?"

Nikki's eyes watered with raw emotion that shocked me into paralysis as she scrambled toward me on hands and knees. "I can't lose him. Please, Liv, think."

Unable to face her intensity, my gaze jumped over her shoulder, landing on my hunk of creedite. The crystal must have fallen during our scuffle, still on the table from . . . the last time I used it! When the haunting picture had first taken shape. "Can you hand me that?"

Nikki's brow rose as she reached behind her and grabbed the coral-rough piece and tossed it to me.

I squeezed my fingers around it, ignoring the sharp points. "I'll try." Taking deep, calming breaths, I tapped into what I'd once called my spirituality but now knew as my abilities. Veronica had said the power lived inside me. She'd meant healing, but why not the rest as well?

Sometimes visions appeared like a vivid dream, so alive and intricate they were a breathing organism. Other times they were foggy and distorted, like memories. But this one appeared like a movie, playing out right in front of me.

A broken green mailbox swung off a rotted stud rooted into the ground. The whipping wind spun the red plastic flag, and the hinges screeched. I looked behind my eyelids at the vision. Where were the numbers? Then I walked around it and saw them on the other side: three, seven, nine.

I shifted my head, and the image turned into the cabin I'd drawn. *That's it.* Now I needed a street, but all I saw was the road. Where it met the property line, I spotted a lone phone pole with a loose wire swinging from the gravel driveway into the trees.

I remember that from when—

A door swung open, hitting the house, and I circled back around. Bradley raced past where I stood rooted, looking over his shoulder like he feared pursuit. He ignored his car and ran into the woods.

I blinked my eyes open and jumped up from the ground.

"What?" Nikki stood with me and grabbed my shoulders, shaking me. "What did you see?"

"I have no freaking idea. But I have a house number for the cabin. Three seventy-nine. I've been on that road before; I just can't remember the name, but I think if we drove it, I'd remember. And"—I paused for a breath—"I saw Bradley running from it. He looked freaked out. He's in trouble. I know it." I latched on to Nikki's arm and charged up the stairs with her in tow.

We barreled through the basement door and continued straight into the living room, where Pepper, Jazzy, Doc, and my dad sat. Jac was still passed out in her room.

I threw my phone at my father. "Take Bradley's contact info and have your guys track his location. I think he's being chased through the woods. This might lead us to his father." I turned to Doc. "It's a hunch, but I believe I know where Liam is."

Doc popped up from the La-Z-Boy. "We need a plan. Jazzy, go collect our hunter kits. Someone needs to stay with Jac. Matt should call . . ." The rest of his words were drowned out as I turned to Nikki.

"You with me?"

Her smirk turned playful. "Do you even have to ask?"

The two of us grabbed our jackets from the hooks and shot out of the house, not waiting for anyone. I slipped my dad's keys to his police cruiser into my pocket before shutting the front door.

When Nikki saw my car selection, she lit up. "Please tell me we're running the sirens."

I gave her a look that said, *You're damn straight.*

We jumped in and pulled out of the driveway, tires screeching. My dad ran after us down the street. The red lights illuminated his pinched, angry face.

Nikki peeked over her shoulder, then twisted back to face the front, smiling like the Joker. "You realize you're going to be grounded forever for that move."

"It's worth it."

Nikki flicked my arm. "You mean he's worth it."

I smiled. Nikki might hate me for my role in Liam's life, especially when it came to his judgment, but she loved him with a ferocity that ensured we'd always be on the same team when it came to his safety.

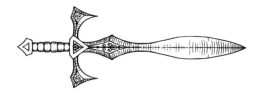

31

LIAM

I tasted bile when her voice echoed between my ears. Mom. She'd lured me to this abandoned house using Bradley as bait, she'd beaten me up, and now she had me tied to a chair for who knew what type of interrogation.

"Bradley mentioned your little romance. I didn't believe him at first. Then I followed you when you went to meet Fenton and saw it for myself. I never had any intention of showing myself until I saw you with her. I don't know what I thought you'd be like as a nineteen-year-old, but I never imagined I'd find you in love."

I clamped my teeth together and tried to calm my pulse, reminding myself she was just another monster. My grip tightened around the chair arms as she strolled into my sight.

She looked like she always did: jeans, white T-shirt, and brown leather jacket. A gun sat on her hip. Dim lights illuminated her high cheekbones, the ones she passed to my sister. If I hadn't known the lycanthrope disease ran through her veins, I'd assume she was a hunter. My stomach hollowed out at the thought. But she wasn't, and I couldn't lose sight of that no matter how familiar this felt.

She flicked an eyebrow up, questioning me. "Hard to hate me when I don't look a thing like the demon you've conjured in your mind. Huh, kiddo?"

I found my voice. "Oh, trust me. I hate you all right. No matter what you look like."

She headed to the island and pushed herself up to sit on it, crossing her ankles. For a while she just stared at me. Her eyes trailed over every injury bestowed by her clan. I watched her gaze trace my swollen face. One of my eyes was barely open. By the time she made it down to my feet, her jaw popped so hard, I thought it might crack.

"The boys went a little overboard with their beating." She glared at Fenton.

He shrugged a shoulder. "They might have had a little too much fun. I'll remind them this was a one-off, and it won't happen again." He smiled. "Maybe I'll even repay them a little. I haven't boxed in a while. Might be fun."

"You do that." Mom returned her attention to me. "Do you hate me because I'm a werewolf or because I shot Olivia Davis?"

At the mention of Olivia's name, I growled, and my mother snickered.

"I'll assume both since we don't have as long as I had hoped. I need something from you, and if you give it to me, I will take out the were-wolves killing in this area."

A rogue chuckle slipped through my lips. "We don't need your help eliminating the monsters." My brows knitted together. "You do realize you're one of them, right?"

"There is no way you'll be able to take Mark and his boys down. They aren't an easy crew to dispose of." She eyed Fenton with a pointed accusation.

The equation started adding up. The only way she'd know who they were, what brought them here, and the details of their end game was if they had been a part of her megapack. "Wasn't this pack once one of yours?"

She bobbed her chin. "Yes. But that's a long story we don't have time for. Are you interested in hearing what I want?"

"No."

"Let's pretend that was a rhetorical question then. I need my notebook."

An unexpected request, but it wouldn't change my answer. Like hell I'd ever give her anything she asked of me. "No."

"Really getting tired of hearing that word from you, kiddo."

I itched to cross my arms. She'd always hated that, called it a blatant act of defiance. "Kill me now, because there is no way I'm bargaining with you. You have nothing I want or need. The sooner you realize the only thing I still need from you is your death, the sooner we can move on from this conversation."

Mom wagged her head. "I was afraid you'd say that." She jumped off the counter and leaned back against the breakfast bar, legs crossed at the ankles and arms folded at her chest. "If you give me the book, I'll give you your dad."

Sheer fear crept up my spine like the bone-deep cold of plunging into an ice bath. Knowing full well, I asked in a shrunken voice, "What are you talking about?" I'd lost my bite.

Dad had been missing. Fenton had taunted me, saying that my dad couldn't kill my mom. And now this? They had him, and that dawning realization's vice grip on my heart made it stutter.

She huffed. "Have you heard from him lately?" It wasn't even a real question. She knew I hadn't. "Didn't think so." She nodded to Fenton. He reached into his pocket and pulled out his phone. He pressed a couple buttons then flipped the phone in my direction so I could see the screen.

Dad lay in what looked like a hospital bed with wires attached to him, his eyes closed. I'd never seen him look so peaceful. "Is he . . ." I couldn't even finish the sentence. Was he in a coma?

"He's fine, just under the knockout drug." She meant the sedation medication she and Dad used on Jac when they needed to knock her out for a while. Dad was right; Jac wasn't always made for this world. My parents knew it long before she even started hunting. "He's suffered nothing more than a knot on his head. If you give me my binder"— she held up her finger—"with all the contents inside, I'll make sure he wakes up in a real hospital. The official report will read he was mugged and suffered a concussion, then was placed under an induced coma as a precaution to avoid permanent damage. He won't even need to know it was me that did it to him. Sound fair?"

"Nothing about this sounds fair," I gritted out.

"Kiddo, life isn't fair. Haven't I taught you anything?"

Fenton's phone rang. He checked the screen, then pointed to the front door. "I'll take it outside."

Mom nodded. When we were left alone, I asked. "Don't you love him anymore?" I couldn't say don't you love us or me. No matter her answer, that would dump way too much on my head right now. But if she ever loved Dad, how could she do this to him?

Mom's eyes softened, the way they did when she used to comfort Jac or boost my spirits when I shot poorly at the range. They'd always spoken more than her mouth ever dared.

"Of course, I do. Aw, kid, I'm doing this for you, for him, for Jacqueline." Her voice wavered, but only for a second. "I need that book, Liam. I'm not asking."

"Let him go now, and I'll give it to you."

Mom smiled our smile, the same one that used to make me feel like the most special child in the world. "Liam Noah Hunter, I've known you since you were in diapers. Don't you dare play me for a fool. But"— her smile widened, like she wanted to make an exception for me—"I'll make you a compromise. I'll have him transferred to the nearby hospital, Chicago General."

"Deal," I hurried to answer.

Her smile faded as fast as it appeared. "Liam, I have people everywhere there. If I don't get the book by tomorrow night, I'll make it a real coma."

Before I could reply, Fenton charged back into the house. "We have to leave, Ronnie."

Ronnie?

Mom nodded as if she'd expected as much. Fenton took off the way he'd come, but Mom walked right up to me. She cupped my chin, her thumb running over the edge of my jaw. "You grew up to be one fine hunter. I'm proud of you, kiddo. No matter how much you hurt right now, I hope you can take that and put it somewhere in your heart. You've made me so damn proud." She leaned down and kissed my cheek. Then whispered in my ear, "Keep loving Olivia. Don't let my situation hold you back from the most important experience in your life. Love. It *is* everything. You won't find what you have with her again. Don't run away from it." She pulled back. "She needs you, more than you both know."

Mom never cried. She never showed emotion. Yet, when she swallowed, I swore tears shimmered across her lower lids.

"I am not the enemy. But I will destroy all who have made me appear that way. Every last one of them."

She dropped her hand and jogged out of view, taking a part of me with her—a chunk yanked right out of my heart.

32

OLIVIA

The drive consisted of Nikki and my mingled breaths, accompanied by the gentle hum of the cruiser's engine and the vibration of Nikki's cell phone. Doc had called at least a dozen times, all ignored. I knew all too well that he would end up tracking our movements, but I also had a hunch that his primary focus would shift to Bradley, leaving Nikki and me to shoulder the responsibility of finding Liam. Call it a premonition or just a new understanding of good strategic policing, but I doubted even my father would follow knowing Bradley could lead him straight to the werewolf pack. The road curved exactly where I had hoped, offering a silent confirmation that we were on the right path. Though I could vividly picture the surroundings, the name of the street remained elusive, slipping through the cracks of my memory like grains of sand. As we rounded the second bend, the swaying power line from my vision appeared, and I swerved off to the shoulder.

"What are you doing?" Nikki wagged her head. The cabin remained hidden from our view, but the green mailbox proved we had arrived.

I pointed toward the gravel driveway, where Bradley's car still sat parked. "This is it." A mixture of certainty and unease tugged at my words.

For most of the night, I had managed to keep myself composed as best I could. I'd found an inner safe place in which to hide, distracting myself with chores and Nikki's antics. But now that sanctuary shattered at a stunning speed, giving way to a torrent of overwhelming emotions. Fear surged through me, vivid and raw, its intensity painting my world in shades of red. Anticipation loomed like a suffocating cloak, enveloping me in its dark embrace. The guilt burned brightest, though, searing and blinding in its white-hot intensity. I had foreseen this moment weeks ago, but I'd lacked the power to prevent it. What if we were too late?

"Let's go." Nikki's door opened and closed.

Her words hammered against the layers of pulsing fear encasing me, breaking my thoughts and propelling me forward. I tracked after her, my legs on autopilot.

We didn't duck or hide. There was no need for stealth or concealment. We'd plow down anyone who stood in our way. Truth be told, I no longer cared about my own safety, and I imagined Nikki didn't either. We were here for one reason. Liam.

Gun grasped in her firm hands, Nikki jogged along the path and bounded up the steps. I slowed, taking in my surroundings. Drops of blood covered the stairs as if it had rained red. The fight started out here. But how and why?

Nikki flung open the door, and I trailed in her wake. She veered right, clearing each room. Nothing but our footsteps sounded. I left her and ran straight for the kitchen, following the vision that had become etched in my mind, as familiar as the constellations of freckles on my skin. My feet came to an abrupt stop as I spotted Liam in the center of the room. He struggled against his restraints, veins popping in his forearms and grunts slipping through his teeth as he tried kicking out with his bound legs. Streaks of blood swept across his figure in wide strokes like an artist's paintbrush.

My teeth sank into the tender flesh of my cheek, the metallic tang of copper flooding my senses. Liam had managed to stay alive. Though his wounds appeared grotesque, they weren't fatal. Relief drew a strangled cry from my throat.

"Liam."

His head snapped up, his eyes wide like those of a child. A deep gash marred his jawline.

I rushed to his side and dropped to my knees. "What happened?" I reached out, my trembling fingers caressing his bruised cheek. Coagulated blood had crusted at the wound, flaking off at my touch.

"An interesting reunion with my mother." Liam managed to conjure up a smile, as if a joke might alleviate my distress.

I twisted my head toward approaching footfalls.

"You look like shit." Nikki fought a grin as she leaned against the doorway, relief evident in her relaxed shoulders.

"Compliments will get you nowhere. I'm spoken for." Liam looked at me, a hint of mischief dancing in his eyes—or at least, I thought so. His right eye had swelled considerably, making it difficult to discern his exact expression. "So, are you two planning to untie me or do you enjoy staring at me like some wild animal at the zoo?"

"I think we've had enough wild animals for a while." Nikki secured her gun and pulled out her knife. She joined me on the floor and, one at a time, sliced Liam's restraints. "Your Alpha mum do this?"

"The one and only." Liam massaged his freed wrists while Nikki worked on liberating his legs.

I reached for my back pocket and retrieved the blended ointment composed of crushed crystals, healing herbs, and arnica—the same concoction that had aided my recovery from my gunshot wound, also compliments of Veronica Hunter. "This should heal you. Just stay still. I don't want to hurt you if I can help it." Adrenaline still sped the beating of my heart. A crash would soon follow. But I steadied my fingers and unscrewed the cap.

Liam dipped his chin as I covered his wounds, starting with his puffed eye. The mixture left a glossy sheen over his skin, its magical properties subtly at work. I moved down to the gash, then worked the substance over his wrists.

"What did she want?" Nikki cut into the last rope, her eyes narrowing with suspicion.

Liam stretched his liberated legs and groaned. "One of her old ledgers."

Nikki's eye squinted. "What? Why?"

Liam shrugged. "Not sure. I've been through the pages so many times, I could recite them. But she thinks there's something in there worth revisiting, so I'll read them again and see what I can figure out." He pushed himself up from the chair, cracking his neck from side to side. "Fenton got a call and then they just left me here, bleeding and tied up." He then surprised me by intertwining his fingers with mine, an open display of affection that left my eyes widening. In front of Nikki, no less. Perhaps the near-death experience had prompted this unexpected gesture, or too many hits to the head, but I wasn't complaining or fighting it. I needed the connection just as much if not more than he did.

Liam guided me toward the sink, saying, "You guys will never believe this, but Bradley and his family are all—"

"Werewolves. We know." Nikki placed her knife back in its ankle sheath.

Liam's gaze volleyed between us as he turned on the water. It sputtered orange before finally settling into a clearer flow.

I released his hand and reached for a rag placed by the basin, running it under the faucet. "Dad and Doc looked into Bradley's dad's murder case like you asked. The park where detectives found his DNA happened to also be a werewolf feeding ground. Instead of killing Bradley's dad, Mark, they turned him." I gently dabbed the soaked cloth across Liam's face, removing the streaks of red. The emollient had already begun its work, miraculously knitting his wounds with fresh, untainted skin.

"Bradley lured me here. Apparently, he knows my mom. They have some kind of beef. It's unclear what, but I'd wager his mother's death has a part in it." Liam leaned against the stained countertop.

I released a weary sigh.

"I'm just happy we got rid of Liv's pet wolf." Nikki winked.

"Your comedic prowess never fails to amaze me." Liam threw the words over his shoulder, a small smile tugging at his mouth. He turned to me, a hint of remorse lingering in his blue irises. "I'm sorry. I know you considered him a friend."

I shrugged, my gaze drifting to the bloodied footprints on the tiles, a reminder of the turmoil Bradley had caused. "I've decided from now on I'm giving all my future friends silver friendship bracelets just to be sure."

Liam's smile warmed, and he pressed a gentle kiss against my forehead. "Sounds like a foolproof plan to me," he whispered, his breath caressing my skin like a bayside breeze. "Thank you for coming for me."

"Always." I leaned into Liam, melting like butter in a saucepan.

"You two ready? Or would you like to use one of the upstairs bedrooms before we go?"

"She really does think she's funny," I quipped.

"I told ya." Liam squeezed me into his side. "But she's definitely not."

"Definitely not," I agreed.

"I can hear both of you. You know that, right?"

We piled into Liam's car. Liam took his place behind the wheel, steering with a white-knuckled grip and jaw clenching with a mixture of resolve and restrained anger. The lines etched on his forehead and the tightness around his eyes spoke volumes. Seeing his mother face-to-face couldn't have been easy, especially when he hadn't fulfilled his vow to end her life. But now wasn't the time to discuss it. We had to find Bradley and the other werewolves before they did any more harm to the innocents in Falkville Falls.

I sank into the passenger seat's leather upholstery, allowing it to cradle my weary body. Fatigue settled deep in my limbs, making my shoulders droop. The corners of my mouth tugged downward with the weight of our next move. Soft amber lights illuminated the car's dashboard, casting an ambient glow that offered a touch of solace amid the madness. As Liam's hand reached out to rest on my thigh, my insides turned to goo. This touchy-feely Liam had come out of nowhere, or so it seemed, but maybe it made sense. When you were worried about your lack of a future, the present became all the more important.

From the front seat, I heard Doc yell through the speaker of Nikki's phone. When I turned, I found Nikki's face scrunched. Her lips were pursed as if around a retort, but she never fought him, only listened. Part of me wondered if she agreed with his account of our hasty actions. Not that I thought she'd have done it differently.

"So, you rescued me without a plan or any backup, huh?" From the bits and pieces of Doc's tirade on our recklessness, Liam got the gist of what transpired.

"I brought Nikki."

Liam side-eyed me.

"Hey, she's pretty badass, and she didn't care to procrastinate any longer either." I waited for the inevitable reprimand, but instead Liam's next gaze touched the corners of my mouth as a soft smile lifted his.

"Thank you." He gave my thigh a swift squeeze, and butterflies danced a jig in my belly.

"Welp, Uncle Harold is pissed," Nikki chimed, her voice tinged with annoyance. She pushed her nose up against the partition. "They tracked Bradley to a house, but no one's there. They found several people's belongings, so they figure it's his pack's den. They're staking it out. Someone's bound to come home."

"Who's they?" I asked.

"Uncle Harold, Jazzy, and your dad. Pepper stayed at the house in case Jac woke up from the drugs." Nikki sat back in her seat and huffed.

"You sedated her?" Liam looked in the rearview mirror.

"Yeah." Sadness coated Nikki's tone. "We didn't want her to know her Alpha mum joined the party and that her brother might be dead."

"Good." Liam dipped his chin.

"Drop me off at the rental house. Uncle Harold's on a rampage. He claims I'm grounded." Nikki scoffed. "And apparently, Matt said, and I quote, 'Tell my daughter if she even thinks of leaving the house, she won't see daylight till she's thirty.' He also threatened to never let you get a car or some bullshit like that because you took the cruiser. Which I guess we'll need to retrieve later. Honestly, at that point I tuned them both out, so I don't even know the rest of the terms."

My father's warnings paled in comparison to the unsettling unknowns looming over us. Bradley's family's ties to Veronica and their deadly actions in Falkville Falls plucked at my brain waves, creating a gritty horror-movie soundtrack of building violins and power chords. If we couldn't uncover their whereabouts soon, the consequences would be far graver than my own transgressions. Innocent lives were on the line, and the more I melded into the Hunterland team, the more that daunting responsibility tightened around my throat.

33

OLIVIA

After dropping Nikki off, we pulled up to my darkened house. An eerie stillness hung like a shadow over everything. Liam parked the car and leaned in, his warm breath tickling my ear as he whispered, "Stay with me tonight." He pulled back, his searching eyes making the plea he couldn't. A silent invitation to find solace in each other's arms like we had done before.

I nodded in agreement and followed him out of the car and into the house. With a gentle touch on my lower back, he led me down to the basement, where Doc's former studio apartment now served as Liam's sanctuary. Handing me one of his long shirts, he turned away, giving me privacy to change. I shed the burdens of the day and slipped into the soft fabric, its familiar scent wrapping around me like a comforting embrace.

As I faced him, my gaze fell on his discarded, soiled clothes hanging haphazardly over the back of a chair. He stood before me, clad only in his boxers, a silhouette against the moonlit room. The solid muscles in his arms flexed as he pulled back the covers. My eyes trailed down his body and landed on a patch of black and blue dotting across his rippled midsection. His mother's clan had done a number on him. I shook my head, caught between wanting to heal it and knowing Liam wouldn't want to shine a light on the situation either. Not right now. He needed another form of healing.

With a shared understanding, we slipped beneath the blankets

Nestling on the pillows, we twisted to face each other. I tucked a hand under my cheek and stared back at him, the only sound our mingled, soft breaths. After a while Liam's eyes fluttered shut, exhaustion winning the battle between gazing at me and sleeping. The soft glow of moonlight filtered through the window, casting ethereal patterns on his face, highlighting the subtle lines of fatigue etched into his features. Thankfully, the cuts, blood, and bruising along his cheekbones and lips had started to fade away, courtesy of my salve.

An hour passed, sleep eluding me to accommodate the tears streaming down my face in a relentless downpour. I tossed and turned, my back now facing Liam, allowing me concealment as I let the pent-up emotions flow like a fizzing torrent from an uncorked bottle. Any attempt to choke them down resulted in a drowning sensation, like I had been cast overboard, shackled and sinking.

I tried restraint, to allow Liam to find rest, but residual fear lingered, gripping my heart's edges and yanking in opposite directions. *We could have lost him tonight.* I still had no clue what had transpired between Liam and his mother, only that she wanted her book. But why would she hurt Liam? Didn't she know her son wouldn't cave from a beating, no matter how brutal?

Then there was the acidic taste of Bradley's betrayal, burning whenever I tried to swallow it. Had I been so blind to his intentions because I craved a normal friend to patch the hole in my heart Jessica left behind? Was I that naive? I wasn't exactly sure I could answer that. And then the icing on the cake: we still hadn't found the clan killing our townspeople. Would our team take them down unscathed or fall victim to their revenge? I still hadn't heard back from my father or the others.

The bed shifted, a gentle dip that pulled the breath from my lungs. Liam rolled toward me and draped his arm heavily around my waist, drawing my back closer to the warmth of his bare chest. It had been over a month since we'd lain like this, and uncertainty hung in the air. I held my inhale, waiting for his response, his touch, his words. His hand enveloped my wrist, his thumb tracing delicate circles across my palm.

"I'm okay," I whispered on my exhale, offering him an escape from the emotional labor. I knew exhaustion weighed him down, both mentally and physically. How could he not be weary? If it were me, even a bulldozer wouldn't be able to wake me. "I swear, I'm fine."

"Liar." Liam's chuckle rumbled against me as his snort tickled my ear. "No, you're not. But that's okay. Neither am I."

I brushed away the tears with the heel of my hand. "Do you want to talk about what happened with Veronica?" I didn't dare refer to her as his mother. While I yearned for him to share his burden—to let me shoulder half the weight—the thought of him shutting me out now, when he'd just cracked the door back open for me, was almost unbearable. A reminder that his own flesh and blood caused this mess might make him padlock himself back behind that barrier I'd come to hate these past weeks.

To my surprise, Liam's voice resonated through the darkness. "Seeing my mother, hearing her speak . . ." He paused, and for a fleeting moment, I thought he might not continue. "You were right. She's not the monster I imagined her to be. I still despise her, and I know we have to end her life, but this . . . this makes it so much harder. Because the woman I encountered tonight was the same mother I buried five years ago, and I'm not sure I can bear losing her all over again."

His confession wrenched my heart and left my lips quivering. When my own mother had resurfaced as a vengeful spirit, there had been no trace of the woman I had known and loved, making letting her go easier that second time around. Yet, Veronica retained all the qualities and traits Liam cherished. How could her son bring about her demise without sacrificing a part of himself in the process?

"I've thought about it. I'm going to give her the binder," he rasped against my ear as he nestled closer. "But for now, I'm not telling anyone but you. Until I figure out what her end game is, I think the less people that know, the better. Are you with me on this?"

My body stiffened. My answer came easy, but I longed to know more and didn't want to discourage Liam from sharing his scheme by asking too many questions. This wasn't my first Liam Hunter rodeo, and he could easily push me away as fast as he had just pulled me back in.

"Yes. Do you have a plan?"

"Kinda." His arm moved over my waist as I felt him shift onto his back. "I'm going to copy every page of her notebook and keep the duplicates hidden. Then, I'll wait."

"Wait?" A shaky breath shuddered from my mouth as I rolled onto my side, facing him. "Wait for what?"

Liam turned his head in my direction. His blue irises darkened like the night sky. "For her to find me again. Because she will. She won't stop until she gets what she wants. We have that in common, ya know. When we Hunters desire something, it's impossible for us to let go." Liam's eyes traced my lips as I wetted them, wondering if we were still talking about his mother.

The air around us shifted. The reminder of what his lips felt like on mine rode through my body on a slow-rising tidal wave. I lifted my hand to his bare chest and wrapped my leg around his torso, pulling him closer to me. "And what do you want?" I sounded like I hadn't used my vocal cords in days.

"Not what, who."

Clearing my throat, I tried again. "Okay. Who do you want?"

Liam's hand grabbed my thigh, spreading his fingers wide. They dug into my skin, both a possessive claim and an unspoken answer. He glided his hand up to my hip, then pulled me on top of him in a rush that went straight to my head.

"Does this answer your question?" Liam's hand gripped my backside as he pushed me against his center. My insides erupted in flames as I felt what he wanted to show me. A gasp slipped through my lips. I leaned forward, my hair falling on both sides of my face like curtains sheltering us. Want, anticipation, and excitement formed in the shape of wings beating inside my chest, trying to break free of their cage.

Liam removed one hand from my waist and cupped my face. "I hate that I've been trying to stay away from you."

I winced. Knowing and hearing it were two different things. And what insurance did I have that he wouldn't do it again?

His brows furrowed. "I know that look."

"What do you mean?" I tried to glance away, but Liam's caressing palm against my cheek insisted I stay.

"You're afraid I'll push you away again because I can't handle balancing my dedication to you and my vow to Hunterland, and you'll get hurt for a second time because of it."

His truth rocked through me, parting my lips.

"I can't promise I'll always do the right thing. But I can try. I want to make it work if you'll have me." His husky voice and flexed chest muscles confirmed he wanted more. "Do you want that? Am I even asking for something you'd like?"

A single tear rolled down my cheek as I nodded. That was all the encouragement he needed. Liam's hand dragged down my body and met his other hand at my waist. He flipped me onto my back and hovered over me. His lips caught my gasp as his mouth covered mine.

Our kiss deepened, and his tongue begged for entrance. A whimper escaped me as his hand went underneath my arching back, drawing us closer. We'd kissed before, but this one felt different, like the start of something real. The warmth from his lips traveled all the way to my toes, and I pulled him closer. Gone were the anger of our first kiss and

Claire

the sadness of the second. In that moment, I kissed him with a raw and undeniable passion, no longer seeking escape but a way to express the depth of my true feelings.

Liam trailed his hands up and under my shirt, caressing my bare back as his lips explored my neck in sweet, tender kisses. His touch sent electric currents coursing through my veins, awakening every nerve ending. His hands' gentle exploration blazed a trail of fire. Caught in the raw, intoxicating contrast between the soft caresses on my back and my skin's remembrance of the earlier possessive grip on my hips, my head buzzed, heart racing with anticipation and breath quickening with longing.

My skin pebbled under his feather-light touch, and I shivered, but for once it wasn't out of fear from impending danger. A whirlwind of thoughts and emotions collided. Was this really happening between us? Could we share a future together? Was this what he wanted, or was it the lingering effects of his traumatic day talking? I fought to push aside the doubts, to surrender to the moment, but my spine stiffened.

Liam stilled and looked up, his eyes soft. "It's okay if you don't want . . ."

I stared at the boy who had captured my heart the day he shot up my room thinking he saw a ghost. His cocky attitude had slithered under my skin and had never left, infiltrating my heart with his deep regard for my family's safety, especially mine. I might regret walking away from him someday, but I'd never regret loving him. I caught his bottom lip between my teeth and sucked it into my mouth before pulling away with a smile. "I've never wanted anything more."

His reservation vanished as his lips took a possessive hold of mine. He kissed me, hard and eager, and the explosion it sent rocketing up my spine in colorful bursts shone so bright the world faded by comparison. Our tongues syncopated in a fire dance that left starry trails behind my eyes. My fingers found the elastic of his boxers, nervously running along the gathering of the fabric.

Liam sucked in a breath and freed a strangled moan unlike the pleasurable ones he'd been releasing. My gaze darted down to his lower abdomen, and I gasped. Beneath the flipped band of his boxers deep purples coated his stomach like splotchy spray paint. They were worse than I had thought.

"Oh my God, Liam." With speed I didn't know I possessed, I jumped off and hovered over him on my knees, indenting the mattress. My hands fluttered over his as he cradled his stomach. His eyes were pinched closed.

"I'm so sorry." My hand flew to my mouth. His body looked worse than raw meat.

Liam's chest heaved, but his eyes soon fluttered open. He pulled my hand down and kissed the tip of each finger, one by one, until his hand closed around mine in a fist and squeezed. "I'm okay. But I think I need to slow down. Maybe I should heal up a bit."

He rolled to the side, propping himself up on his elbow and sucking in a breath from the movement. "It's clear Veronica's guys have some anger issues. Now that the adrenaline and serum are completely worn off, I feel it more. Apparently, they used me as their personal punching bag. I hope I get to repay them one day."

"I can't believe she let that happen." I traced my fingers lightly over his chest, scared to further hurt him.

"I don't think she was there for it. Not like that's an excuse."

"Let me get my emollient." I jumped out of bed and returned with the container from my purse. With light, dexterous touches, I applied it to the spots I hadn't had access to before.

Liam tucked wild strands of my hair behind my ear. "I never thought we'd get to this place . . ." He cupped my cheek.

"Me neither." I continued my pursuit, covering every inch of his exposed skin to ensure he'd heal everywhere. His breathing slowed, and by the time I finished, he'd succumbed to sleep's embrace again. I screwed on the cap and placed the mixture on the night table, then slipped back under the covers. My mind wandered to Bradley. I was still uncertain about his role in all of this. Was he really the bad guy or a pawn in his father's crimes? I reached for my phone on the nightstand and tapped out a message before I could second-guess myself. If the team couldn't find him, then I would

Tell me the truth. Did you use me to get to Liam? What are you trying to accomplish here? If you want to stay alive, I am your only hope.

I set the phone back on the table and snuggled into Liam's arms. Uncertainty pooled in my gut as I thought about how Liam would feel when he learned about my message. Would he see my text to Bradley as betrayal? Or would he trust my intentions?

Maybe Bradley would write me back. Maybe he wouldn't. But I had to try. If for nothing else but to end the murders in Falkville Falls. At least that's what I told myself.

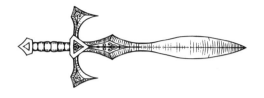

34

LIAM

After a fourth humming sequence began from the nightstand, I rolled over Olivia and reached for her illuminated phone. Who the hell would be calling incessantly at five o'clock in the morning? Unless it was the team, and they were in trouble. It wasn't like they could reach me on my broken phone.

"Hello." I rubbed the sleep out of my eyes.

"Well, well, Liam. Looks like you evaded Mommy Dearest's grip." The voice's cool amusement prickled my skin. "How'd you manage to escape her clutches? That woman has claws like I've never seen before. She makes grown men cry."

I slipped my hand out from under Olivia's head and sat up. "Why the hell are you calling Olivia? Where are you?" I snarled, cautious of my volume.

"Actually, she messaged me. I was only being a gentleman by responding."

I took the phone away from my ear and tapped her last message. It popped up and I read: *Tell me the truth. Did you use me to get to Liam? What are you trying to accomplish here? If you want to stay alive, I am your only hope.*

So, she did reach out to him. Why was she trying to protect him? Did she not realize how dangerous he was? Did she not believe he'd used her? Her flagrancy for dangerous circumstances yet again drove my blood pressure to soaring heights. She never thought through the consequences.

"I think your girlfriend actually cares about me. What do you think?" Bradley taunted.

"I think you're a dead man."

He snickered. "Your mom gave me the same warning when I left her clan for my dad's pack. You don't even know the half of what your mother's done. Do you know how I was infected with the disease? Do you know why I am in this situation to begin with?"

"The better question is, do I care? And in case you're wondering, the answer is no. I'm still going to kill you." I scooched to the end of the bed, careful not to wake Olivia.

"You'll have to catch me first."

"I don't do foreplay with werewolves. Give me a time and a place and let's settle this." I wrestled my jeans on in the dark, the phone held between my shoulder and ear. Would Bradley give up his location? Probably not, but then again, he didn't seem like the most intelligent wolf I'd ever met either.

"Why not? Livy did say you and I should be friends."

I zipped up my pants and clasped the button, looking for a shirt. "Name the time and place."

"The abandoned airfield on the outskirts of Falkville Falls. You've got one hour, or I'll make it my mission to kill every single hunter you love, starting with your sister. Maybe outside biology. Or the school parking lot. Or maybe on Livy's couch. I know the address. Just remember: you so-called hunters invited me in."

The line went dead.

I grabbed my shirt from the floor. *That son of a bitch.* The smart move would be to call the cavalry and tell them, but I knew they were in the middle of their own mission watching over Bradley's pack. Besides, I could handle one little werewolf, especially the one who'd handed me over to my mother like a prized pony. It was more important the team took out the others while I dealt with this.

I grabbed my pistol, leather jacket, silver blade, and extra rounds of silver bullets. Then opened my top desk drawer and took out an extra syringe. I might not be calling for backup, but I wouldn't go without all my arsenal, and after the beating I took, I knew I needed strength. I pressed the needle into my skin as I pushed the serum into my veins. I squeezed my eyes closed as I sucked in a deep breath.

The burn of power itched under my skin until settling into a menthol-like cool. I tossed the syringe into the wastebasket and snatched a pen and paper.

Before slipping out the door, I left Olivia a note.

Your friend Bradley called, and I'm meeting him at the abandoned airfield on the outskirts of Falkville Falls. Oh, and I took your phone since mine's been smashed. We will be having a talk about monster stranger danger when I'm back.

—L

I shot one more look at Olivia. Strands of her chocolate hair spilled over the pillow where my head had rested just moments ago. Her bare leg wrapped around a bunched pile of covers as if it were my body. Soft breaths escaped from her half-smiling lips, and I hoped she was dreaming about us. Tomorrow we'd talk, but for now, I prayed for sound rest. After the week we had all had, she needed it.

It took less than twenty minutes to arrive at the dilapidated airbase. The sign stood as a weathered sentinel at the entrance, its faded blues and reds broken up by patches of exposed metal. The base itself screamed neglect, the framework rusted and corroded. Had he chosen this location because no one frequented it, or because he watched too many horror movies and wanted to play Jason? The guy had more than one screw loose; I'd favor the second guess.

I parked the car and jumped out. I'd have to walk the rest of the way. Rounding the Bronco, I opened the tailgate and grabbed my hunter kit, making sure the contents matched the enemy. I pocketed a few extra rounds of bullets for the pistol tucked at my back and one in my ankle holster, then grabbed a shotgun for good measure and closed the door. I slipped a silver blade into my other leg sheath as backup.

After securing the car, I traipsed through the foliage till I got to the rusted fence, where an opening had been cut. Whether loiterers or Bradley did it, I was going in regardless.

I crossed over the main runway, a desolate strip of faded asphalt that stretched out like a ghostly path. Where landing gear had once touched down stood a crumbled and cracked tarmac that no machine could travel over. Vines slithered across the ground like serpents, ready to ensnare any unsuspecting intruder. The wind howled through the skeletal remains of landing-strip lights, casting eerie, flickering shadows that only added to the sensation that every step I took was being monitored by unseen eyes.

Come on, Bradley. Show yourself.

Abandoned hangars rose ahead like ancient tombs, the unsteady light giving impressions of foggy figures dancing before them in some forgotten ritual. Each creaking sound, each rustling leaf had my eyes darting. My gaze shot up. A broken window rattled. I hesitated. This screamed trap, but what alternative did I have?

I opened the door to a hangar and walked in. Two old planes sat in the middle of an empty room. Every step, every breath felt like a gamble. He was here watching, but—

An arm wrapped around my neck and jerked me backward, pinning my shotgun between us. "Were you trying for the element of surprise? You're not very stealthy. This is the second time you've been tricked. Does Olivia know how dumb you are?"

I bent down and reached for my ankle gun.

"Don't." Bradley warned, bicep compressing my neck until I thought it might snap. "You try that again, I bite you, and this fight will end with you using that gun on yourself."

Slowly, I lowered my leg, hands clenching into fists. In the seconds needed to unholster the weapon, Bradley's teeth could tear clean through my skin. It wasn't a chance I would take.

"Let's have a chat." Bradley kept his firm grip. "Livy always wanted us to hash out our issues. Why not now?"

"Did you really like her, or was she a means to an end?" I gritted out between gasps of air. The question left my lips without thought. I didn't know why I asked, maybe because I was protective of her heart. I knew that the way Bradley used her to get closer to me had hurt her on a deeper level than she admitted.

"She showed me kindness in a time I needed it. She surprised me. I've never had someone care like that. So yeah, I didn't hate her." He cleared his throat. "But you, handsome, have always been my end game." He breathed in my ear. The moist heat grossed me out more than the smell of vamp breath. "You know what your mother did to me? How she ruined my life? Took my family away from me?"

He tightened his hold as the anger rose in his voice, and I coughed. Getting my windpipe broken hadn't been my plan. I had just evaded death, but now I had it toying with me for a second time in less than twenty-four hours.

"She killed the only person who ever loved me."

"She killed your mother?" It was an educated guess. After hearing all the details of his mom's story, I had wondered if she was my mother's supplier. It added up.

"You take the fun out of everything," Bradley moaned. "Yes, she killed my mother. But her evil didn't start there. Did you know she turned me into a monster?"

I tensed.

For all the time Fenton spent defending my mother, hearing this reignited my fear of her intentions.

"A couple months after she was bitten, she took a healthy nibble of my neck." He flexed harder, and my airways contracted. "Do you know how painful that first transformation is? It's like someone lit your skin on fire, like bathing in a volcano, your flesh melting right off the bones until those break to reform. Your *mother* did that to me!"

"Why?" I breathed. That was the million-dollar question. Why would my mother infect him? There had to be a reason. Or maybe I just wanted one.

"Why?" Bradley echoed. "Don't you see? She wanted a son. She tried replacing you."

My mouth dropped open. That couldn't be true. Why would she want to hurt an innocent fourteen-year-old? And even if it were true, Bradley and I were nothing alike. It didn't make sense. I might be biased, but he made for a lousy replacement.

"Does that make you sad, knowing you weren't that special after all?"

"You can have her." I spit on the ground.

"Oh no. I'm done with her now. She threw me out of her pack. She tossed my entire family out. So I'm going to ruin her family. Starting with you." Bradley loosened his grip a fraction, and the explanation came in the form of a canine fang touching my skin. My heart plummeted to my belly. Being turned into one of them, I couldn't stomach the thought. Bile rose in my throat.

"Don't."

Bradley and I both snapped our heads upward.

Veronica.

"Let go of my son," she ordered. Her hands were raised in surrender like she wanted a truce, but I'd never known her as a peacemaker.

Bradley laughed. "You're kidding me, right? You have the balls to ruin my family and then ask me to save yours?"

"I did not ruin your family. Your family did that to themselves." My mother's hard gaze darted to me for a brief second, betraying no emotion, but I knew her. She did a quick assessment and stayed on task, putting feelings aside for later. "I adhered to your mother's wishes. That's all." Mom took a step closer. "She asked me to turn you."

Bradley's heart pounded against my back as he labored to breathe. Hell, my own kicked up a notch. His mother wanted him infected? Why?

"She would never."

Mom took another two steps toward us and swallowed. "She did. She thought . . ." Mom shook her head. "*We* thought if I didn't turn you and take care of your first shift, you'd end up being turned by your father and suffering bloodlust. Then we'd never be able to save you."

"You're a liar!" Bradly roared. My ears rang from his outburst.

"Bradley, she sought me out. You know this. Your father had turned. She was trying to help him, but at every tiny provocation he'd threaten to infect you. It was only a matter of time before he hurt you both."

"Even if that's true, why kill her? So, he wouldn't hurt her? How does that make sense? You brutalized her. *You* hurt her!"

"No. I never would have killed her. Moana was my friend." Veronica kept her hands high. "Your father did, though. I can prove it. I have the security footage from that night. Let me get it from my front pocket." She pulled out her phone, and Bradley tightened his hold on me. "Just watch."

She held it so the illumination faced us. A video recording started to play, angled from the ceiling. Although it was blurry, I spied two figures, a surgeon's table, a computer, desk, and a cabinet filled with what looked like medicine. The grainy sound vibrated through my bones as the two people spoke.

You promised all the hearts would be here. Tomorrow's a full moon. We're all already going crazy with bloodlust. Where are they? The man spoke in the deep baritone of a life-long smoker.

I gave them all to Ronnie. She has them. I told you this, Mark. You need to leave. You're not yourself right now. A petite woman around my mom's age backed away from the man, her pin-straight blond hair brushing the desk's surface. She tried to conceal her shaking hands behind her back, but the trembling of her arms and shoulders gave it away.

If you don't give me a heart right now, I'm taking yours.

We watched as the man transformed into his beast shape. The woman shook her head—a silent answer to his question or shock over his appearance, we'd never know. It was the last move she made. He pounced and within seconds tore the woman to shreds, eating every one of her organs. Blood splattered against the walls like finger paint. Screams echoed in the hangar as if in surround sound.

Bradley whimpered in my ear, and his trembling arm sagged away from my neck. But my brain stuttered as the male voice from the video suddenly crooned from my left.

"Oh, Ronnie, love. I wished you hadn't shared that." His legs dangled off the wing of one of the abandoned planes. Like Whac-a-Mole, three other men popped up.

"Now, Liam," Mom shouted.

I elbowed Bradley in the gut, and he lost his footing. He anchored himself with my shotgun, pulling the strap off my shoulder but giving me the space to dart behind a stack of crates in the corner. Shots sounded in the distance. Men yelled.

"Find her. And her son."

I grabbed my gun from my back and held it to my chest. Before I could poke my head up and assess the situation, Mom rounded the crate and sat next to me.

"Hey, kiddo, fancy meeting you here." She winked. "Interested in killing some werewolves with me?"

My mouth dropped. To say the last couple of days felt like a dream was an understatement. I stared at my monster mother asking me to fight by her side like we had done a hundred times before.

She used two fingers under my chin to shut my mouth. "I need your head in the game. You with me?" When I didn't respond, she slapped my cheek. "Liam, pull yourself together. There are five werewolves out there, and it'd be a hell of a lot easier to take them out if I could count on you as a functional teammate."

I snapped back to the moment and found words—not the ones I necessarily wanted to lead with, but close. "You mean six, present company included."

Mom smiled. "All right then. Six. But I am hoping you'll just help me kill five." Without waiting for confirmation, she continued like an army captain detailing a mission. "Mark is Bradley's dad. He's their leader. Then there's Gabe, Daryl—who you met—and Toro. Big guys, barely any weaknesses. They'll stay in human visage, half-turned; it's their preferred fighting form. Mark carries a gun on his hip loaded will silver bullets; Daryl, a silver blade. He thinks the irony is funny. Gabe fights with his claws; Toro, his teeth. Ready?"

Ready? No. But did I understand her rundown? Yes. "And Bradley?"

"He's never eaten a heart from a living person before, nor killed anyone. He's not motivated by bloodlust, only revenge and pain." Her lashes lowered, curtaining the brief flash of sadness that streaked across her eyes. Bradley either meant something to her, or he had, and she'd take no pleasure in killing him. "He'll probably use whatever he can to stay alive." A hint of hurt tinged her voice.

I pulled out my gun and racked a bullet into the chamber. "Ready."

"On three. One. Two . . ."

We both popped up before Mom finished her count.

Two men charged at my mother. I assumed Gabe and Toro, given that one swiped with his claws and the other snapped his elongated canines.

Daryl stalked me, blade at the ready. "Nice to see you again, hunter. Wish I had known who you were at the motel. Might have tried harder to kill you." He increased his speed to match my own. Steadying my gun with my nondominant hand, I had pulled the trigger halfway when a bullet dinged off my piece, knocking the weapon from my grip. It slid along the concrete behind me and out of reach. At a thudding on the beams above, I tilted my head up to find Mark running in the opposite direction, gun in his hand. I searched the hangar high and low for Bradley, but he'd disappeared.

Daryl, still charging at me, jumped into the air with his blade brandished. With swift and calculated precision, I reached for my own knife and spun clean of his slash in a crouch, bringing my own blade across his collarbone in an upward strike as I rose. It would've been his heart, but Daryl, agile as a serpent, dodged and melted away with a swiftness that deceived the eye. He jumped up on the crates behind me, and I followed. Adrenaline surged me forward.

"You're gonna die tonight"—he spat the declaration like venom—"and that will kill Ronnie more than any death."

"Spoken like a true beta wolf." I snickered. In a lightning-fast motion, I lunged forward, but the crate below me shifted, and I crumpled to the concrete, hitting my head hard against the floor. My free hand flew to my skull, now moist with blood. Daryl took advantage and leaped off his crate, punching his knife through my shoulder. The steel lodged into the bone, and I growled. I think it hurt. It should have. But I didn't feel a thing.

All I knew was anger.

With a steadying breath, I kicked the heel of my boot into his shoulder. The force threw him backward without his weapon, and he crashed into a pile of tools. The clang of metal radiated through the echoing building. I bucked up, regaining my footing, then tore Daryl's blade from my wounded flesh by the hilt and cast it aside. "Guess you won't be needing that anymore."

I ran as fast I could and pounced on top of him. Grasping my silver knife, I slashed him across the chest, not once, but twice. He hissed in pain, a hand pressed to the wound as if he could erase it.

"Cut me over and over again. See if I care. All I want is to put you into an early grave and give your mother exactly what she deserves, exactly what she gave our family when she abandoned us."

"And what's that?" I quirked an eyebrow. What had my mother done to piss everyone off?

"A broken heart."

Beneath his hardened exterior, I detected a glimmer of something— a sliver of agony, a fleeting taste of humanity. But it was not enough to warrant his life.

"Catch!" My mother's ringing voice cut through the chaos. I pivoted, reflexes honed, catching the gun she tossed in my direction. As she fought her own battles with her claws, I leveled the gun.

"Let me alleviate your pain." I pulled the trigger, the bullet finding its mark in whatever shattered fissure he claimed his heart bore. He crumpled, collapsing onto the cold cement floor, his torment finally extinguished.

I pivoted. My mother stepped over Toro's carcass, continuing to grapple with Gabe. She sliced his cheek open with her claws, and he stumbled backward. Her gaze locked with mine over his shoulder. I nodded.

She dove out of the way as I aimed and shot him in the back three times, knowing at least one pierced his heart. When she stood, she wore a smile backlit with pride. And then a shot rang out, and she crumpled to the ground.

35

OLIVIA

I reached out for Liam but clutched a lumpy, cotton-stuffed mass instead. My eyes peeled open, adjusting to the dark room. Liam was gone, a pillow left in his place.

"Liam." I swung my legs over the side of the bed and stood. The light in the bathroom was off and the door open. He couldn't be in there. My gaze flitted to the nightstand. My phone. It had been right there. Instead, a piece of paper beckoned.

As I finished reading it, my heart sank into my stomach. I ran up both flights of stairs, bounding two at a time, until I reached Pepper's room. I swung the door open, and she shot up from her bed.

"What the hell?" She looked around, her blue hair sticking up straight as if she'd attempted a hairspray mohawk. "Is he dead?"

I almost forgot she didn't known Liam had safely returned with us. That at one point this evening, he'd lain in bed right next to me. "No. We found him. Beaten, but alive." I shook my head. "But now." I sighed, closing my eyes for a moment. "Now, I don't know. I need your phone." I grabbed it from her night table and dialed Nikki. Once, twice, then got her on the third try.

"What the hell, Pepper?" she grumbled.

"Liam is going after Bradley and I'm going after him. Call everyone. He has my phone." I didn't wait for her to speak. Instead, I hung up and ran to my room, Pepper hot on my heels. I pulled a sweater from the closet and jeans from my drawer as Pepper assaulted me with questions.

"Livy, what's going on? Why the hell would Liam meet up with Bradley? Where's Dad?"

I ignored the onslaught and grabbed my coat and scarf off the back of my desk chair.

"I'm coming with you," Pepper said from somewhere behind me.

I swung around. "No. You need to stay here in case Jac wakes up." My pulse picked up a notch. Jac. What would she even do if she found out we saved her brother from her mother only to lose him again to another werewolf? "And I don't know why he went alone to meet Bradley, but I'm going to find out. Nikki will call Dad, and they'll meet me there." I slipped Pepper's phone into my back pocket.

Pepper clasped my shoulder. "Okay. Just breathe. It's Liam-freaking-Hunter. He always makes it out alive."

I swallowed and forced a half smile.

"I'm just confused. How did he even talk to Bradley?"

Me. This was all my fault. I'd texted Bradley. "I have no idea of the details. Just that it has something to do with my phone."

Pepper stayed silent. It was probably best that she did. Having my foolish actions voiced aloud would give them life and weight, and if anything happened to Liam, I'd never forgive myself. If he died tonight, I'd have no reason to live.

I ran down the stairs and out the door, back into the cruiser's driver's seat. It felt like days ago, not six hours, that I'd sat here with Nikki on a Liam rescue mission.

Adrenaline coursed through my veins as I throttled the steering wheel. My mind raced. Go, or wait for backup confirmation? Liam had left the safety of our house to go after Bradley alone. I couldn't sit back and wait. The darkness of the night paled in comparison to the uncertainty that loomed over my head. In the distance, the sun grazed the horizon but not enough to shed light on the road.

Pepper's phone rang, and I picked it up.

"I'll call for a ride share and meet you there. Uncle Harold said no one's been to the house, which makes me think this is an—"

"If you say *ambush*, I will throw up."

"How the hell did he talk to Bradley and split without you knowing?"

I wanted to lie to Nikki, but what was the point? Eventually everyone would know. "I texted Bradley. Told him if he surrendered to us, I could help him, but I needed to know the truth."

"Are you out of your ever-living—"

I hung up, knowing exactly where that was going. She'd blame me, and this time she'd be justified.

Pepper's phone rang again, flashing Dad's name this time. "Are you okay?" The fear in his voice reminded me of the last time he'd asked me that—the day after Mom tried to kill Pepper.

"I'm fine."

"Good. Because I'm still pissed about the cruiser. Don't think that conversation is over with, young lady." He half grunted, half sighed. "But I understand your reaction. Even now. We are on our way to the airfield. You need to wait for us."

"Dad, I love you, but I am not waiting."

There was a brief pause on the other end of the line, and I could almost sense my dad's internal struggle between wanting to protect me and understanding the gravity of the situation. Finally, concern straining his voice, he said, "We haven't seen Bradley, his dad, or his supposed three brothers, which makes us think Liam's walking into an—"

"Oh my God, I know, Dad," I interrupted, my irritation bubbling to the surface. "An ambush. I got it, all right! That's exactly why I am not waiting on anyone else. The second I get there, I'm going in."

"Did you bring a gun with silver bullets?"

I strangled the wheel instead of my own dumb neck. Weapons! How could I be so stupid? I'd run through the house like my hair was blazing at the ends, totally forgetting to bring anything to defend myself. My heart pounded in my chest, fighting the python of panic constricting it like prey, but I quickly gathered my resolve, releasing a sliver of tension. At least if Liam died tonight, I had a high probability of going with him to the grave.

"There's a shotgun in the trunk." My dad broke through my macabre thoughts. "Use it. We will be there soon."

I pulled up to the abandoned airfield, the cold wind cutting through my coat, its bite inducing shivers. The dark silhouette of the deserted place loomed before me, an eerie backdrop for bad decisions. Best-case scenario: Bradley had shown up alone, and Liam and he were battling. Worst case: I'd walk into a cemetery. The whoosh and thump of my pulse thickened the odd quiet, leaving me half deaf and jumpy.

On an inhale, I exited the car, my legs like noodles. The urgent concern for Liam's welfare pushed me forward, fueling my determination. With every step, the impression of walking into a crypt increased, but I couldn't allow fear to consume me. Liam needed me, and I wouldn't back down now.

I popped the trunk and grabbed my dad's hefty shotgun, now more thankful than ever that he had taken me hunting with him years ago. As I approached the airfield's entrance, I clutched the weapon tightly and stayed within the shadows. With each stride, the darkness gave way, a lighter sky pushed through, and flecks of orange and yellow skimmed the distance. I entered the abandoned airfield, inching the door open, and immediately heard gunshots. Heart lodged near my collarbone, I ducked low and slunk inside, rounding behind a stack of crates for cover.

"What the hell are you doing here?" Bradley hissed, hunkered behind the same barrier. His clothes were covered in dust and dirt like he'd rolled around with Pigpen from Charlie Brown.

I looked at him in complete disbelief, then around the stacks, then back at him. "What the hell are *you* doing here?" I pointed. "Who's shooting?"

He pressed his mouth together before answering, the hard angles of his face severe in the dim light. "You're gonna get yourself killed."

I gaped. "Seriously?" The word cracked in my chest. I gripped the gun like it was tethered to my sanity. If Bradley was the enemy, hiding in a corner and pretending to care about my safety was a poor show of his wrath. "What the hell is going on? Why are *you* not trying to kill me?"

Bradley laughed, but it lacked the sunny humor I knew from school. "You have nothing to do with this. Why would I kill you? Hell, you might be the only real friend I've ever had." He motioned with his head toward the report of gunshots. "It's the Hunter family I want dead. Or wanted dead. I don't even know what I want anymore." He rested his head against the wooden box behind him, baleful gaze toward the ceiling.

"Wanted?" I lifted a brow.

Bradley pulled his knees into his chest, forearms wrapped around his shins. "The short version? I thought Ronnie was responsible for everything bad in my life. But apparently my dad's the one who killed my mom, and even though Ronnie infected me, she didn't do it to control me. She thought it could save me from a worse fate."

I covered my mouth with my free hand. "Wow. I'm . . ." What could I even say to that?

He waved me off. "I'm not overly surprised. My dad's as evil as they come. Daryl has always felt more like a father to me. It broke his heart when Ronnie threw us out of her pack, but we didn't know my dad had committed such a heinous crime. We just thought she didn't want us anymore, after my mom's death, that she felt guilty for what she had done. That's what my dad said anyway." Bradley shrugged, but I could tell the betrayal stung by the way his lashes lowered, fluttering as if to keep tears at bay.

Another shot sounded, and I jumped, worry seizing me again. "Who's out there shooting then?"

"Your boyfriend and his mother against my family."

My jaw slackened. *Did he just say that Liam and his mother had teamed up?*

"You heard me correctly. Liam and Ronnie are fighting..." Bradley paused. "Actually, I don't know who's left anymore. No way they're all still alive after that many fired rounds."

I pressed my fingers to my temple. Veronica and Liam were out there. "Okay, well, I'm going in."

Bradley's hand swung out as he grabbed my forearm. "The hell you are. They'll kill you. I'm not letting them take you too. You're all I have left."

I ripped my arm out of his hold. "Friend or not. I'm not going to let them kill Liam either."

Bradley ground his teeth. "Fine. I'll go with you."

The shots stopped. A women cried out. Bradley lifted his chin toward a strangled howl, and he peeked around the crates. "Shit. Veronica's hit." He grabbed the side of my arm and jerked me upright, jostling the shotgun out of my grip. "I'm getting you out of here."

"Oh, I don't think so, son." Metal pressed into my back. My heart rammed against my ribs, my breathing picking up. "Walk, girl."

"Dad, no." Bradley pleaded, holding his hands up in surrender. "Take me. Not her. Please, haven't you stolen enough people from my life? I'll do anything."

I pinned my eyes on Bradley, silently asking him what I should do. My racing pulse sharpened the world but fogged my brain with a sound like crashing waves in a storm. If Mark could kill his wife, I didn't doubt for one second, he'd put a bullet through my back. But better that than be used as a lure to bait Liam to his death.

Mark, more beast than man, pressed harder into my spine, pushing me forward. "Don't make me repeat myself. Walk."

"Just do what he says," Bradley answered, giving me a slight dip of his chin for reassurance. Not that I believed we had any.

The three of us trekked toward the middle of the hangar. Veronica lay on the ground clutching her bleeding arm. Liam sat behind her, his jacket lying next to him and his long-sleeved T-shirt in his arms. Blood was smeared around his shoulder and crusted down his bicep and elbow. His glistening chest shone in the light filtering through the now illuminated windows. The sun had met the sky, and morning had found us. Too bad my father and the others hadn't.

"I think I have something you both may want," Mark growled.

Liam paused with his ripped shirt in mid-wrap around his mother's wound.

"Mark," Veronica hissed, pushing herself upright with her good arm. A muscle in her jaw ticked.

Liam's head snapped up. Rage ignited behind his irises like a blue flame.

"I'm fine." I tried to comfort him, but his shoulders tensed in response, the muscles along his chest flexing. More blood seeped from his wound.

Liam finished wrapping his mother's arm and stood, blocking her with his body. "Let her go, or I will kill you." The structure of his face shifted, the words barely escaping his taut mouth.

"Dad, let her go." Bradley echoed Liam's command, stepping closer. "I'll do anything you want."

"Anything I want, huh? Where was this attitude when I first asked you to leave Ronnie and come away with me? You said no then, right?"

Bradley nodded, tears forming along his lower lids.

"But now, when you're the one asking me for the favor, you think pulling the family card means I have to say yes, huh?"

Bradley swallowed.

Mark's deep chuckle raised the hairs on my arms. I heard the click and braced myself—knowing what a gunshot felt like already—but the bullet zinged into the meat of Bradley's arm instead. His body lurched backward with a spurt of blood. Tears wetted his red-darkened cheeks as his wolf side emerged. His teeth elongated and claws broke through his nailbeds as he hissed like a cat. His paw-like hand clutched his injury, blood dripping between the webbing.

"Mark, stop it," Veronica commanded.

"I don't work for you anymore, Ronnie. Keep your ass down and shut the hell up, or the next bullet is yours."

"Don't talk to her like that," Liam shouted.

My eyes widened. Whether Liam knew it or not, he'd just defended his monster mother. I hoped we'd have a chance to revisit that . . . in this life, preferably.

Bradley bared his teeth. His eyes glowed, the pupils thinning into black slits. "I said, let her go."

"Well, since you asked nicely."

Everything happened so fast. A hand knocked me forward, and a thunderclap of gunfire pierced the air. I landed sprawled on the hard ground before I realized I'd fallen. Someone fired another shot, then a third. The ringing in my ears echoed like a gong beaten right in my face. Someone screamed. I think it was me. I closed my eyes, thinking I'd taken at least one hit, but no pain arose other than my mildly bruised front.

"Are you okay?"

My eyes snapped open. I clutched my chest. It pounded but was still intact. Liam's breath punched in and out of his lungs as he stared at me, waiting for my answer.

"I . . ."

A crumpled body lay in a pool of blood several feet from me. I whimpered, the person's slack face blurring as hot tears gathered at the corners of my eyes. "What happened?" The words broke on a sob.

"He saved you." Liam cradled my head in his hands. "Mark pushed you at him, planning to shoot you in the back, but Bradley jumped in between you. The bullet must've been silver. It got him straight in the heart."

Grief and guilt cut deep into my gut, nicking a paralyzing nerve that arrested my heartbeat. Bradley's green eyes stared lifelessly back at me. Blood bubbled out from his mouth, covering his pale lips in a stark, shining red. The heat of a tear trailed down my cheek.

Liam used the pad of his thumb to wipe it away. "I don't think he used you. Somewhere in all this mess, he really did care for you." Liam turned my head away from the devastating scene and pulled me into his arms. I went willingly. "Bradley's distraction gave me the time to get my ankle gun, and I shot Mark, a couple times for good measure."

"Veronica?" I pulled out of Liam's arms and stood, frantic. We both swiveled around and around.

She was gone.

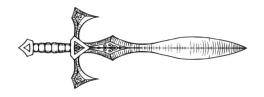

36

LIAM

A month passed, and Veronica didn't show her face. I knew she was biding time. Although I copied every page in her notebook, ready for her to come and take the original, she never turned up. Each night I'd read another section, desperate to find what she sought in all those writings, but nothing stood out to me as strange or notable—the main issue being I had no clue what to look for or even which section to focus on. Did she want details about an old case, a Hunterland clue, or something else completely? I had no idea.

My phone buzzed in my pocket. I slid it out and tapped on the message.

Meet me at the Bronco before the final bell.

Olivia. That was another secret. We'd been sneaking around for weeks as a couple, or at least I thought we could call ourselves that. I'd never been in a real relationship before, so I wasn't certain. The one time I tried to talk about it, she'd hushed me saying it wasn't the right time to go public. Between my Dad still roaming Chicago looking for answers, and my sister still clueless on the details of my capture and later ambushing, Olivia felt like the timing wasn't right for our team.

Dad had showed up in the hospital just like Mom promised, even though she hadn't retrieved her notebook. When I finally talked to him, I told him everything, including Mom's request. Both Olivia and I had hoped he'd know what information she wanted so badly, but he, too, was at a loss.

Fenton's claim that Dad had failed to take his chance to kill Mom turned out to be real. When Dad confided in me, I didn't fault him. Mom had surprised him one night at his hotel. She only stayed long enough to deliver a message: *Stay away. It's not safe.* Then she'd fled. He said the warning had thrown him off guard.

By the time he'd made sense of her words, she had disappeared into the night. But now he was even more determined, feeling responsible for letting her go. A second time. I knew the feeling. I'd fought by her side, even helped her. The way she'd acted made it hard to think of her as what she really was, a monster.

I raised my hand and asked the teacher if I could be excused to use the restroom. Then I rushed to my locker, grabbed my leather jacket and bookbag, and dashed out of school to meet Olivia in the parking lot. We'd been knocking off early to rendezvous here for the occasional make-out session before our sisters joined us for the ride home. Keeping our relationship quiet had turned into more of a chore than I'd thought. Sure, it was exciting, but I was ready to tell the world.

I rounded the bend, taking in Olivia as she leaned against the Bronco, her bottom lip trapped between her teeth, something she did when she couldn't wait to nip mine. The sun caught a few strands of her hair, enriching the chestnut color with auburn strands. The wind chill to her cheeks made apples on her snow-white skin. God, she was beautiful.

"Waiting for someone?" I asked as I approached.

She smiled so wide it touched every cell in my body. My stomach dipped with want, and my tongue primed my lips. The hell with hiding this, I wanted her, and I hated waiting until the coast was clear each time we were together. I wanted to push her up against the lockers and devour her, take her in my arms while watching a movie at home, smother her with kisses in between training.

Her blush darkened from pink to red as if she'd read my mind. She rubbed her gloved hands together and blew into them. "You took long enough. I got your text thirty minutes ago. Were you trying to keep me in suspense or letting me freeze so you could warm me up?"

That snapped me out of my fantasy. "What text? You texted me."

"No, I didn't. You said to skip last period and meet you by the car."

My brow rose. "I—"

A man's deep cough interrupted us.

"Technology isn't very secure, is it? Makes you wonder what our government has access to."

I swung around to see Fenton leaning up against a blue Oldsmobile parked across from the Bronco. He wore jeans and a gray Henley the same color as his aging hair, as if it were sixty degrees outside.

I reached for the gun hidden at my back only to brush a warm hand already snatching it away.

"Sorry, kiddo. This might not kill us, but really don't feel like bleeding." Mom's voice pierced my heart in more ways than one. I spun. Each time I saw her, it never got easier. She wore her usual hunter garb and mom grin.

"Olivia Davis." She inclined her head as she retreated several steps. She tossed the gun to Fenton, and he put it in his waistband, under his shirt.

"Why do you always call me by my full name?" Olivia asked as she shifted to stand shoulder to shoulder with me as a unified front.

Mom winked. "Now that is a good question." She refocused on me. "But I don't have time to answer that right now. The ledger, Liam."

I crossed my arms over my chest, teeth grating together. "How do you even know I have it?"

Mom chuckled. "You've been carrying it around with you for the last three weeks. Now open the bag."

Of course, she'd been following me. How dumb was I? She'd been waiting for the most opportune time, provided courtesy of my little secret meetings with Olivia. But I cared less about her surprising us and more about the job.

Right now, we had our sights on information, not her death. Not yet. Letting her live to figure out her end game had become the new mission. We just needed her to take the bait.

"What are you looking for?"

"Answers." Mom reached out her hand, and I stared at it. If I gave the leather-bound book up too easily, she'd know we had a copy and were letting her take it. *Play hard to get*, Dad had said.

"Oh, come on. A deal's a deal. I gave you back your father without even asking for the notebook first. Your locker isn't a vault, Liam. And that bag," she pointed to the strap over my shoulder, "has been in it more than in your possession."

I narrowed my eyes. "Which means you could have taken it at any time if you know all that. So, what's with the meet and greet?"

Mom smiled, the one I hated but also deep down loved because it was hers, the one that ran through all the best currents of my early life. "Bradley was part of an experiment."

"What?" Olivia stole the word right out of my mouth.

"Moana, his mother . . ." Mom sighed, running a hand through her blond curls. "She's the reason Mark was turned at the state park. Moana had been doing research on werewolves' DNA for me. We met at a medical conference. She was the keynote speaker. When I showed her my other form, she grew interested. Instead of fearing me, she wanted to help, to be a part of the solution. To this day I'm still surprised her love for science outweighed her trepidation. She always treated us as equals." Mom pointed at Fenton and herself.

Fenton pushed up onto the trunk of the car behind him, his legs dangling. "Moana acted as our heart supplier for years, researching a cure for our disease and helping with bloodlust. But Reginald and the other two Origins weren't very happy about it. They convinced a wolf pack to go after Mark as a warning to Moana."

"Why?" Olivia chimed in.

"Because he expected the werewolves to kill Mark, thus killing any chance of Moana continuing to help our pack, letting him regain control, with us less focused on hunting down his vampires. But Mark made a deal with his attackers. If they didn't kill him, he'd get them all the hearts they needed whenever they wanted. So, they took the deal but made him a wolf to give him extra incentive to hold up his end of the bargain."

"Oh God." The pieces started to take shape. Mark was a pawn in a chess game, strategically played. He was their insurance.

"Toro, the one I killed back at the airfield, was part of that pack before I challenged their Alpha and claimed the members," Mom added. She unzipped her bag and pulled out a thick file folder. "Everything is in here. It'll show all Moana's research. Give it to Doc." She held it out to Olivia, who stepped forward. Once she had it, I grabbed her arm and pulled her back. Mom chuckled, shaking her head. Olivia tucked it away in her bag.

"Moana knew Mark blamed her for his situation. He held Bradley over her head, constantly reminding her of what he could do to their son if she didn't make him happy. She asked me to turn Bradley before Mark did and make sure her son would never kill out of bloodlust. He'd be our first experiment. We ran tests before I turned him, during his transformation, and after. I never let him take a life. I watched over him for almost five years. He never felt the raw power of the disease." She swallowed and looked away—the little muscle in her jaw ticked, but when she returned my gaze, her features held no trace of emotion. "Eventually, our relationship angered Mark, and when Bradley wouldn't leave with him, Mark took advantage and convinced him I'd killed Moana. Before I even knew about the lie, they had fled."

"How do you know Bradley didn't end up hurting anyone? That he didn't join in the deaths here in Falkville Falls?" I'd already had a suspicion someone killed for Bradley. But who?

Fenton jumped off the car. "Daryl made those kills for the kid. He might not have known who really butchered Moana, but he knew Bradley was innocent and made sure to keep him that way. Daryl thought of Bradley like a son; he was a better father than Mark ever was."

It all made sense. Daryl had been the wolf killing for two; he got Bradley out of the motel room before I entered; he made sure Bradley never turned into . . . a what? A monster?

"It's a lot to take in, I know," Mom said as if reading my thoughts. "I need the ledger, Liam."

I'd played coy long enough. Mom probably suspected I had a copy. Why wait any longer? I opened my bag and tossed the leather-bound book to her.

The school bell rang, and Fenton's head snapped up. "We gotta go, Ronnie."

Mom nodded.

"Wait." I stepped forward. "Why do they call you Ronnie?" The burning question slipped through my lips without thought. No one I knew had called her that, not even Dad.

"Liam Noah Hunter," my sister's voice sounded in the distance. "Where the hell are you?"

"Something is totally going on with them," Pepper's voice echoed.

"I'll stall them." Olivia darted out of sight.

Mom's eyes trailed over my head. "How is she?"

I didn't even have to ask to know she meant my sister. It was written in the worry lines on my mother's face. "She's fine."

"Does she know about me?"

"No."

"Good." Mom started to walk away, but I stopped her with a hand clasped around her forearm. Her eyes trailed to the touch.

"Tell me why they call you that."

She looked up, tears gathered in the corner of her eyes. In all the years I'd known her I'd never seen her cry, but she didn't hide these. She let them fall, unabashed. And that gutted me more than any blade.

"I tried to kill myself that night." She swallowed.

My hand dropped, numbed by her admission. "The night you were bitten?"

She nodded. "But the wolves had left me too injured." She looked away. "I didn't have the strength to get the job done. Fenton found me. He asked me my name, but I couldn't really speak. One of the wolves had taken a chunk of my jaw."

I choked as if I'd tried to swallow a melon. She had been missing part of her face? I didn't . . .

"All he heard me say was *Roni*. So that's what he called me. Ronnie." She turned back to look at me one last time, her eyes red. I blinked away my own tears, and when I refocused, she was gone. Again.

37

OLIVIA

During our training sessions, Liam tried to stay all business. But every now and again, he'd let a grin slip when he thought I stopped paying attention. But, let's be honest, I *always* had my eyes fixed on him.

Sparring with Liam rather than Nikki presented a new sort of challenge. Liam had a habit of fighting shirtless. His glistening, sweat-covered muscles demanded attention. I couldn't help but admire his ripped arms, sculpted abs, and defined chest flexing with his graceful movements.

Meanwhile, I struggled to maintain my own balance. Imagine a ballet dancer meeting a toddler mastering their first steps—that was us. I literally had no idea how he still found me alluring after all the flailing, squawking spills I had taken, but by the kisses he peppered on me at school in darkened corners and the secret ones he snuck at the house, I'd be a fool to think he wasn't head over heels. He'd done a complete one-eighty, and I was still adjusting to all the touchy-feely moments.

Both Nikki and Liam contributed to my progress. I managed to gain some muscle, which Nikki acknowledged in her own way. She pointed out that my toothpick legs had become "drumsticks." It wasn't the most poetic compliment but one, nonetheless. If only she hadn't adopted it as my new nickname.

Sundays became Liam and my designated training day, while Saturdays were still dedicated to Nikki. With my progress, I'd expected to be ready for fieldwork soon. However, every session boiled down to Liam and Nikki telling me I wasn't ready. So today, when I started swinging the machete around and Liam groaned in response, I wasn't surprised.

"Are you out of your mind? You'll end up taking off my head. And I'm rather attached to it." He pointed to the blade, which reflected the sunlight coming through the windows. "Put that back where you found it. We need to work on your kicks."

I rolled my eyes. "It's been a month of kicks." I had healed enough bruises and puffy toes to prove it.

Liam folded his arms. Today he wore a gray T-shirt that looked one size too small for his chest. It stretched as if begging to be pulled off.

"And we will work on it for another month if you don't get any better at it." He waggled his fingers. "What if you injure your hands in combat? You need to learn how to use your feet and legs as defense."

"Seriously, you think I'll incapacitate both of my hands. What are the odds of that?" I returned the blade to its designated table. "I'm tired of you twisting my ankle. I'd be a much better student if you gave me something fun to do."

"I'll give you something fun to play with, after we review kicks."

My brows rose. "Oh, which weapon? Stakes, swords, the new gun you got with silver bullets?" I held my hands in prayer at my heart.

Liam shook his head, biting his lower lip to suppress laughter. "I meant me."

I grimaced.

Liam released a soft chuckle as he approached me. His hands interlocked behind my back, pulling my body closer to his. I melted into his embrace. He kissed the side of my neck and moved his lips over my jaw and up to my ear. I shivered. "I was hoping you'd be a little bit more excited that I was your reward. Who knew custom weapons would trump me?" I lifted my chin, giving him better access for more pecks, not really paying much attention to his words. "But if you don't want me"—his lips brushed over mine as he continued to pepper kisses on the other side of my face, bringing his mouth to my other ear—"then I guess . . ." He pulled away and clapped his hands. "Kicks it is."

I bristled. *Jerk!*

"Okay, let's start."

"You're mean." I stuck out my tongue. Liam responded with a smile, and I assumed my position, ready for the next move.

Liam walked me through the kicking maneuvers he wanted me to replicate, demonstrating a fast roundhouse kick—just like the one Nikki favored to take me down.

"You ready?"

I shrugged. "Sure." Without waiting for him to get into a fighting stance, I charged forward. Executing a powerful kick, just as he had taught me, I aimed for the vulnerable spot beneath his rib cage. Perfect execution. So fluid, so balanced, I almost squealed.

But my heel never landed.

With a swift swipe of his arm, he knocked me to the mat. Standing above me, he sported a smug smile. "Nice try. Do it again, and this time see if you can actually make contact. A monster won't give you a pass for effort."

I propped myself up on my elbows and smirked back at him. "Bradley did."

A low growl escaped his lips, precisely the response I had aimed for. "Not the same," he grumbled, turning away. Seizing the opportunity, I took advantage of his exposed backside. With the heel of my shoe, I delivered a powerful kick to the back of his knee, and he buckled beside me. I burst into laughter, rolling back and forth in amusement.

Faster than I'd ever seen him move, Liam flipped me onto the mat, my back hitting the cushion hard. Our eyes locked in silence. Was he mad?

"That was the hottest thing you've ever done." He licked his lips, drawing my attention to his mouth.

My brows pulled inward. "Taking you to the ground?" Liam surprised me regularly, but this was new. I hadn't thought we were flirting, but hey, what did I know about seduction?

His gaze drifted to my mouth. "Yes." He lowered his forearm and let his free hand cup the curve of my cheekbone. My pulse thrummed as his tense stare followed his fingertips' trail down my face to graze my parted lips.

"Do you know how hot it is, sparring with you?" he whispered, his warm breath sending shivers down my spine.

I shook my head, or at least I thought I did. Honestly, gawking like I was, I couldn't really be sure of anything.

"It takes all my willpower not to kiss you every time you land on this mat, but I promised myself I wouldn't until you took me down." Voice husky, he leaned forward and rested his cheek against mine, spreading hot tingles as his lips moved against my ear. "But now you did, so . . ."

I lifted my hips, eliciting a deep sound in Liam's throat. His hand slid down and around my side, tightening until a soft moan escaped me.

Liam's lips brushed across mine—gentle and sweet at first, but soon the kiss deepened, becoming more fervent and unrestrained. I was tugging on the hem of his shirt, ready to get rid of the barrier keeping me from his chest, when his phone rang.

We both looked up at his cell resting next to his keys and wallet on the circular table. "I should get it." Liam pushed off the ground to stand.

"Why? There's no monster in Falkville Falls anymore. Can't you finish this"—I waved at my body still waiting on the mat—"then call them back?"

"What if it's my dad?"

After the hospital released Agent Hunter, he'd decided to come back to Falkville Falls but wanted to scour the trail on his way back, searching for Veronica and clues about Reginald. He refused to let it rest, and because of that, neither did Liam.

Liam answered the phone. "Hello."

The voice on the other end made Liam scowl.

"Yeah, she's here. What do you want, Veronica?" Liam placed the phone on the table and put it on speaker as I jumped up from the mat. We had no idea when Veronica would reach out or even if she would. The past couple weeks since she ambushed us at school had eaten away at Liam. I couldn't be sure what she'd told him when I left to intercept our sisters, but whatever it was had rattled him.

"Is that any way to talk to your mother, kiddo?"

"She can hear you now. What do you want?" Liam plopped into a chair in front of him and ran his hands through his hair, pulling on the ends.

"So, Olivia Davis, have you decided?" Veronica said with a chuckle.

"Decided what?"

The sounds of Willie Nelson played in the background. "Are you a hunter?"

I pressed my finger against Liam's lips to make sure he wouldn't interrupt. Veronica Hunter might be a monster, but she was also the answer to our questions. And we had plenty.

"Yes." I paused, and when she didn't speak, I continued, "Why do you keep using my full name?"

"It's important you know who you are and where you came from. Your full name will lead you there. You have a bigger place in this world than you know, but you have to ask the right questions to find it."

"This isn't a game," Liam said between clenched teeth.

"No, it's not, but there are things you both will have to uncover on your own."

"Why?"

"Because if I come out and just tell you, you won't believe me. But if you find it, you'll have your proof." A siren in the background wailed as a car horn honked. She sounded like she was outside. "You were onto something that day we met in the woods. Keep digging. Ask your questions and don't stop until you get the answers. You're a hunter now, and we always get what we want."

I thought back to that day in the forest. I had asked about how Hunterland started, and she'd told me about . . . "I want to know more about Danica Davisa."

Veronica chuckled. "The information is there. You've had it all this time. You'll find it."

"Where?" Liam pushed back his chair and screamed at the phone. He couldn't help himself. "Stop playing with us. Where?"

"Where it's always been. In Hunterlore."

Acknowledgments

First and foremost, I want to express my heartfelt gratitude to all my reviewers, book tour participants, and my street team, Dana's Darlings, as well as you, the reader, for choosing *Hunterlore* and embarking on this paranormal adventure by my side. Your love and support for my monster hunters mean the world to me. Thank you from the bottom of my heart.

To my beta readers—Heather, Tia, Kylie, Penelope, Ashley, Belinda, Leslie, Laura, Jenna, Rachael, and Melissa—you all are simply amazing! Your invaluable feedback and constructive advice helped refine this story into what it needed to become. I am perpetually inspired by your comments, unwavering encouragement, and affection.

To Hannah Sandoval, your steadfast support is the pillar upon which my writing stands. I am truly grateful for your patience in accommodating my unique working style.

To Elana Gibson, our partnership has been nothing short of fantastic. Our developmental editing sessions were a blast, and I dedicate two chapters solely to you, your vision, and your commitment to making *Hunterlore* the best it can be. Thank you once again for everything. I cannot wait to embark on the next installment with you.

To Katherine Bountry, who this book is dedicated to, thank you for believing in the *Hunterland* series and for bringing it to a new market. Whatever happens, I know we gave it our all, and without you none of it would have been possible.

To my loving author friends Ginger Scott, Heather Hildenbrand, Katie Cross, and Jennifer Eaton, thank you for being such wonderful human beings. Your love for *Hunterlore* means more to me than you will ever know. I'm forever grateful for our friendship and guidance. Without you ladies, writing would be a lonely endeavor.

To my father, who never lets me back away from a challenge—your belief in the impossible has shaped my journey. Because of you, I continue to strive for my next goal, knowing there are no limits.

To my mother, whose legacy I carry, I am driven each day to make you proud. In your absence, I make it a point to cherish every experience, honoring the ones you missed.

To my husband, Jason—my best friend, soulmate, and the embodiment of a perfect romance—thank you for taking care of me, loving me, and reminding me that there are no mountains I cannot climb. Our love story will forever be the greatest of all.

ABOUT THE AUTHOR

Dana Claire is an award-winning author whose stories explore identity, fate, and destiny in the crossroads of romance and adventure. But her writing career didn't begin when she published her first book, *The Connection*, in 2020. It started as a young girl when her mother, an elementary school teacher, inspired her to create imaginary worlds between the pages.

Dana's love of romantic tension, the supernatural, and nonstop action has elicited positive feedback from many readers, as their online reviews reveal her flair for spine-tingling action and unforgettable characters. But it's not just readers who love her; literary critics have also taken note, and Dana was given the Children's Moonbeam award for *The Connection* in 2021, and the Children's Moonbeam award, PenCraft Award, and eLit Award in 2023 for *War of the Sea*.

Dana is now sharing her stories through speaking events and book signings, introducing more readers to the worlds she created. She lives in Los Angeles with her adoring husband, living her dream: writing books, telling stories, and changing the world, one reader at a time.

If you enjoyed
Dana Claire's *Hunterlore*,
please consider leaving a review
to help our authors.

And check out
Gwendolyn Womack's
The Premonitions Club.

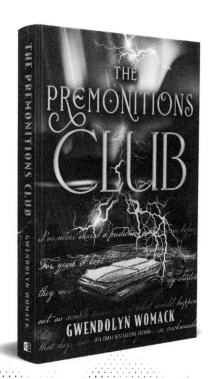

1

LIV

Premonition:
A strong feeling something is about to happen

L iv Hall didn't believe in knowing the future before it happened. If she did, maybe she would have sensed her stepdad had been cheating on her mom all year. Or maybe she would have known they'd divorce when Bodhi finally confessed, so he could go live with his new girlfriend. Or maybe she could have foreseen she and her mom— who was busy having a nervous breakdown—would leave New York City to go live with her grandfather in Hyde Park. And maybe, just maybe, she would have had the inkling to know her grandfather would pass away peacefully in his sleep two months later, leaving her mom the house and everything in it.

But life hadn't been predictable. It had come at them full speed, an eighty-mile-an-hour chain of disasters. They packed their bags in early spring and came to Hyde Park where she was forced to finish out her junior year, all two and half months of it, at Roosevelt High School as the new girl. "That girl from New York" with the funky jewelry and silver armband.

The night before her first day of school she slapped green dye on her long auburn hair in a shade appropriately called Manic Panic and wrote "New Girl" on a white T-shirt in black sharpie to make sure everyone knew how she felt about it. The only thing that kept her from completely losing it was that at least she had one friend at school, Winnie, the daughter of her mom's old friend.

Growing up, whenever Liv had come to town to visit her grandfather, her mom always signed her up for "summer fun" classes with Winnie. Liv's favorite activity had been the baking classes at the Culinary Institute of America, which had its main campus in Hyde Park. To Liv, the building and grounds looked like a magical castle. The institute was where Hazel, her mom, had met her stepdad. Hazel had come to campus to write a freelance article for a food magazine. Bodhi had fallen hard for the struggling-writer single mom, and they were married by the end of the year. Hazel continued to write articles on food and wine. Over the years she became the queen of reviews from bean-to-bar chocolate to artisanal cheeses, to gourmet specialty products around the world. Bodhi Hall was a big name in the food industry too, a superstar chef who owned a restaurant in Manhattan.

Liv hadn't talked to her stepdad since he left, and her mother didn't blame her. Bodhi had destroyed their family as if the last ten years together meant nothing. During the worst of the breakup, at the height of the yelling and her mother's tears, Liv would hide out in her room making jewelry, her longtime hobby. She'd stay up late, bent over her worktable with a soldering iron, as if she could somehow weld her life back together again.

The most intricate piece she made for herself was a silver armband. It looked like braided rope, but really it was a chain of *triskelions*, an ancient Celtic symbol of three triple spirals joined together. She found the symbol in a design book, and making the armband had gotten her though that last horrid month of the divorce. Now she never took it off.

After the move, her mom had barely kept it together. At night she watched sappy rom-com movies and powered through Kleenex. She retreated into the house in Hyde Park like it was a fortress, locking herself in her bedroom and rarely coming out. Liv's grandfather had welcomed them with open arms, shuttling Liv around town and managing all the cooking.

Even with the tragic end of Hazel's marriage, Liv could tell her grandfather was happy to have them come live with him. Clement had been alone, Liv's grandmother having died before Liv was born, and he'd had almost three precious months together with Liv and Hazel before he passed away. Now he was gone, and his house had suddenly become one big ghost of a memory.

Her grandfather's estate attorney had called and left several messages that they needed to come and go through some things. Her mom had been putting off returning their calls, saying it was too soon. Liv agreed. She wanted to look through her grandfather's things before a stranger did. She decided to start with the attic, not ready to tackle her grandfather's bedroom or closet yet. Her mother said she was only interested in keeping antiques or family heirlooms and trusted Liv to make the call.

Winnie had come over to help. It was Sunday and they planned to spend most of the day going through boxes. The attic was huge, the kind that could be turned into a spare bedroom or an office loft. It had a pitched-roof ceiling with enough room to stand, and an old-timey circular window looked out onto the street below. Sunlight streamed in through towering oak trees. The house was a two-story Cape Cod and sat in the heart of town. Her grandfather had lived there forever and amassed enough stuff in the attic to prove it.

Liv and Winnie spent all morning opening old boxes and making piles to donate. They laid out old blankets on the floor to sit on, and when it got warm around noon, Liv brought up a fan. She was wearing cutoff jeans and a tank top which showed off her armband, and her long hair was up in a hasty twist, secured with a hair clip that liked to slip off every hour. True to form, Winnie was *not* in let's-go-through-the-attic wear. She always wore black skirts, no matter what, and dressed in a unique style that had a vintage Gothic flair. Her hair was the star, a 1920s pageboy blunt cut, dyed jet black with the edges ringed in sapphire blue, framing perfect black eyeliner, siren red lipstick, and her cat-eyed glasses.

"I think there's more boxes behind this thing." Liv stood on tiptoe and tried to peek over the top of a six-foot wall of wood panels that were tied together and draped with a black tarp. She twisted her falling hair back up and secured it with the clip again.

Winnie fanned herself. "Sorry. I draw the line with heavy lifting. It will completely destroy the manicure I got yesterday." Her nails were painted silver with purple stars and moons stenciled on them. "Maybe Matty could help? He should be here soon."

Liv raised her eyebrows without comment. Matty was Winnie's best friend. He was even shorter and skinnier than she was. He also liked to dress like a fashion designer on *Project Runway* and had already told them he refused to touch anything dusty today.

She looked out the window down below at her neighbor across the street, who was washing his car, an old Ford Mustang, in the driveway. He was wearing board shorts, a work-out tank, and flip-flops. The tank showed off every muscle on his arms.

"I bet *he* could." Liv nodded to him.

Winnie joined her at the window. "No way. You live across the street from Forester Torres? How did I not know this?" Forester went to their school, but Liv had never talked to him. He had thick, wavy black hair, deep brown eyes, and was ridiculously tan. He reminded Liv a little bit of Bodhi.

Maybe that's why she was feeling so fearless. She started to open the window.

"What are you doing?" Winnie sounded alarmed.

"Asking for help. He looks like the Hulk down there. He can totally move this thing."

"Wait!" Winnie tried to stop her. "Forester Torres is one of the most popular guys at school. He's captain of the football team."

"So?" Liv turned to Winnie, surprised. "I thought you didn't buy into social cliques."

"I don't. I'm not. But you haven't lived your whole life here going to school with some of these people."

At school Winnie was a loner and sometimes hung out with the drama club along with Matty. Liv didn't know where she fit in with the scheme of cliques and cool status, and right now she was beyond caring. All she wanted to do was move this stupid wood.

"Maybe he's really nice, and like you said, we need help." Liv cranked the window open with the handle before Winnie could stop her and called out, "Hey! Hello down there!"

Forester looked up, and Winnie ducked down to hide. "I can't believe you're doing this."

Liv laughed and yelled down, "I'm your new neighbor. I'm clearing out the attic with my friend, and we need help moving some wood panels. Think you can come over for a minute?"

Winnie was laughing now too. "What's he saying?" she whispered.

"He nodded and put down the hose."

"You're kidding me."

"No, he's coming over." Liv grinned and closed the window back up. "See? That was easy."

"I hate you." Winnie picked up the electric fan and blasted her face to cool off. The doorbell rang and Liv ran downstairs, knowing her mother was sound asleep in her room after an all-night Netflix binge. She whipped open the door, a little more violently than she intended.

Forester took a step back with a friendly hand up. "Whoa there."

"Sorry." Liv smiled up at him, trying to play it cool. Forester was huge, well over six feet. "Hi. Thanks for coming over. I'm Liv."

"Yeah, I know." Forester gave her an easy grin. "The new girl." He motioned to his T-shirt, mimicking where she'd written it on her shirt that first day.

"That's me." Liv grimaced. "I really appreciate the help."

"No prob. Let's do it." He shrugged off the thanks and followed her up the stairs.

When they got to the attic he gave Winnie a friendly salute. "Yo yo."

Winnie raised her eyebrows in surprise. "Yo yo yourself."

He asked them, "So what are we moving today?"

"That." Liv pointed to the wall of wood.

Forester circled it. "I see what you mean. Why don't you guys take one end and we can try and angle it over this way."

"Sorry team," Winnie announced, shaking her head regretfully. "I gotta sit this one out. My nails." She flashed them at Forester.

"It's fine, Win." Liv rolled her eyes with a smile. "We got it." She and Forester each took a side and tried to lift it together, barely getting it to budge.

They made several attempts, until Forester finally said, "I think we need more muscle." He pulled out his cell and speed-dialed someone.

Liv looked to Winnie in alarm. *What* was he doing?

Whoever he called picked up on the first ring. "Yo dude. You still stopping by? I'm at the house across the street from mine. We need help moving some wood. It'll just take a sec. Think you can come over?"

Winnie was looking at Liv in alarm too. *Who* was he calling?

Forester hesitated, listening to whatever the person was saying. "Seriously? She is? Whatever, man. I don't care. She can come." He sounded annoyed.

Winnie was silently communicating to Liv: *Who is* she, *and what is happening?* Liv shook her head, mystified.

Forester hung up. "Jax can help. He'll be here in five minutes with Nebony." He said it casually, when it was anything but.

Liv stared at Winnie in absolute horror.

Jaxon Coleson and Nebony Price were coming over here? To her house? Even Liv, in her new-girl bubble, knew who they were. If there was an exclusive club at school, then Nebony and Jaxon were the heads of it. Nebony was *the* most popular girl. Alpha head cheerleader and social-media superstar, she had a gazillion followers online from all her cheerleading posts, not to mention she was a physically perfect goddess. Nebony and Forester had been a hot item all year, until they broke up over spring break. It was a mystery who had been the one to pull the plug. Rumor was Nebony and Jaxon were going out now, the added drama being Jaxon was Forester's best friend.

Liv had noticed Jaxon on her first day, when she and Winnie had pulled into the parking lot in Winnie's car. Jaxon had been nearby, talking with his friends at his Jeep. He was standing still, his eyes hidden by reflective shades, his brown hair more gold under the sun. The moment Liv saw him, she felt a visceral reaction in her gut and had to force herself to look away.

When she crossed the parking lot, she could have sworn he was watching her—but when she glanced back, he wasn't looking. She quickly discovered he was not in any of her classes. But every day she found herself looking for him. In the parking lot. At lunch. On the field. She rarely saw him—only the taillights of his Jeep zipping in and out of the school lot with the top down. Sometimes Nebony was in the car with him, her long hair flying in the wind. Liv never told Winnie about her secret crush. Was it a crush? It was more like a strange fascination, really.

And now they were both on their way over to move her granddad's old stuff?

This was a nightmare. She tried to do damage control. "You guys don't have to help. Really. My mom will get some movers to do it. Why don't you call him back?"

She did *not* want Jaxon Coleson here—or Nebony Price. Today was supposed to have been a mellow Sunday. She couldn't even remember if she had brushed her teeth this morning.

"Relax, it's no biggie." Forester waved off her concern, already heading down the stairs. "Got anything to drink while we wait for them?"

"Uh . . . sure." Liv had no idea what to do. "I have lemonade?"

"Awesome sauce," Forester shot back, heading to the kitchen, and Winnie and Liv hung back to talk.

Winnie whispered, "Did he just say 'awesome sauce'?"

Liv whispered back, "What do we do?"

"Roll with it. You started this, *dude.*"

Liv tried not to laugh, but her heart was now racing. The impulse to call out to Forester from the window was having an unforeseen ripple effect. The enormity of which she had yet to realize.

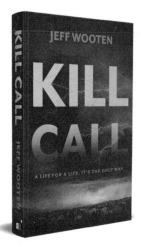
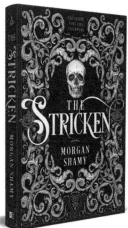